P9-DXF-762

The Figgs

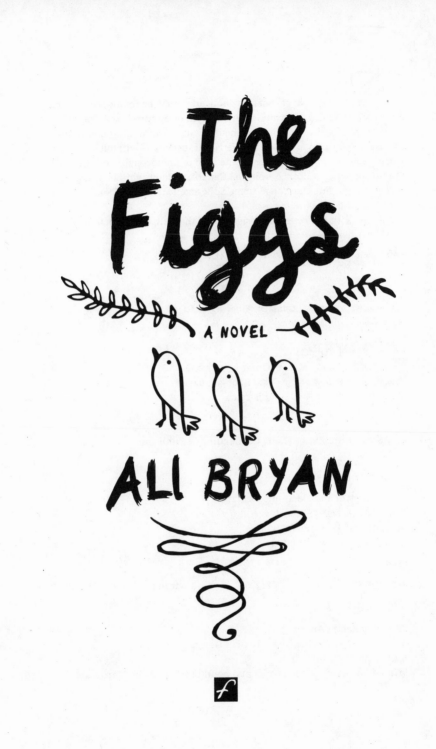

The Figgs

A NOVEL

ALI BRYAN

© Ali Bryan 2018

All rights reserved. No part of this publication may be reproduced, stored in a retrieval system, or transmitted in any form or by any means, graphic, electronic, or mechanical — including photocopying, recording, taping, or through the use of information storage and retrieval systems — without prior written permission of the publisher or, in the case of photocopying or other reprographic copying, a licence from the Canadian Copyright Licensing Agency (Access Copyright), One Yonge Street, Suite 800, Toronto, on, Canada, M5E 1E5.

Published with the generous assistance of the Canada Council for the Arts and the Alberta Media Fund.

Canada Council   Conseil des Arts   *Alberta*
for the Arts   du Canada   Government

Freehand Books
515 – 815 1st Street sw   Calgary, Alberta   T2P 1N3
www.freehand-books.com

Book orders: LitDistCo
8300 Lawson Road   Milton, Ontario   L9T 0A4
Telephone: 1-800-591-6250   Fax: 1-800-591-6251
orders@litdistco.ca   www.litdistco.ca

Library and Archives Canada Cataloguing in Publication

Bryan, Ali, 1978–, author
The Figgs / Ali Bryan.

Issued in print and electronic formats.
ISBN 978-1-988298-25-2 (softcover).
ISBN 978-1-988298-26-9 (EPUB).
ISBN 978-1-988298-27-6 (PDF)

I. Title.

PS8603.R885F54 2018   C813'.6   C2018-900104-6   C2018-900105-4

Edited by Kelsey Attard
Book design by Natalie Olsen, Kisscut Design
Author photo by Life Photo
Printed on FSC® recycled paper and bound in Canada by Marquis

To my always Mom,
for being my mom, always

To my Dad, for without the
Weedon family crest, there
may not have been a story

1

June stood in the middle of the basement. It was a mess. Tom had been spilling orange pop on the carpet since 1995. There was a stain in the corner that still smelled faintly of rum and spaghetti, where Derek had puked after a school dance. At some point, Vanessa had drawn a lipstick happy face and covered it with the couch, and there was a trail of hardened wood glue stretching from Randy's workshop to the bathroom. He blamed the glue on Tom. The plan had always been to replace the carpet when the kids grew up and moved out, but they were still here, all three of them, and now a third of the basement had been swallowed up by two decades worth of stuff.

"I'm ready."

"Jesus Murphy, Randy, you scared me." June clutched her chest. Her husband stood behind her in rubber gloves and a respirator.

He pulled the mask down around his neck. "What do you think?"

"Do we really need facemasks?" June wrestled on a pair of rubber gloves. There were two more sets on the ping-pong table for Tom and Vanessa.

"I had them in my workshop." He tossed her a garbage bag.

June tucked it under her arm. "Where are the kids? I told them we were starting at nine."

"They're finishing their pancakes."

"You made them pancakes?"

Randy was engrossed in trying to peel apart a garbage bag. After several attempts it opened and he flapped it up and down. He looked like a children's entertainer, all hair and hysteria and mismatched socks.

June marched to the base of the stairs. "Tom, Vanessa, get down here." She looked at the clock above the TV. "It's already after nine."

Vanessa yelled, "I'm not coming down until I have coffee."

"Where do we start?" Randy was already digging through a box balanced on an old weight bench. He held up a bag of beeswax pellets and a container of wicks.

"Those are Vanessa's." June pushed her limp bangs out of her face. "From her candle-making phase."

Randy moved the box to the side as Tom lumbered down the stairs, a ribbon of syrup on his cheek. His hair was big like his father's, and he was still wearing last night's work shirt with the cartoon mop embroidered on the lapel.

"Gloves are on the ping-pong table." June pointed.

"Why's Dad wearing a mask?"

Randy sat cross-legged in the corner, the respirator secured over his face, flipping through a yellow picture book.

June's nose twitched. The basement's usual scent of floppy disk and microwave popcorn had been replaced by Go-Kleen Now! — the industrial cleaning products Tom imported from China that smelled like schoolyard orange peels.

"How long is this going to take?" Vanessa stood at the

8

bottom of the stairs, her eye makeup thick in shades of death, the rest of her skin pale as a scone. Her blue-black hair was slicked beneath a headband with ears.

"However long it takes."

Vanessa's pet cockatiel, Jerry, stood on Vanessa's shoulder with his head cocked. June thought he looked like a small chicken. He had a slightly deformed beak that made it look like he was always smiling.

"I have a friend coming over at ten."

"But you knew we were cleaning the basement today." June made fists. "And why is Jerry here?"

"He didn't want to be alone." Vanessa petted Jerry's head.

Tom rifled through a bin of comics. "How come Derek doesn't have to do this?"

"Yeah," Vanessa said. "How come?"

Randy removed his facemask. "This is such a sad little book." He hugged it to his chest.

June sighed and looked at her two oldest children. "Because Derek had to work this morning."

Vanessa stormed across the basement like a yeti to where Randy sat. "Derek gets out of everything."

"He'll go through his things later. Just focus on your own stuff." June felt the beginnings of a hot flash. "There's garbage bags over there and anything you think you can sell, put it over by the washer and dryer."

Vanessa dug into a laundry basket and held up a CD. "Michael Bublé?"

"Never mind," June bristled. "The stuff in there is mine. That big microwave box by the storage closet is yours. Sort through that."

Vanessa hovered over the basket. "What the fuck is this?"

"Vanessa, language." Randy hauled himself up from the floor.

"It's a personalized travel journal," June said. "One of the technicians gave it to me at my retirement party."

"You don't even travel." Vanessa replaced the leather book. "And before you say anything, road trips don't count."

"Why wouldn't they count? Besides, when have I had time to travel? I've only been retired five months."

Tom emptied the contents of an old pencil case into a garbage bag.

"Still," Vanessa balked, "it's not really your thing."

"Well, it might be," June argued. "If we can ever get out of this house and move into something smaller."

Vanessa had found her flute and was busy assembling it. "And what about Dad's workshop?"

June studied Randy for a response, but he was still in the corner holding the yellow picture book, looking like he had been abducted and placed in a sad Ukrainian library.

"What is that?" June said.

Randy flipped the book around. *You Were Chosen.* The title was written in bleak uppercase letters. A homely baby sat alone beneath it, grasping what resembled a stone tool. Then the subtitle: *An Adoption Story.* That part was written in a fancy script. June remembered tracing it as a child. She recoiled.

"Where did you find that?"

Randy held up an open banker's box.

"Leave that," she waved. "That's all Mom's stuff. We'll do that last."

On the other side of the room Vanessa stood amongst a mosh pit of stuffed animals and played the flute. June didn't recognize the song.

"Smells Like Teen Spirit," Tom said.

Vanessa stopped, "Correct!" and then continued playing.

June surveyed the room. They were fewer than fifteen minutes in, and it was twenty times worse than when they started. There was no place for anything. Tom leaned against the ping-pong table reading a yearbook, and Vanessa looked like she was trying to make the stuffed animals and a Cabbage Patch Kid levitate.

June hollered over the flute. "You guys really need to start taking some responsibility. I mean . . ." She paused to kick a board game out of the way. "You should not all be living at home still." June looked for Randy's support but he was in the corner doing bicep curls with ancient metal dumbbells. "Randy?"

"Huh?"

"Back me up here."

"Right." He placed the weights on the ground. "Your mother has a point."

June moved a set of badminton rackets to the sell pile. "You know I read the other day it's actually now a *syndrome*. When adult kids still live with their parents. Like toxic shock or restless leg. Something like *adult entitled dependence disorder* or *entitled dependence*. Psychologists are treating it like a *disease*."

Randy looked worried. "A disease?"

"What kind of disease?" Tom asked. "Like herpes?"

"Gonorrhea," Vanessa said.

"No," June scolded. "More of a trend. Like gluten-free diets."

"Or anal bleaching," Tom said.

"Thomas!" June said.

"But Marty and Dawn still have Elijah living with them," Randy said.

"He's in his fourth year of med school."

"What about the Dekkers then? Don't they still have two living at home? And I'm pretty sure the girl is older than Tom."

"She's in a wheelchair." Tom played with a protractor.

"So?"

"Dad, she can't feed herself."

"She can't?"

"She has a feeding tube."

Randy frowned.

"Are there any more pancakes?" Vanessa snapped the flute apart.

Randy brightened. "I can make another batch."

"I'll have some too." Tom held up a compass. "Can you do half blueberries half chocolate chips this time?"

June glared at her husband.

He froze en route to the stairs. "Yes. But not until we get some more done around here. Tom, put away the geometry set and get to work. Vanessa, do something with all your friends."

Friends. That's what those stuffed animals had been. June exhaled and tried not to think of those years of Vanessa's life. "Thank you," June muttered, picking up her ukulele and moving it to the clear side of the room where she'd set up a chair and a music stand. The ukulele had been an impulse buy. The salesman had a lovely beard and told her retirement was for making music. She ran her fingers across the fretboard before setting it on the chair. So far, she could play "Three Blind Mice."

June took a step back and bumped into a caramel-coloured spring horse. It had been hauled out of the closet and now trembled in its frame. She stroked its rippled mane. "Vanessa, remember this? This was your all-time fave."

Vanessa threw a graffiti-covered binder in the garbage. "Who, Percy?"

"Yes, Percy. That was it." June petted the chocolate saddle, the plastic smooth. "Remember I made you a bunch of cowgirl outfits to go with it? All those little plaid shirts with the tassels and the sequin pockets? And you always wore the hat with the beaded band even though it was too big and you couldn't see out of it?"

"It was my favourite, until Tom sat on it naked."

"I didn't sit on it naked," Tom piped in. "That was Derek. I *peed* on it."

Randy was wearing blue swim goggles that were too tight. "Why would you pee on Percy?"

"I don't know," Tom replied, carrying a stack of comics to the sell pile. "I was five."

June wiped her hand on her pant leg.

"Mom?"

"Derek?"

June looked up to see her youngest son at the top of the stairs. He was the tallest of her children, arguably the most handsome, with a lean body and a touch of her ginger coloring.

"Aren't you supposed to be at work?"

"I need to borrow the car."

Randy interrupted. "How about taking the bus? Or your bike? It's a nice day for some responsibility." He looked at June for approval.

Derek ignored his father. "It's important."

"What's wrong?" June recognized the worry in her son's face. She'd memorized it from years of bedside conversations about war and death and lice. Nights the hall light had to be left on.

"I need to get to the hospital."

"What for? Is someone hurt?" June's heart rate quickened. "Is something wrong?"

Randy took off the goggles.

"Marissa's having a baby."

"Who's Marissa?" Randy asked.

Derek gripped the handrail. "Can I just take the car? The contraptions are really close."

"Give me two minutes." June tore off her rubber gloves. "Your father and I will drive you."

Derek looked sickly.

"Wait for us upstairs."

Vanessa chased Derek up. "Blond Marissa or Asian Marissa?"

June had never seen Vanessa move so fast.

Derek didn't reply.

"Who's Marissa?" Randy asked again.

"Did you hear that?" June brushed bits off her shirt. "The *contraptions* are getting close."

"Yeah, but he's nervous," Randy said. "His friend's having a baby."

"His friend's not having a baby, Randy." She took the stairs two at a time and stopped at the top. Randy hurried behind her. She turned to her husband, a stair below, nearly knocking him over, and looked him in the eye. "Derek is having a baby.

Marissa and Derek are having a baby. Together." June clasped her hands into a ball. "Your son is about to become a father."

"Derek's having a baby right now?" He touched the wall to steady himself. "You can tell all that from him wanting to borrow the car?" He scratched his neck and looked back for Tom. "I don't even know who Marissa is. Do you know her?"

June darted through the kitchen searching for her purse. "No. Maybe. I don't know. Get your shoes on."

Randy sat down at the table, pulled on a pair of sneakers, tied them, and slumped back in the chair. "But why is he only telling us now?"

Tom had joined them upstairs and was switching his wallet from an old coat pocket to the one in the jacket he'd just put on. "I'm guessing he just found out."

"Derek," June hollered in all directions. "We're ready. Where are you?" She looked out the window to see if he was waiting outside. A red Civic was parked out front. "Whose car's that?"

Tom looked out the window and shrugged.

Vanessa thumped into the room and returned Jerry to his cage. She'd put on her Petland uniform and was fixing her nametag to the shirt. "There's a red car out front?" She jostled Tom out of the way and threw open the curtains. "Leslie's here. Give me a sec." She picked up her boots and ran out the door in her sock feet.

"Derek," June shouted.

"I'm right here," he said from behind her, annoyed. "Can we just go?"

"Yes," she said. "We were all waiting for you."

Tom was first out the door, with Derek right behind him.

"I'll drive." June barrelled past both of them and pressed the door-open button on her key, more times than necessary.

"I can't believe I'm going to be a grandpa," Randy said.

Someone had parked too close to the hedge, and the Figgs had to shuffle down the driveway in single file. As June approached the van, Vanessa was already in the back row with her friend. One side of Leslie's head was shaved, while the rest of her hair was arranged into a blond pompadour. Her hairstyle belied her age. Her body language was much too mellow for a woman in her twenties. June could see laugh lines and sunspots. She recognized Leslie's shirt was from a place where only nurses and women in search of common-sense clothing seemed to shop. Last week, Vanessa had bought pre-ripped fishnets from a store that sold Deadpool backpacks and adult onesies.

"Who's that?" Randy whispered.

June whispered back, "Vanessa's friend."

"Her friend?" Randy peered into the back seat. "She's kind of old, no?"

"At least forty," June mouthed.

Randy grimaced. "Why is she coming to the hospital?"

"I don't know." June held on to the door handle. "Maybe you should say something."

"You say something," Randy argued. "You're better at that stuff."

Derek pounded on the window from inside. "We have to go."

They jumped and wrestled open their doors. June adjusted the steering wheel and mouthed *say something* to Randy.

He fiddled with his buckle. "Hi, Leslie. It's a . . . it's nice of you to join us."

"Hello," Leslie said politely.

June put the van into reverse, the seats behind her full of knees. "Vanessa, honey, don't you have to work today?"

"Not until later. Leslie and I will just hang out in the cafeteria."

The street was empty.

"Who's Marissa?" Randy asked. "Have we met her?"

"No." Derek stared out the window.

"Is she a girlfriend?"

Tom and Vanessa laughed.

"Fuck off." Derek pulled his hat down. "She used to work next door to the depot."

"That's Blond Marissa," Vanessa offered.

"She worked at the Christian bookstore?" Randy tugged at his salt-and-pepper beard.

"The carpet store," June said. Her eyes met Derek's in the rear-view mirror.

"Yes," Derek confirmed. "Carpet One."

June turned left. She knew exactly who Marissa was. Last summer she'd surprised Derek at work so he wouldn't have to take the bus home, and he was having sex on one of the recycling depot's slanted aluminum counting tables. Her six-foot-two baby boy with the skinny girl who worked next door. June had recognized her orange Carpet One T-shirt despite the fact it was bunched up around her neck like a loop scarf, the ends of her blond hair wet like paintbrushes, dangling over her son's chest. Derek frantically sucking on her fingers like a giant baby farm animal. It was not unlike the way he used to breastfeed. And their movements! So jarring, like they were travelling down a waterslide without the water. It could not have been comfortable, but they just wouldn't stop. Their mouths remained open and drawn to the side like they'd each had a stroke, while cases of empty beer rattled and vibrated on the manual conveyer belt flanking the table.

June shivered. "What hospital is she at?"

"Lougheed," Derek replied.

"Turn right," Randy pointed.

June put on the blinker. "I know how to get there."

For a second, she closed her eyes and tried to remember Derek as a child. How he pulled his sport socks up over his jogging pants. The affectionate way he dismantled his Wagon Wheels. His blue pogo stick. That terrible show with the bouncing lemur he obsessed over. But the moment passed, and instead she recalled the red lace underwear that had been draped over his head like a fast-food hairnet. And his sex face. Stroke face. Fist eater. Pervert. Baby boy. Man. Son. Father?

Randy turned in his seat to face his children. "You know all three of you were born at that hospital?"

Derek stared at his iPhone. "She's one hundred percent effaced and five centimetres diluted."

"Dilated," June said.

"Whatever, it says diluted."

"Autocorrect," Tom sang.

Randy looked worried. "You can read, son, right?"

"Yes, I can read! What kind of question is that?"

"Everyone calm," June said.

"Well, tell Dad to stop asking me stupid questions."

"Guilty." Randy raised his hand.

June raced to make a green light. "To be one hundred percent effaced means her cervix is thin." She searched for a better term. "Ripe."

"Like a big juicy peach," Tom offered.

"Love peaches," Randy said, closing his vents. "Remember the peaches we got in the Okanagan that time? They were as big as grapefruit."

"What the hell does five centimetres dilated mean?"

"Means her hole is this big." Tom approximated the size with his hands.

"Tom," June scolded. "Don't do that."

"What? It's true."

June exhaled. "At ten centimetres she'll be ready to deliver."

Randy sat up straight. "I wonder if it's a boy or a girl."

"Did you not know she was pregnant?" June asked.

"I sort of knew. But not until last week."

"How do you *sort of* know?"

"She sent me a text saying she was eight months pregnant."

"And you couldn't see that earlier?"

"I haven't seen her. She doesn't work at Carpet One anymore."

Tom leaned forward. "How do you know it's yours, bro?"

June wondered the same thing. She pulled up to a red light behind a Hummer.

"Because."

June and Randy turned simultaneously toward Derek.

"Because?" Tom asked.

"Because she said it's mine. I'm the only one she was with at the time."

June ignored Vanessa's raised eyebrows in the back seat.

"You are one hundred percent positive that this is your child and not someone else's?" Randy questioned.

"Yes, okay? She won some stupid singing contest last summer and that's all she does now."

"A singer." Randy smiled.

June tensed.

"Go," Tom hollered from the back. "It's green."

June accelerated too quickly, knocking everyone into their headrests. "A singer?"

"What?" Randy replied. "Maybe the baby will be able to sing. It would be nice to have a singer in the family."

"A singer," she repeated. "It would be nice to have a singer in the family. You know what would be nice to have in the family? Maybe someone with a little ambition. A few life goals."

"Like what? Knocking up a carpet rep? Playing the ukulele?" Tom crossed his arms. "Is it not enough that I own my own company?"

June honked at a man texting in the car beside her. "But don't you want to travel? See the world? Buy a house?"

"With what money? You know how many toilets I need to scrub to pay off my student loan?"

"Can everyone just shut up?" Derek said.

June could see the hospital in the distance. The car fell silent, but it hummed with thought. June didn't know what the others were thinking about, but she was thinking about Marissa. Carpet consultant. Berber buyer. Feeder of fingers and illustrator of sex face. Purveyor of red lace. Of grandchildren. And Derek. She tried to guess how much he made in a week working at the recycling depot, counting bottles by fours, and whether it would be enough to buy diapers. How much were diapers these days? She thought about how small newborn diapers were. No bigger than her hand. And then she stopped thinking and started feeling. Dread. Anticipation. There was going to be a baby. A real baby with toes the size of peas and fuzz on its shoulders.

"So, Leslie," Randy said, shifting again to face the back seat. "What do you do?"

"Dad," Vanessa groaned.

Randy looked at June for direction, then at Vanessa. "What? Is that wrong to ask?"

"I'm a carpenter."

"A carpenter?" Randy looked like he'd witnessed the magic of Christmas. "Did you hear that, June?"

"I heard." June changed lanes toward an exit.

Randy turned nearly 180 degrees in his seat, and was practically sitting on his knees. "I am a carpenter," he said proudly.

"I know." Leslie smiled.

Vanessa rolled her eyes. June drove into the parking lot, below the hospital's looming blue H.

Randy repositioned himself. "A carpenter and a singer," he said wistfully.

2

June pulled up beside the ticket dispenser. She rolled down her window, but she was too far from the machine.

"Shoot." She put the van in park, unbuckled her seatbelt, and climbed partially out the window. The machine made a pleasing mechanical sound that Randy mimicked. June slipped the ticket in the sun visor, and accelerated. The engine revved, but the van refused to move.

"You're still in park," Randy said.

June changed gears, her face hot.

"Seven centimetres!" Derek shouted from the back seat. He had already taken off his seatbelt.

Tom approximated the size with his hands. "That's about this big."

June started driving at the same time the black and white control-barrier gate swung down to its closed position.

Randy shielded his bushy head as the van crashed forward, crudely severing the gate from its post. It landed with a thud on the cement surface of the parkade, splintered and bent, before June slowly rolled over it, everyone bracing for the rise and fall of both sets of tires. An automotive waltz.

Tom slow-clapped.

Randy was speechless, his hand wound tight around the handle above his window.

"That wasn't my fault." June looked for an arrow to tell her which way to turn. "It closed before I had a chance to drive through."

"Because you took too long," Vanessa said, twirling gum around her finger. June went the wrong direction and ended up at a dead end.

"You'll have to back up," Randy suggested.

June attempted to put the van in reverse but instead turned the windshield wipers on high speed.

Tom leaned forward between his parents. "You know they probably have cameras that saw you do that."

"Thomas," Randy said sternly. "Zip it." Randy pressed his thumb and pointer finger together and pretended to zip shut his own lips.

Tom looked out his window. "Just sayin'."

June inched backward until she could turn in the correct direction.

"Eight centimetres." Derek gripped Randy's headrest while gazing wide-eyed at his iPhone. "Stop, Mom. I'm getting out."

Derek left the sliding van door open and made a beeline to the corner stairs.

"Wait!" Randy called after him.

"I'll meet you in there," Derek replied, without turning around.

June crept up two levels of the parkade and pulled into a spot flanked by vacant spaces. She poured sweat and searched for something she could use as a fan. Randy got out of the van and started running. *You Were Chosen* was left behind on his seat. June tried to stuff the book into the glove compartment, but it wouldn't fit. She waved it in front of her face as Vanessa and Leslie climbed out of the back and headed toward the hospital's main entrance. A page fell out of the book and onto June's lap. The paper was yellowed. The text read *"Everyone has a birth mother."* June jammed the page back inside the book and shoved it into her purse, clambering out of the van and closing Randy's door.

The parking garage air was ripe with exhaust and spring. Ahead, patients smoked in wheelchairs. A jaundiced man played the harmonica. He had no legs.

June caught up with everyone when she reached the main reception desk. It was manned by a volunteer wearing a red vest.

"I'm looking for Marissa," Derek stuttered.

The volunteer scanned a sheet in front of him. "Last name?"

"S-s-s-simms or Simmonds . . . Simons! Simons?"

Randy frowned. "You don't know her last name?"

"Labour and delivery," June interrupted.

The man raised his eyebrows. "Third floor." He pointed toward the elevators.

Randy rushed ahead to push the button, and then positioned himself so that he was equidistant from both elevators. Vanessa and Leslie headed down a corridor marked *cafeteria*.

"Tom, text me," Vanessa said, before rounding the corner. She paused and looked at Derek. "Good luck, little brother. Break a vagina."

When the elevator to Randy's left dinged, he charged towards it.

"Dad," Derek said. *"I'm* the one having the baby."

Randy stepped back when the door opened, but then hurried in before a nurse and a patient hanging onto an iv pole were able to get out. He held the door and ushered the remainder of the family inside. Before June had a chance to turn around, Randy had already pressed the *close door* button and was staring hopefully at the floor indicator lights.

There was a notice promoting a breastfeeding clinic fixed to the wall. It was written in four different languages. Was Marissa going to breastfeed?

The elevator opened on the third floor. June grabbed Randy by the elbow as he attempted to get off first.

"What are you doing? It's not like you can go in the delivery room."

Randy stopped and waved for Derek to go ahead. Tom followed, texting as he walked.

"He needs to do this on his own," June said.

Derek stared at a series of wall placards. Behind him, Randy was motioning wildly toward the labour and delivery reception desk. Derek used his finger to scroll down the sign.

"There," Randy jumped in. "Reception. That way." He pointed down the hall.

June smacked his arm.

"He was taking too long," Randy whispered.

Derek set off for the double doors and stopped at a desk that was still decorated for Easter. A row of pastel eggs, like paper dolls, dangled from the front, and a green and pink woven basket was set to the side. It was filled with grass and a family of stuffed chicks. June plucked one out of the basket and separated the coarse yellow fur around its face. "Where are its eyes?" she asked, placing it back and examining another.

"Mom, what are you doing?" Tom unwrapped a stick of gum.

"These chicks don't have eyes." She went for a third chick but was interrupted by a long hideous groan, followed by intermittent yelps.

Tom froze. "What the hell was that?"

June put the chick back in the basket and buried it, along with its siblings, under the grass. The noises continued. This time from another woman. First screaming, followed by a long droning growl. Like a Doberman was trapped in her diaphragm.

Tom laughed loudly, arousing sneers from a clerk stationed behind the desk. She balanced a phone between her shoulder and ear.

June raised her finger. "That," she pointed, "is the sound of labour. Respect it."

"It's just . . . did you hear the last part?" Tom imitated the growling sound.

June ignored him, and looked around for Randy and Derek. "Where did they go?"

Tom peered down the opposite hallway from the noise and shrugged. June went around the other side of the desk where another hall branched out in two directions. To the right, she saw Randy on his toes, straining to see inside a delivery room. June joined him.

They heard a woman's voice. "You're ten centimetres," she said. "In a few minutes, we're going to start pushing this baby out."

A sob. "I can't."

"Marissa," the woman continued. "I need you to listen to me. It's time. You can do this. Just remember to breathe, and don't push until I tell you to."

Marissa cried. June pushed the door open wider. From this angle she could see Derek. He had taken off his hat and was standing at Marissa's side, his fingers splayed across her shoulder. She could only see a bit of Marissa's face, which was puffy and wet and terrified. June was suddenly angry. Where was Marissa's mother? Her father?

"Okay," a different voice said. "On the next contraction I want you to push down as hard as you can. Like you're having a bowel movement."

Tom repeated, "Like you're having a bowel movement," and laughed.

"Go wait with your sister," June ordered.

Tom surrendered, and left.

June hugged herself. "Where is Marissa's mother?"

"I don't know." Randy pushed the door open a little further.

"On three," the voice commanded. "One . . . two . . . three. Push, Marissa! Come on, Marissa."

"Come on," Derek added faintly.

June looked up and down the hall nervously. "Are we allowed to be here?"

Minutes went by. The cheerleading continued. There were messy exhales and clenched forearms. A nurse left the bedside and returned seconds later with a cloth. Underneath the bed, amongst the clogged feet of Marissa's team, was a pair of black Converse sneakers with neon orange laces that were dirty and frayed. June wondered if they were Marissa's. Her Carpet One sneakers? Her singer ones? Her playground shoes? She worried they would be left behind. She focused on the sneakers.

"I see some hair, Marissa!"

"Hair?" Marissa repeated, her voice like a pixie.

"Lots of it," the doctor replied. "We're getting there, Marissa. I need you to stay with me. Focus."

Focus, June thought. She zeroed in on the shoes again, tuning out Marissa's whimpers. Randy jumped beside her. "It has hair!" he whispered jubilantly. The rubber toes of the sneakers were supposed to be white, but one of them had been coloured in pink, and there were ink lines drawn on top. Were they words? A symbol? She squinted. Imagined what was there, and then she blinked, and when she looked again she saw Derek's face. Why was Derek under the bed?

"Derek!" June cried, grabbing Randy by the arm. "He fainted."

A nurse attended to Derek.

June nudged Randy. "Go, help her!"

"How am I supposed to help her? I can't go in there."

"Go!"

Randy pushed the door wide open.

"That's my son," he announced.

The nurse acknowledged Randy with a nod. "It's common," she waved. "Some of them faint."

"The head is almost out," the doctor said. "On this next push, Marissa . . ."

The nurse returned to the foot of the bed and grabbed one of Marissa's feet.

Derek propped himself up on his elbows. His face was greenish white. An awful colour, like the dirty aquarium glass at Vanessa's work. Pistachio ice cream. June summoned for Derek to get up, but Randy misunderstood and grabbed his son by the ankles and attempted to drag him out of the delivery room.

"What are you doing?" June crept into the room.

"I thought . . ."

"Derek, get up!"

He looked stunned.

"Come on," she said. "It's almost time."

June helped her son into to a seated position. She kept her eyes down, wanting to respect Marissa's privacy. How awful, June thought. Marissa couldn't be more than twenty. Instead of a singer, she would be a single mom. Did she own a car or would she be one of those single moms who had to take public transit in the middle of winter, pushing her stroller to and from bus stops, bags of canned goods and homogenized milk dangling from the handles, a gas-station coffee in her hand? And what about work? Who would look after the baby? Would Marissa and Derek trade off, or would she ask a neighbour down the hall who smelled like sausage and was always home because he was under house arrest?

Without another thought, she turned to look at Marissa and came face to face with the baby. A little face with pebble-sized features and the hair of an orangutan. The orangest hair she'd ever seen. The smallest ears. Tiny treble clefs. The rest of the baby's body still shrink-wrapped inside Marissa.

"Oh my gosh," she whispered. "Derek, honey, look. That's your baby." But Derek was on all fours crawling to the bathroom, where Randy was waiting for the delivery to be over. The retching started immediately. Like an idling Mac truck. And distracting. June spun around. "Can't you be a little quieter?"

But Derek continued, and when she turned back around, Marissa was empty. There was silence for one second, two.

Then as though it had been orchestrated, Derek and his offspring commenced a duet. He on the stomach tuba, the baby on a tiny broken reed.

"It's a boy," the doctor announced.

"I'm a grandpa!" Randy shouted from the bathroom.

June looked at Marissa, who was sobbing, alone, as nurses attended to the baby on a nearby table. She approached the bedside and took hold of Marissa's hands. Her trembling hands, and for a moment June thought about her own birth mother. Had her hands also trembled? Had she, too, given birth alone, her church shoes all scratched up and toppled under the bed, while her father was back in the suburbs building a bicycle ramp?

"You did it," June said, exhaling hard and squeezing Marissa's hands. "Like a pro."

Derek groaned from the bathroom, while Randy ruffled his son's hair. June took a Kleenex from her purse, a soft one with lotion, and handed it to Marissa. Marissa wiped her eyes, while the baby screamed on the table, fists suspended in the air. Derek attempted to stand. He was on one knee, hanging onto the bathroom doorknob. June motioned for Randy to wait outside. He obliged, sidestepping with his back to Marissa while the placenta slipped out, completing the birth.

"Sit down, Derek." June turned the room's only chair to face the bed.

He stumbled over and fell heavily into the moss-green vinyl cushion.

"Six pounds, eight ounces." The nurse wrote on a chart. She picked the infant up, swaddled him into a tidy bundle and handed him to Marissa. "Here you go, Mom. He's a beauty."

June stood beside Derek and watched Marissa, who held the baby awkwardly up by her shoulder. Marissa wept quietly and mouthed the word *mom* as she stared at the little face.

"Can I hold him?" Derek asked, and for a second June was ready to answer. She was the mom. It was her permission Derek normally sought.

"Go ahead," Marissa replied.

Derek stood up and reached for the baby, his arms long and veiny, and then he carefully sat back down in the chair, cradling the baby's head like it was a glass ornament. "He's so small."

"He has your red hair," June said. "My hair."

"Can I come in?" Randy called politely from the hall.

Again, June held her tongue. Marissa, blanketed from the waist down, nodded.

"Yes," June replied.

Randy rushed into the room and stared at his grandson.

"Marissa, he's perfect!" Randy said.

"Perfect?" she repeated.

"One hundred percent."

One hundred percent, June considered. An elephant's faith according to Dr. Seuss. Perfect. But it wasn't perfect. Derek and Marissa weren't even in a relationship. He worked in a bottle depot. Marissa was someone else's daughter. Another grandma would dispense advice, and maybe it would be wrong and her grandson would end up with a flat head or rotten teeth. Or maybe he, too, would be chosen.

3

When Marissa decided to breastfeed, Derek saw his parents out.

"We'll be in the cafeteria," Randy said.

June gave Derek a Gravol as a porter wheeled a patient into the room across the hall.

When they reached the elevators, Randy and June stood for a minute before either thought to press the button.

"I can't believe it." Randy stared into space. "Our son has a son."

"I know," June held her face. "It's almost unreal."

"Except he looks just like Derek."

"Exactly like him."

Randy looked worried. "Do you think they'll raise him together?"

"I don't know." The elevator opened. "I don't know anything."

Randy took her hand, and it helped her breathe. They went in silence to the ground floor of the hospital, passing sad-eyed people on stretchers and clumps of families wielding foil balloons. The cafeteria smelled like fries and disinfectant.

Randy looked around. "Do you see the kids?"

June saw Leslie's platinum blond hair lit by a sunbeam. "By the window," she pointed.

Randy brightened and hurried to the table. "It's a boy!"

"I can't believe he has a kid," Vanessa said. She was halfway through a plate of pasta. A piece of wet penne dropped from her mouth to the floor. Next to her, Leslie ate orange Jell-O with a plastic spoon.

"Jell-O," Randy said. "I haven't had Jell-O since Tom had his wisdom teeth out. I'm going to get some."

"Does the baby have a name?" Tom flapped his shirt to air out his armpits.

"No," June replied. "At least, I don't think so. Randy, does he have a name?"

"Not yet." Randy pulled a twenty-dollar bill from his wallet. "Do you want anything?"

"A salad, please." She turned to Vanessa. "He has red hair."

Tom called after his father. "Can you grab me a slice of pizza?"

June unzipped her purse and pulled out a bottle of water. She wondered if Marissa was going to let Derek have any part in naming the baby. She hoped he would have a normal name. Nothing too trendy, like Jayden or Braden or Caden.

"Will Derek have the baby on weekends?" Vanessa asked.

"What do you mean?"

"Like visitation rights," Tom explained.

"They're not divorced."

"You know what I mean. Is he going to get to see the baby?"

"I hope so."

Randy returned with a tray of food.

"Do you think we can go see him?" Vanessa pushed her empty plate to the side and placed her hand on top of Leslie's. Leslie had taken off her plaid shirt, revealing a sleeve of faded Celtic tattoos. Vanessa traced a harp with her fingertip.

June stared. Vanessa had always been single. In front of her was a couple.

"Why don't you text him?" Randy wrestled a blob of Jell-O into his mouth.

Vanessa squeezed Leslie's hand and then pulled out her iPhone. The case had a picture of a cat wearing a dress and bonnet. Her daughter tapped away at the phone's surface. Seconds later, it pinged.

"He says we can see him, but it has to be quick because the nurse wants Marissa to rest."

Randy said, "Ask him if the baby has a name."

Vanessa obliged. The table waited in silence for the reply. Vanessa slid her phone into the middle for everyone to see. For thirty seconds, nothing. Then a pale grey speech bubble appeared around an ellipsis. And then the name: *Jazz*.

"Jazz?" June questioned.

But another speech bubble appeared. *Not Jazz. Jaxx.*

"Jaxx?" Randy said.

"With two x's?"

"J-A-X-X," Vanessa read aloud.

"Why not just one x?"

"I like it." Tom drizzled salad dressing on his pizza crust. "Sounds like a porn star."

June frowned.

"That Jell-O was better than I remembered."

"Let's just go," June said. "Before it's too late."

"But you've barely touched your food."

"I'm not hungry. Are you coming?"

Randy cleared the table. "Why don't I stay with Leslie and you three go."

"Fine. You can get the van."

June led her kids to the elevator. It was empty.

"How big is he?" Vanessa stooped to see her reflection in the elevator's mirrored panel.

"He's little. Six pounds. And he has the tiniest features. The reddest hair," she said, watching Vanessa preen. She noticed that her daughter was wearing blush. Vanessa usually wore makeup with colours called "black mould" or "anthrax." The swath of pink was refreshing. "You know, that really lightens your face."

Vanessa reddened and adjusted the ears on her headband. "Leslie gave it to me."

"It's pretty." It had been a while since June used the word *pretty* in association with her daughter. "You and Leslie seem very close."

"Maybe." Vanessa was coy, but her happiness was palpable. As if Santa's workshop was operating inside her chest.

Tom read his phone. "Shit," he said. "I missed a delivery."

"Go-Kleen!" Vanessa said, mimicking the Go-Kleen info-mercial.

"No, something else." He swore.

The elevator opened, and June led Vanessa and Tom down the hall to room 316. The door was ajar.

"It's just us," June whispered. "Mom and Tom and Vanessa." She could see Derek rummaging through a bag. He held up a diaper shirt covered in sailboats.

"This one?" he asked Marissa.

Marissa replied, "Sure, whatever."

Derek waved them in.

"Marissa, this is my sister, Vanessa, and my brother, Tom."

Marissa and Vanessa looked at each other with vague familiarity. Tom fondled a bag hanging from Marissa's IV pole.

"And this is Jaxx." Derek pushed the plastic bassinette toward his sister like it was a room-service cart. Vanessa bent down to stare at her nephew, and she did something that surprised everyone in the room. She cried.

4

When they returned from the hospital, June flopped on the couch, unable to face the basement.

Tom stood in the fridge and ate leftovers. He'd changed into a new work shirt. "Can I take the van tonight? It's a new client. Got to bring the shop-vac." He wiped coleslaw from his chin. "It won't fit in the car."

"You can, or I'm sure your dad will drive you. Weren't you supposed to be getting yours back today?"

He shook his head. "Still waiting for a part. They had to order it in from Florida."

June forced herself up and finally removed her coat. "Your father's downstairs. Give him a heads up."

Tom nodded, closed the fridge door, and drifted away. Outside, Vanessa said goodbye to Leslie. June watched them from the window. They leaned in at precisely the same time to kiss. Then they hugged, and it was the kind of hug June would have wanted to clap and cheer for, if it hadn't been between Vanessa and a woman old enough to be her mother.

"I'd say they're more than friends." Randy rested his chin on her shoulder. He smelled like yogurt.

"Looks that way." June turned from the window and went back to the kitchen.

Growing up, Vanessa had shown no interest in boys or girls. She spent her time raising money for no-kill shelters and holding funerals for roadkill in the front yard. Her only crush had been on the SeaWorld mascot.

"It's good, right?" Randy tossed the yogurt cup and pulled himself up on the counter, his back hunched into the letter c. The overhead track light illuminated the wool hairs on his socks.

"I mean, yeah. It's great that she seems to finally be in a relationship with someone, but why does Leslie have to be so old? Why couldn't Vanessa have found a young, energetic lesbian? Like that nice Ashley who teaches kickboxing down at the community centre, or the produce manager at Sobeys."

"I don't think it's that big of a deal." Randy opened the fridge. "I'm just happy she's not alone. Remember her prom?"

June put her hand up. "Don't talk about the prom." She wiped crumbs from the counter. "I just always pictured Vanessa with a really nice, bright man. Like an activist. You know? Someone like Don Cheadle."

"Don Cheadle? You mean with a man."

"Yes, I mean a man. But also a man like Don Cheadle. Or the guy who does the six o'clock news and organizes all those charity runs for animals."

"Brent Barry? Geez, I think he's gay." Randy slid off the counter. "I'm just happy Leslie isn't a stuffie. Remember Vanessa wanted to marry Ralph the elephant?"

"He was a rhinoceros, yes. And Brent Barry isn't gay."

"Ralph was a rhinoceros?" Randy put his arm around her. "I like Leslie."

June freed herself to put away the can opener. "You should have seen Vanessa when she saw Jaxx. She actually cried. Real tears. When's the last time you saw Vanessa cry?"

"Babies have that effect on people. How could you not look at a newborn and be in total awe? Did you see how tiny his fingernails were? And his feet?" Randy cupped his hands together like he was holding a wounded bird. "It really takes a miracle — the timing, the conditions — everything. I mean *everything* has to align perfectly."

June sighed. He was right. She thought of Jaxx's heaving chest and his waxy wrinkled lips. His string-bean fingers. She smiled. It was probably exactly what Vanessa felt when she looked upon her nephew. That he was a miracle. June tried not to think of the perfect conditions that led to his creation — the slant of the depot's counting table, the angle of Derek's bare white hips, the arch of Marissa's back. "You think Vanessa will ever want kids?"

"I don't know." Randy paced. "Haven't ever really thought about it."

The back door opened. Vanessa barged through and dumped her jacket in the entryway. "Mom, you parked in the hedge again."

"I did not," June said.

"I pretty much had to crawl over the hood."

Randy placed a head on his daughter's shoulder. "Hello, Aunt Vanessa."

Vanessa went to Jerry's cage. "If I ever get to see him."

Randy frowned. "What's that supposed to mean?"

Jerry danced on his trapeze.

"Dad, they're not even together. You really think we're going to get to see him?" June wondered if this was why Vanessa had cried at the hospital. Maybe it was true. They'd all be shut out and Jaxx would have his own family. Marissa's family.

"Do you know Marissa?" June asked. "At the hospital, you seemed to know her."

"Not really. Asian Marissa was in my chemistry class. All I know about Baby-Mama Marissa is that she used to work at Carpet One."

Randy changed the subject. "Is Brent Barry gay?"

"The news guy? Does all those marathons and wears those stupid motivational headbands? No."

"Huh." Randy crossed his arms.

June poured herself a drink. "Told you he wasn't gay."

Vanessa ate a handful of peanuts. "Fuck, no." She flicked open the latch on Jerry's cage. Her fingernails were painted purple. "As for Marissa, I've met her a few times. Carpet One donates their scraps to Petland. We use them to line the rabbit cages and some of the cat enclosures at work." Jerry climbed onto her shoulder. Vanessa pursed her lips. A tiny whistle escaped. Faint but harmonic. A hobbit's kettle.

"But Derek's the father." Randy reasoned. "Of course we'll see him. Fathers have rights . . . right?"

"Not if they're not married." Vanessa took another handful of peanuts. Jerry puffed his back feathers and pecked at the string of hardware in her ear. He seemed to be turning the tiny ship's wheel at the bottom of her lobe.

"I don't think they have to be married," June offered. "I think his name just has to appear on the birth certificate."

"Well, did he do that?" Randy touched his pockets for his phone.

Vanessa petted Jerry's head. "Dad, chill. He was only born an hour ago. Anyway, if you haven't already figured it out, Leslie and I are together. I thought you guys should know so it doesn't get all weird and shit."

"It's not weird." Randy put on his coat. "She seems very nice, and *hello*, she's a carpenter."

"I knew you'd like that." Vanessa kissed Jerry's beak and transferred the bird onto her finger.

"What's weird is that your mother thought you'd want to marry Don Cheadle."

"I said someone like him," June corrected.

"Don Cheadle? He's, like, fifty."

"And how old's Leslie?" June slipped a piece of lettuce into Jerry's cage.

"Tom, let's go!" Randy hollered.

Vanessa didn't respond. She ushered Jerry back onto his dowel trapeze. "I'm goin' upstairs."

"Wait." Randy followed. "Do you think Leslie would help me make a cradle for Jaxx? I haven't made one in years."

"Maybe." Vanessa pulled her phone out and proceeded up the stairs with less stomping than normal.

"Thomas!" Randy yelled. "Let's go."

June flinched. "You're driving him, then?"

Tom appeared from the hall, shop-vac in tow.

Randy struggled to slip into his shoes. They were still tied. "Yes, and then I'm going back to the hospital."

"What for?"

"To make sure Derek puts his name on the birth certificate."

Tom kissed June on the cheek. "Bye, Mom."

"Have a good shift," she said, following him through the back door with the shop-vac cord.

June watched them get into the van, Randy's feet still not completely in his shoes, and then she slumped back onto the couch. She thought about Vanessa and Leslie. Up until now the word *lesbian* was just a word with a lot of curves that got stuck in her throat. June repeated it in her head so many times it became other words — thespian, amphibian, librarian. She thought of that hug. Their kiss. How their fingers linked into a fat baseball and the way their forearms touched. Now the word had meaning. Now it had life. Vanessa Joy Figg, *Lesbian*. To go with Derek Arnold Figg, *Father*.

5

Someone had already made coffee when June got up the next morning. She poured herself a cup and tied her robe. Randy called from the living room, "Honey, come check this out."

June yawned and went to Randy. He was sitting in a faded green sandbox shaped like a turtle, and dressed in his woodworking clothes.

"Remember this?" He leaned back and caressed the edges.

"Yes," June replied. "What's it doing in the living room?"

"I was working on the basement and found it tucked in the crawlspace under the stairs." He was pleased. "I was going to throw it out, but instead I'm going to clean it up and save it for Jaxx. The kids loved it."

June remembered. Derek in particular. He had pushed his blue dump truck through it with the sound effects of a vehicle travelling in reverse. A slow and high-pitched *beep, beep, beep*, though he always moved it forward, crushing things in its wake. Plastic shovels, Vanessa's lumpy legs. Tom's Millennium Falcon.

Randy heaved himself out and beckoned June to follow him to the kitchen where he poured himself cereal.

"Want some?"

"No, thanks." She carved a grapefruit in half. "Did Derek come back yet?"

"He was going to spend the night at the hospital."

She touched Randy's shoulder. "Why were you up so early?"

"Well, aside from working on the basement and fixing up that sandbox, I'm building a cradle. I found a great design online. Wanna see it?"

She sprinkled sugar over the grapefruit and nodded.

Randy put down his spoon and dug out a piece of paper from his pocket, placing the drawing in front of her. It was a traditional-style cradle. Pencil measurements were scrawled all over it.

"I don't think people use these kinds of cradles anymore."

Randy snatched the paper back. "Don't use cradles? Of course they still use cradles."

"Not wooden ones. They use bassinettes that vibrate."

"That's silly," he said, heading for the basement. "It's probably not that people don't use them anymore, it's more likely that nobody knows how to make them."

June shrugged and slurped her coffee. "Wait," she called. "Did Derek get his name on the birth certificate?"

"Not yet," Randy thumped down the stairs. "They hadn't received the paperwork, but he will."

June went to the fridge for cream, when Derek barrelled through the door. His eyes were bloodshot, and last night's T-shirt was stretched and sagging beneath his unzipped coat. There was something white on his hat.

"Diaper paste," Derek explained.

"Coffee?" June held up the pot.

He shook his head and grabbed a can of Mountain Dew from the pantry. "I'm so tired, Mom." He gulped crudely. "Marissa puked all over the bed, and Jaxx was up every two hours. Plus, they stuck this big fucking needle in his foot."

"That's all normal," June assured. "It's not easy, but normal."

"That's what the nurse said." Derek belched. "Excuse me."

June refilled her coffee. "How's Jaxx eating? Is Marissa breastfeeding?"

"Heck, no, he hated it. Totally prefers a bottle."

June cringed. "Breastfeeding takes time, Derek. It's not that Jaxx doesn't like breast milk; it's more that he has to learn how. Babies have to learn how to latch."

"Nah, Marissa said some babies just don't like it. Can you make me an omelette?"

June collapsed into a chair. "Let me finish my coffee first."

"Thanks, Mom." He took off his hat and ran his fingers through his hair. "I'm taking a shower."

June cracked eggs into a bowl. She thought of Jaxx drinking formula because he didn't like breast milk. Where were the nurses? Why weren't they helping Marissa breastfeed? Why hadn't the La Leche League surrounded Marissa's bed the way they had circled hers? Next Derek would be feeding him Sunny D through a syringe.

Randy tapped her on the shoulder.

"Randy, you have to stop doing that."

"Are you crying?"

"They're feeding him formula."

"Honey, formula isn't the end of the world. You gave Vanessa formula."

"Only because I couldn't produce enough milk. Marissa's convinced Derek that Jaxx doesn't like breast milk. What next? Is she going to tell him that Jaxx prefers to sleep on his face or that he prefers riding his car seat shotgun?"

"He'll be fine, June. Millions of kids drink formula every day. In fact, you probably drank formula." He paused. June knew it was true.

"I mean, most of us did at some point," Randy fumbled. "Besides, it's better now than it used to be."

June ate a handful of chocolate chips.

Randy placed a hand on her back. "Can you help me?" He thrust a different cradle pattern in front of her. "What does this part say?"

June squinted at the small print. "Thirty-two-point-five inches."

Randy grabbed a marker from the junk drawer and wrote the measurement in large numbers. Sawdust covered his plaid shirt like autumn snow. "That's what I thought." He kissed her and retreated back to the basement.

June dabbed her eyes with a tissue and chopped a tomato. She pulled a slab of ham from the fridge and picked apart slices. The phone rang over the buzz of Randy's table saw. She waited for a break in his work, then picked up the cordless, hands smelling like pig, a smattering of tomato seeds on her robe.

"Hello?"

"June!" It was her friend Birte. "Earle and I were just sitting here at the breakfast table and it occurred to us that we haven't seen you since Christmas."

June plucked the seeds from her robe. "Has it been that long?"

"How about dinner tonight?"

June stared at the ribs she'd taken out, thawing on the counter. "Sure. What time?"

"Whatever works," Birte replied. "We're just going to order in. Earle's knee's bugging him again. It keeps giving out. Honest to God, it's fine one minute and seconds later he's limping like I don't know what, something that limps." Birte's voice faded. "Earle, what's something that limps?"

June set a pan on the stove. "Dinner sounds great. We'll bring dessert."

"Perfect," Birte replied. "We bought some new lattes for the Keurig."

June hung up and pushed the eggs around the pan. Birte and Earle were one of those happy couples that met later in life, making them both grateful and smiley and affectionate. They held hands when they grocery shopped. He watched her paint. And they kissed all the time. June had noticed the latter at their Christmas party. No other couples kissed, let alone like bus-stop teenagers. Instead they only nudged each other to top up a wine or find a heartburn pill.

Derek returned to the kitchen barefoot.

"Here's your omelette," June said, sliding it onto a plate.

"Thanks." He slicked his hair under a toque and finished in three bites. "I was starving."

"Are you heading back to the hospital?"

"Yeah, but I have to go get a car seat first. Can I borrow the car?"

"Keys are hung up." She gestured to the wall. "Do you know how to buy a car seat?"

"I ask for an infant one, because apparently there's different kinds."

"Do you have money?"

"Yeah."

"You sure?"

"Yes, Mom." He pulled his toque over his face the way he had as a child when he was irritated.

"Dad and I are going to Earle and Birte's tonight, but I'll throw something in the slow cooker."

He grabbed his jacket from the back door and took the keys off the pegboard Randy had built. "Cool. I'll text you later."

June cleared Derek's plate. The sound of Randy's table saw had been replaced with the radio. She warmed her coffee in the microwave and carried it to the basement. Vanessa's stuffed animals had not been put away and were having a séance. She called, "How's the cradle coming?"

There were a dozen planks strewn across the workshop floor and a half-eaten pear balanced on the drafting table. Meatloaf bellowed from the radio.

"I'm on the computer," Randy replied.

June kicked away the same board game she'd moved yesterday. "Are you looking for another pattern?"

He jumped a little, and swivelled in his chair. "Trying to figure out how to do something." He tipped his head up and down as though his glasses were an obstacle, and then punched the keyboard with his finger. He spent hours trolling online woodworking forums with the screen name WOODNINJA. "I don't like the head and footboards on the last one I printed." He closed the screen.

June picked up a ping-pong racket. The rubber coating had been scraped off. Someone had set the other paddle on fire. June tugged at the net. "Wonder if we should put this in a yard sale?"

Randy unbuttoned his shirt and placed it on the back of the chair, his face flushed.

"You okay?"

"It's hot down here." His undershirt had sweat marks. "Had the saw going all morning. Is Derek still here? I want to show him this new pattern."

"He went to get a car seat."

"How's Jaxx, other than drinking formula?"

"Fine, I think. They're all just tired." June replaced the lid on one of the boxes containing her mother's belongings. There were about six boxes in total, most of them jam-packed with old photographs, faded recipes and papers, the furniture long gone when they sold her house and moved her into the nursing home. "Birte and Earle invited us for dinner tonight. I said we'd bring dessert."

Randy placed a ruler on the crib pattern. "Should I make cookies?"

"I'll just pick something up."

"But I always make them." He took his glasses off and cleaned the lenses. "I need a break from the cradle. It's more intricate than I thought."

"What are we going to do about this baby?"

Randy threw his hands up. "What can we do?"

June looked around the room. "I guess I'll keep working on the basement. Can you send Vanessa down to help?" She picked up Randy's plaid shirt and tossed it in a laundry bin.

"I can try."

June put on rubber gloves and opened a bin filled with Lego. She fished out an empty chip bag and a hardened sock and moved the bin to the sell pile. She opened another box full of old computer stuff. A noose of cords, a keyboard, and a mouse the size of a catcher's mitt.

"What am I supposed to do with this?"

"With what?" Vanessa was at the bottom of the stairs eating a cinnamon bun.

"These computer parts."

"Make Tom deal with it. Most of that stuff is his." She tied her Petland apron and batted her hair away from her face. "I only have fifteen minutes."

"The stuffed animals," June pointed. "Do something with them first."

"I'm not getting rid of them."

"Then pack them up and find a place for them in your room. They're not staying down here."

Vanessa sat on the floor and shoved the animals into a garbage bag.

"What about your candle-making stuff?"

"What about it?"

"Keeping or selling?"

"I don't know, selling, I guess."

"Then move it over there."

Vanessa kicked the box into the corner. "Can I have this?" She held up a blender.

June rifled through a box of winter gear. Some of the hats had pom-poms. "The blender upstairs works better. What do you want it for?"

"I just want it."

"Then take it up to your room."

Vanessa hurled the bag of stuffed animals over her back and tucked the blender under her arm. "I can't do any more today or I'll be late."

When Vanessa was gone, June moved a stack of Tom's unused textbooks into the giveaway pile and removed her gloves. She picked up her ukulele and strummed it. She wished she'd bought the mahogany one. The phone rang. It was Derek.

"Got the car seat. It was two hundred bucks."

"They aren't cheap." She pulled her music stand closer. "Are you back at the hospital?"

"Yeah, and the doctor said Marissa could go home this afternoon as long as Jaxx doesn't lose any more weight. They're going to weigh him again in about an hour."

"That's good, Derek. Keep up with that formula."

June hung up the phone. *Go home*, she considered. Where was Jaxx's home? Did he have a home? Did he have a crib? Why was he losing weight? She still hadn't heard about Marissa's parents. She closed her book of sheet music and placed her ukulele on the floor.

6

Randy stood in front of the vanity in his underwear. His legs were the colour of mashed potatoes. The dresser drawers were open.

"Just something casual," June said. "They're ordering in."

He picked his favourite golf shirt, which was yellow and too long because he bought it on clearance from a store intended for tall men. June put on jeans. They were tighter than she remembered.

"You think we'll have time to see Jaxx before dinner?"

June checked her watch. "Probably not. Derek said they might go home today, but that was hours ago and he hasn't called."

Randy finger-combed his beard. "Well if they're still there, maybe we can drop in on the way back?"

June straightened the pillows on their bed even though they smelled like workshop. "We can call him when we're leaving." She closed their bedroom door and bumped into Tom.

"How come you're home? I thought you were going out?"

Tom shrugged. He was holding a puzzle. "I don't know. What's the point?"

"What's that supposed to mean?"

He shrugged again. "What's the point of doing anything?"

"If you're bored you can come with us to Birte's."

"I was thinking of going to visit Grandma. Thought I'd bring her this puzzle." He held up the box. It was of an English garden. June had found it yesterday in the basement closet.

"I'm sure she'd love that." June fixed the collar on her shirt. "You know, she finished the little barnyard one I brought her last time in only two days."

Tom forced a smile and wandered down the hall.

Randy tucked in his shirt. "What was that all about?"

June grabbed her purse. "I don't know. He seems kind of depressed."

Randy waved goodbye to Jerry and then followed June to the driveway, carrying a container of macaroons. "I think he took all that ambition talk personal."

"It wasn't aimed at him, specifically." The sun was blinding, so June put on her big sunglasses.

Randy pulled down the visor. "He's working a ton of hours, and he's nowhere close to paying off his debt." He gazed out the window. A man was jackhammering the sidewalk. "I think he's struggling a bit with his masculinity."

"Tom? But he's very masculine."

"In the traditional sense, yeah. But it's different now. Men of our generation were raised to provide. To figure things out. To get things working."

June bumped over a pothole and stopped at a red light. Hadn't they raised Tom to do the same? "He fixed the suction problem in the upright vacuum," she said. "And he taught himself how to make a panini."

"I taught him that."

June frowned.

"It's more than that. Men nowadays don't have enough to provide even if they wanted to. Why do you think they all still live at home?"

June immediately worried about Derek. Wasn't it worse when you didn't have enough to provide when there was actually someone who needed provision? "At least he doesn't have a baby."

"That might be part of the problem. Tom has nothing to define him. Our grandfathers had war. Our fathers got jobs straight out of university. Tom has a vacuum."

June pulled into Birte's driveway, troubled. Earle was on the front steps watering a bush.

"I just found my ring." Earle set down a watering can, held up his hand and showed off a thick gold band. "Thought I'd lost it, but found it right here when the snow melted. Been there all winter." Earle polished the ring with the flap of his dress shirt, exposing a ring of brown belly.

Randy stared and sucked in his gut. "Earle, you must have lost thirty pounds."

Birte pushed open the screen door and wrapped her arms around her husband from behind. "Doesn't he look great?" Her body was egg shaped, her limbs small and thick. "Hi, Junie." She winked.

Earle kissed Birte on each cheek, leaving wet marks. "Come on in."

Inside, Birte peeked from the galley kitchen, holding up a bottle of white wine. "Can I get anyone a glass?" The couple's tabby padded by, licking its chops.

"Sure," Randy and June replied in unison.

Birte disappeared from view and returned with two glasses of wine. She set them on the coffee table. "So, what's all the news?" She plunked down on a loveseat and tucked her knees up. Earle rested his hand on her thigh.

"Actually, we have some exciting news to share." Randy stood up and then hunched over the coffee table to make a drum roll.

Earle, about to eat a chip, paused.

"We're grandparents!" Randy said. "We have a grandson!" He clasped his hands together.

"Well, congratulations!" Earle dipped his chip. "Fantastic news."

"Whose baby?" Birte asked.

"Derek's," June croaked.

"Derek's? Get out of here!" Birte said. "You never told us he was expecting a baby."

"It was a surprise," Randy offered.

"What a great idea." Earle picked up another tortilla.

"Not that kind of surprise," June said.

Birte raised her eyebrows and lowered her eyes. Her Nordic skin flushed a deep pink. Blood on snow. "Who is she?"

"Her name's Marissa. She and Derek used to work near each other."

Birte asked, "Is he still at the depot?"

"Yes," Randy replied.

"He's good." Earle took a handful of chips. "Fastest one there. I was in a few weeks ago, got Derek, and I was finished before the two people that were ahead of me in line."

June tuned out. She watched the cat, whose name she'd forgotten, weave in and out of the sheer curtains that covered the dining-room window. The cat stopped to lick its front paw, the curtain draped just behind its short triangular ears like a veil, and for a moment June thought back to the day Jaxx had been made on the counting table. The slip-slide of Derek's long body. His sucking Marissa's fingers down to their knuckles. The angle of his knees. She drank her wine.

"Birte and I have some news too," Earle said.

"We do?"

Earle leaned over and whispered in Birte's ear.

"Oh, yes!" she giggled. "We do."

"We're putting the house up for sale and moving into an apartment."

"An apartment?"

"Because —" Earle continued.

"We're buying a place in Phoenix!" Birte interrupted. She let out a small shriek, and then both she and Earle puckered their lips and engaged in a long, hard kiss that bent their noses sideways.

June glanced over at Randy, who had a spot of salsa on his yellow shirt. He leaned forward and shook Earle's hand.

After the Chinese food was delivered, June joined Birte in the kitchen, removing lids from foil containers as Birte emptied the bag.

"So will Derek and Marissa be living together?" Birte arranged the eggrolls on the plate to form a flower.

"I don't know," June said. "We don't know much of anything right now. This all happened yesterday. Last week he was vaping in his room and playing Grand Theft Auto, and today he went out to buy a car seat." June put down a container of chow mein. "But you should see him, Birte. The baby. He looks just like Derek. He's got the red hair and the long limbs."

"I'm sure things will work out." Birte took a wonton. "Derek's a good kid. A responsible kid."

"I just wish things were different."

Birte gave June's arm an encouraging squeeze. "We all do. Actually, that's not really true. I don't want anything to be different. But you know what I mean, Junie. Grandchildren are gifts. Gifts from heaven," she said. "Now let's eat."

A gift from a recycling depot, June thought. A gift that Derek might have trouble sustaining. At least he was an adult, she reasoned, and not fifteen. And he had a job. And Marissa seemed nice, and maybe she was responsible. June filled her plate.

Earle proposed a toast. "To Jaxx," he said.

"To Jaxx," the group repeated.

After dinner, everyone fussed over Earle's selection of coffee pods.

Randy chose French vanilla. Earle limped to the kitchen, the floor creaking under his feet. The cat jumped onto his vacated seat.

"I almost forgot about the fortune cookies," Birte said. She pushed her chair back from the table and joined Earle in the kitchen. June looked at Randy. His arms were crossed and he was slumped forward like he'd eaten too much, but there was a hint of something else in his expression. Contemplation.

"Are you thinking about Jaxx?"

Randy folded his napkin into a square. "I'm thinking about Phoenix. Wouldn't it be nice if we had a place there?"

She pushed her plate to the side. "But you don't even golf, and that's all people do there, is golf."

"Earle doesn't golf."

Earle lumbered into the dining room. "One French vanilla cappuccino," he announced, setting a mug in front of Randy.

"Merci," Randy said.

Earle bowed, tilted his head to the side like an oversized minstrel, and returned to the kitchen.

"And you're not particularly fond of the sun either," June added.

"I like the sun."

"We'd have to sell our place and get an apartment. Could you live in an apartment?"

Randy shrugged. "Any word from Derek?"

June pulled her phone out of her purse. "Nothing. They must be still at the hospital."

"And when are we going to meet this dear grandson?" Birte set a bowl of fortune cookies on the table.

June looked at Randy.

Earle ferried the remaining coffees to the table. He shooed away the cat, and it plunked to the floor with the grace of a bull.

"Ladies first," Birte said, cracking open her cookie. "*Never underestimate the power of the human touch.*" She leaned over the table, and grabbed Earle's face, thumbs pressing into his cheekbones. He leaned in too, cupped the back of her fair, thinning hair, his fingers, thick and mottled brown, pressing into her skull with just a touch of pressure. Finger on an iPad. June turned away and opened her cookie. The resulting cap-gun snap separated Birte and Earle.

"*Love can turn a cottage into a golden palace.*"

Birte clapped. "Isn't that the truth?" she said. "You do have a golden palace. How blessed are you to still have your three kids at home?"

June thought about the golden palace. The hoard in the basement. Vanessa's blue-black hair that clogged the tub. The boys' sneakers that were too big. Elephant shoes. The econo-sized tub of parmesan cheese in the fridge. A wood-panelled palace? A golden institution? She slid the piece of paper under her plate and realized she'd missed Earle's fortune. She gathered by the laughter it had been amusing. Maybe it was irrelevant. Maybe it was generic. Maybe it was true.

"Your turn." Earle slapped Randy on the back.

Randy used a knife to pry open his cookie as though it were an oyster. *"A pleasant surprise is in store for you tonight."*

"Ooh!" Earle laughed.

Birte gently pushed his shoulder and said, "Earle!"

"Not from me," June said over a yawn.

Earle laughed again.

"On that note," Randy said. "We should get back to the golden palace."

June unbuttoned her pants and ate the remainder of her fortune cookie in the van. Randy drove past an art piece that had been carved from a tree stump on someone's front lawn. "See that?"

"Kind of," June said. "It's too dark."

"Leslie did that. It's magnificent. Vanessa said it took Leslie two weeks to complete."

June glanced at the side mirror. A cyclist lit up with a helmet lamp was pedalling furiously behind them. She did not want to go back to the golden palace. She wanted to go where the cyclist was going. Away. Wherever it was he was going. Downtown. Phoenix. Siberia.

"Maybe we really should consider downsizing," June said.

"Yeah?"

"I don't know. We retired for a reason. If we sell the house, we can get a small apartment, and maybe we can get a condo somewhere hot, like Birte and Earle."

"I don't know about Phoenix."

"Doesn't have to be Phoenix. Doesn't even have to be a condo. We could go to Europe or Malaysia. We could take a cruise."

Randy looked at her hopefully. "June, I've always wanted to go on a cruise."

"Then we should do it."

"But the basement. The kids."

"I don't mean right away. But soon. We can fix up the basement, paint the upstairs. People are always looking for four bedrooms up. And we're in walking distance to all the schools."

He gripped the steering wheel. "We should. I mean, once Tom pays off his student loan, he's pretty much ready to move out, and if things work out with Leslie, Vanessa . . ." he trailed off, but his eyes continued to speak. A beautiful story that finished with a cursive *The End*. He pulled into the driveway beside the car. Derek was home. A stack of flyers was on the front step. June picked them up and opened the front door, Randy following behind. Sprawled out in the sandbox on the living-room floor was Derek, his legs and arms draped over the sides of the plastic turtle, and on his chest wrapped in a Pepsi towel, Jaxx, fast asleep.

7

June and Randy stared at each other. Neither said anything. June set the flyers down on the bench and kicked off her shoes. Randy quietly closed the door and tossed his jacket over the flyers. He tiptoed toward the sandbox as Vanessa appeared from the kitchen. She jumped at the sight of her father, and placed her hand on her chest.

"Frig, Dad, you scared me." Dangling from her free hand was a bottle. It was small and plastic, not much taller than a shot glass but wider. The obtuse nipple on the end was clear, not brown as June remembered them. "He has to eat every four hours," Vanessa whispered. "I have to wake them up."

"Why are they sleeping in the sandbox?" Randy asked.

Vanessa rolled her eyes, which had been stripped of make-up. "Do you see a crib anywhere?" She gave the bottle a shake, and got down on one knee close to her brother.

"Wait!" June called out. "You shouldn't wake him. You never wake a sleeping baby."

"Derek said every four hours."

"Yeah, but he's fine. At least give him a little more time. He'll wake up when he's hungry."

Vanessa switched knees and sighed. The formula sloshed inside the bottle, grey and un-milk-like.

Randy paced. "I haven't finished the cradle!"

"You can do it tomorrow." June took off her coat.

"He can't sleep in a sandbox!" Randy continued to pace, and stubbed his toe on the coffee table he'd moved earlier to make way for the turtle. He grabbed his foot and winced.

Vanessa stood up from the floor. "Leslie's bringing over a cradle."

"Leslie?" Randy said. He looked at June. "I told you people still use cradles."

June ignored him. "That's awfully nice of Leslie. Did she say when?"

Vanessa set the bottle on the table and moved to the front window. "She should be here any minute. She made it last night."

"She made it? I'm supposed to be making him one."

"Relax, Dad, she already had one started."

"So did I." He made a beeline for the kitchen.

Vanessa looked at her mother, a hint of doubt registering on her pale face. "*Now* can I wake him up?"

June heard the creak of the basement stairs. The sudden onset of machine noise. Buzzing, clapping, assembling. "He's down there trying to build that cradle."

"Yep," Vanessa said. "The milk's getting cold."

"Let me get him." June stood over Derek. His mouth was open slightly, his neck muscles rigid and pronounced. She slipped her hand under Jaxx's body, and, holding his head, gently turned the infant face up and pulled him into her body, the towel all in a bunch. She carried him to the armchair and settled into its worn tapestry. The baby cocked his head slightly and continued to sleep. Randy appeared in the doorway, out of breath. Bits of sawdust peppered his hair.

"Is Leslie here yet?"

"No," Vanessa answered.

"Sshhhh," June said.

"Good." Randy hurried back downstairs.

June looked at Vanessa. "Why don't you sit?" she suggested. "You look tired."

Vanessa shrugged her shoulders and gave the bottle a shake before plunking down on the couch. There was a hole in her Metallica T-shirt.

June adjusted Jaxx on her shoulder, one hand still wrapped around his grapefruit head. Her fingers looked old and bony. She mourned her younger hands, which were soft and able to open anything.

Upstairs the hall light flicked on, and Tom descended the stairs with a blue towel cinched under his belly fat. His hair dripped.

"Phew," he said, relieved. "It's been over four hours. Who fed him?"

Vanessa scratched at the nail polish on her thumbnail. "Mom won't let us," she chirped.

"Mom? He has to eat. The doctor said every four hours. I'll feed him." He twisted a Q-tip in his ear.

"The bottle's probably cold now," Vanessa said.

"You can't waste it. That shit cost me forty bucks."

"You bought the formula?"

"Well, Derek doesn't have any money."

"He bought the diapers, too," Vanessa added. "I got him the towel."

June looked at Tom. Water continued to trickle down from his hair like an IV drip.

"You can't let him starve."

June looked at Tom and Vanessa. "Have I ever let any of you starve?"

Vanessa looked up from her fingernails. "Marissa and Derek decided Derek would keep the baby."

"What?" June replied.

"They decided he would raise him."

June tried to make sense of the arrangement. The nonchalance in Vanessa's voice. As though Marissa and Derek had agreed to who would go first in a card game. Who would get the comfy chair. She felt her blood gallop to her brain. She lost her breath.

"What do you mean, they decided he would raise the baby?"

"She's going away in the fall," Vanessa explained.

"For music," Tom added, "but she'll be home in the summers."

June held Jaxx tighter. She felt a mix of rage and devastation. Hulk-like, as though her fingers might explode. Like her wedding ring might break off and lodge itself in the popcorn ceiling.

"Marissa's just abandoning him?"

"She said she'd help out on weekends until she goes to school," Tom said, twisting the Q-tip, like a pencil in a sharpener, in his other ear.

"Help out on weekends? That's not parenting. You say that like we're talking about planting a garden. What, is she going to come over and water him on the weekends?"

"Don't get mad at us," Vanessa said.

"Yeah," Tom agreed. "It's not our fault."

June said nothing. She covered her eyes as Derek rolled out of the sandbox.

8

It took Derek a second to register that Jaxx wasn't there. Not on the floor, not in the sandbox. He leaned back on his knees, and was relieved to see the baby nestled in his mother's arms. June produced a weak smile. There was crust in her son's eyes. He looked at his iPhone, which had fallen out of his pocket and lay on the floor.

"Fuck, it's 9:40 p.m.," Derek said. "It's been over four hours."

He was good at counting by fours.

He looked at Tom and Vanessa. "I told you to wake me up!"

"Mom wouldn't let us."

"Mom?"

"He was asleep."

"He's going to starve," Derek panicked. He looked at the bottle. "Is that his?"

"No, it's mine," Tom joked, giving the bottle a shake.

"Go upstairs and put some clothes on," June said.

Tom obliged, but only, June decided, because he was cold. Vanessa reached for the bottle on the side table and poured some of the formula on her wrist.

"I can't tell," she said. "Seems a little . . . cool?"

"Let me try." June offered her wrist. Vanessa tipped the bottle over a second time and milk trickled out onto her mother's forearm. "I can't really feel it." It lacked temperature. "Maybe heat it up again?"

Derek rubbed his eyelids. "I'm just going to make him a new one."

"There are clean bottles on the counter," Vanessa said. "I boiled them like you said." Her phone buzzed from her pocket. "Leslie's here." She clambered off the couch.

June watched Vanessa move swiftly to the kitchen, a smile forming on her daughter's face. She got up out of the chair and placed Jaxx on the seat. Then she knelt down in front of him. "Hi, sweet boy," she whispered, "I'm your grandma." She touched his arm with the back of her finger. "Sweet boy," she repeated. The baby stretched his arms over his head, fists clenched, head tilted back, lips like Earle's — big and puckered.

"I got him," Derek said, returning to the room. "Come here, buddy." Derek lifted Jaxx off the chair, leaving the towel behind. His legs remained tucked in, arms still in a stretch position, eyes open. June got up from the floor as Jaxx began to feed. She wanted to yell at Derek and she wanted to yell at Marissa, wherever the heck she was, but instead she watched Derek feed the baby, and for a moment she felt removed from the drama. Away from their weekend parenting arrangement and the sandbox crib. She detached herself from the father-son pair as though they were strangers to her. Subjects in a magazine. *A man feeds his infant son*. Jaxx stared at Derek hopefully, dependently. The way one looks at his mother, except it wasn't his mother. It was his father, who counted cans and wore SWAG T-shirts and Axe body spray. It was like one of those stories from *National Geographic*. Cross-adoption in the animal kingdom — tigers looking after piglets, Derek and Jaxx. Awkward, askew, endearing.

In the kitchen, Vanessa was helping Leslie with a cradle. Leslie wore a K-way jacket and a plaid cap. Tufts of blond hair stuck out from the back like fur. An orange garbage bag was loosely draped on top of the cradle.

"Is it raining?" June asked.

"Sprinkling," Leslie replied, setting the cradle down. She pulled off the garbage bag, folded it neatly, and handed it to Vanessa.

June ran her fingers down the cradle's edge. "It's beautiful, Leslie."

"It swings, too." Vanessa nudged it with her knee so that it rocked side to side.

"So does mine," Randy grunted up the top two stairs holding his cradle at eye level. "And it's solid." He carried it past the island and carefully lowered it beside Leslie's. His stood much lower to the ground.

"Check it out." With two fingers he pushed down on one side of the cradle. It jerked down about a quarter of an inch.

"Isn't it a bit small?" June asked, focusing on the box where the baby was supposed to sleep.

"Nope," he argued. "It's suitable up to twenty pounds."

"Twenty pounds and six inches," Vanessa said.

"It's thirty inches."

June looked at the two cradles. "Are you sure that's thirty?"

"Am I sure that's thirty? I've been woodworking all my life. I know how to measure, and it's thirty inches."

"I think it's thirty centimetres." Vanessa stood over the cradle. "You could rock a foot-long steak and cheese to sleep in there."

"I like the design," Leslie offered. "Kind of reminds me of a sled."

Randy turned to her. "Thank you," he said.

"Or a shoebox," Vanessa added.

Derek hollered from the living room. "Can someone get me a cloth?"

"I'll get it," June said. She pulled open the drawer of linens, removed a dishtowel, took it to Derek, and placed it on his knee. "Will this do?"

Derek tossed it, unfolded, onto his shoulder. The bottle was nearly empty. He moved Jaxx into a burping position and softly thumped his back. "Who's here?" he asked.

"Leslie made Jaxx a cradle."

"She did? Sweet. I was looking at cribs when I went to get the car seat. They're friggin' expensive."

"He'll need one eventually. Cradles are only for when they're tiny."

"Where should I put it?"

"Probably beside your bed."

"In *my* room?"

Randy appeared in the living room carrying his cradle. He held it low, forcing him to take baby steps.

"Leslie made that?"

"I made this one," Randy corrected.

Derek looked at his mother. "I thought you said Leslie made him a cradle?"

"We both did," Randy said.

"Cool. Guess I could put one on each level. Does it rock?"

"Of course it rocks," Randy replied. He gave it a push, but it only wobbled slightly.

"It looks small."

"Why does everyone keep saying that? It is *not* small." He rubbed his moustache vigorously. His post-dinner stomach protruded from his golf shirt like an inflamed joint, and his hair was on high alert. He looked both familiar and unrecognizable.

"Why don't you hold him?" June suggested.

"Yeah, Dad. I just fed him."

Randy reached for the baby and held him to his chest. He softened, but June knew that Randy was anxious. It was a quiet anxiety, arriving with minimal fanfare. Like a spider in a shipment of lettuce. But now she could see it. He paced the room with the imperfect tension of his unfinished cradle, clutching Jaxx with the grip of a first responder, singing "Twinkle Twinkle Little Star," but it sounded off. A broken appliance. Or maybe she'd been wrong. Maybe the anxiety had always been there but simply out of sight because he whistled and made balloon animals, and people who did these things couldn't have anxiety.

"Do you mind watching him for a bit?" Derek asked. "I need to check my fantasy team."

"You go," June replied.

Derek stretched his arms over his head and stood up. "I won't be long."

June sat in his vacated spot and looked at Randy. "What's wrong?"

"Nothing's wrong," he protested. "I'm fine."

"You don't look fine."

"Well, I am."

"You're not."

"Then I probably ate too much Chinese food."

"But you couldn't sing. You can always sing."

"Because I forgot the words."

"You forgot the words? Come on, Randy, something's bugging you."

"Nothing is bugging me."

June rested her chin on her fist. "Fine," she sighed. "Nothing's wrong."

"Thank you," he said, turning to walk Jaxx in the opposite direction. He cleared his throat. "Twinkle, twinkle, little star, how I wonder what you are."

The words pelted out of him like rocks from a lawnmower.

"Something's wrong," June repeated.

"Nothing's wrong."

"Randy . . ."

He turned toward her. The anxiety was physical now. His ears pricked like a dog's and his eyes bulged.

"I have a son." He twisted away so his back was to her again.

"A grandson," June said.

"No," he said. "I have a son."

"Yes," she agreed quietly. "You have two."

He turned to June, his eyes now a wet, blinking mess. "I have another son."

The news trampled her, and she felt breathless and limp, the balance in the room suddenly off. She could not find her footing to get up from her chair so she remained seated. A mannequin.

"What do you mean?"

"I have another son. He was born in 1982."

"1982?" June frantically tried to do the math. Was this before Tom or after? Was it before her? How old was Tom? "How old is Tom?"

Randy, who was swaying side to side with Jaxx, paused. "He's twenty-four."

"I'm not twenty-four," Tom interrupted. His hair was partially dry now, and he stood at the base of the stairs stringing a belt through his jeans.

"You're not?"

"I'm twenty-six."

Randy made a thinking face. "What year were you born? Was it eighty-five?"

"Eighty-five? What kind of math are you doing?" His belt buckle was off-centre.

"1990," June said. "He was born in 1990. Same year your brother got married."

Tom pulled his phone from his pocket.

"Who are you texting?" June asked.

Vanessa barged in to the living room. "You thought Tom was twenty-four?"

"Twenty-four, but that I was born in 1985."

"He also thinks that cradle is thirty inches long." Vanessa gestured to the wooden box and folded a piece of salami into her mouth.

"I think that salami is old," June said.

"Go sit on the stairs," Randy ordered.

Vanessa and Tom both laughed. Tom continued to text. Derek appeared from the kitchen with a palm full of salami. He looked at his father. "Did you try to give Vanessa a time out?"

"No, I just told her to sit on the stairs. She was being rude."

Vanessa said, "Dad couldn't remember how old Tom was."

"Or when I was born."

Randy shook his head, frustrated. June kept thinking about 1982. Were she and Randy together then? She remembered nothing about that year. It was irrelevant. She pulled herself up from her chair and went into the kitchen. Leslie sat at the island with Jerry, who ate seeds from her hand. June hurried downstairs. Her legs wobbled with adrenaline. She sat down on the computer and typed *1982* into Google and there it was at the top. Wikipedia. The year, 1982, like it was a famous comedian or an important trade route. It started on a Friday. This had to be relevant, she thought, because Fridays were celebrated. People dressed down and left work early and had takeout for dinner. But 1982 wasn't a good year, according to Wikipedia. There were plane crashes and car crashes and cold snaps and mudslides. Wars in Lebanon and the Falkland Islands. Viruses in floppy disks. In October, sixty-six people were crushed during a stampede at a soccer game. June tried not to think about the victims because their kind of death horrified her but it was all she thought about. Suffocation. Collapsed cheekbones and flattened ribs and trapped limbs. She felt all of those things.

The reality of the past forty-eight hours sat on her chest. She thought about what would become of Derek. She imagined him going to Chuck-E-Cheese to pick up single moms with cleavage and winged eyeliner, Jaxx in an umbrella stroller drinking Coke from a sippy cup and gumming pizza crusts. And she worried about Vanessa moving too quickly and wondered if being in a relationship might change her. Would she be the quiet lesbian who managed her money wisely and listened to folk music like the nice lady who ran the floral shop, or would she cut off all her hair and dress like a boy? And though Leslie seemed genuine and kind and well-established, she was not the future June had imagined for her only daughter. She felt silly even acknowledging her grief, but it was there, and grief was what it was, relentless and nagging.

And Tom. Poor Tom. She had always hoped he'd grow into his body. But his top half was now bigger than ever, and his legs were still as thin as crutches, both parts exaggerated so that with his moustache and curly hair, he looked like a Tim Burton character. There were no girlfriends. No dates. Nothing to define him, as Randy had pointed out. All he had was an arsenal of cleaning supplies, student debt without a degree to show for it, and a collection of graphic novels where all the female characters had pierced vaginas and koi fish for nipples.

The drizzly timeline of 1982 flickered on the screen in front of her. And now there was another son. Randy's son. Conceived before she and Randy met. She knew this now because 1982 had been the same year Prince William was born, and she remembered watching the coverage with her mother in her parents' farmhouse that Randy had never seen because they sold it that Christmas.

"What are you looking at?" Randy asked, over her shoulder.

"Get off me!" She was breathless.

He stepped back. "I'm not on you."

"Well, I feel like you are."

"Maybe you're having a heart attack."

"I'm not having a heart attack."

"Lift your arms up."

"Randy, I'm not lifting my arms up."

"Just do it. Try to raise them straight up to your shoulders." Randy demonstrated.

"I'm not raising my arms."

"But you might be having a stroke."

"I'm not having a stroke, Randy." She put her head on the keyboard. "How could you have not *told* me?"

"My mother wouldn't let me talk about it."

"Your mother wouldn't let you? That's it? So you just kept it a secret all these years?"

"I tried to tell you about him more than once, but it was too hard, June. You have no idea what it's like to know you have a son out there that you can't see or talk about and you have no idea whether he sounds like you or shares the same mouth or even whether he knows you exist. I never even got to meet him."

June lifted her head from the keyboard. "But I wouldn't have judged you."

"How do I know that?"

"Randy!" June pushed tears away.

"I'm sorry. Look, it's just . . . you won't even talk about your own adoption."

"There's nothing to talk about."

"See what I mean?" Randy looked up at the sunshine ceiling as if for guidance. "I'm sorry, June. It's just not an easy topic to discuss."

June had nothing to say.

"I would have kept him."

She shook her head and gestured. "Look at this place. It's a mess. Everything's a mess."

He touched her arm. "We're not a mess."

"We aren't? Derek's up there with a two-day-old baby. He couldn't even afford formula. Tom had to buy it. Don't you get it, Randy? We're never getting out of here. *This* is our retirement. This house and this ping-pong table and Derek and Tom and Vanessa and Percy and Jaxx. They're our retirement. The golden prison. This is it."

Randy put his hand on the ping-pong table. "Are you sure this isn't about Fergus?"

"Fergus?"

"That's what they were going to call him." He picked up a lost nativity scene shepherd. "That's all I know about him. His name and that he had a large head."

"No. This is not about Fergus. I mean, you should have told me about him. You absolutely should have, but I can't worry about him, because I'm too worried about everyone else. What if Vanessa is moving too quickly?"

"Why do you think that? They only just started dating." Randy spoke quietly and held June's shoulders.

"Yesterday she wanted the old blender."

"What does that have to do with Leslie?"

"I think she's gathering stuff to move out."

"You've been telling her for a year it was time to move out, and now you think it's too soon?"

June opened the Game of Life and shook the pieces into the garbage.

"And our grandson up there? He doesn't have a mother." She lowered her voice, "And I think Tom's addicted to porn."

"He's not addicted to porn."

"Then what about all those magazines in his room, huh?

I saw one the other day with a double-page spread of two vaginas fighting over a piece of cake."

"Who won?"

"Randy!"

"Sorry, I know. That was inappropriate. But seriously, I wouldn't worry about Tom. The magazines are just a phase. He's doing all right. A few more clients and he'll be good. And maybe a girlfriend. Or a date."

"Well, what about all these toys, then? I'm sick of looking at them."

Randy looked at the plastic spring horse. "Even Percy?"

"Even Percy."

"You can't get rid of Percy. That would be like getting rid of Jerry."

"No it wouldn't, because Percy is a toy and Jerry is a bird." She lunged at the horse's neck.

Randy backed away. "What are you doing?"

"I'm getting rid of it." She held Percy in a headlock and yanked him forward, but the toy's steel frame had attached itself to Randy's ab roller.

"My ab roller!" Randy shouted, as it bumped along behind Percy.

June looked her husband in the stomach. He frowned and sucked in. She made it halfway up to the kitchen, when the ab roller got caught on the railing, wedging the horse into the wall. June tried to kick it free. She hammer punched his head. Bits of drywall flitted to the floor like powdered sugar. She mounted the horse in an attempt to crawl over to push it from behind, but she only made it partway. At the top of the stairs, Tom stood with his iPhone pointing at her. He summoned Vanessa.

"Come see this. Mom's trying to ride Percy up the stairs."

"I think you should turn that off," Randy suggested, but the phone stayed fixed on June.

"Shit, Mom, what are you doing?" Vanessa had joined her brother. She'd changed into black yoga pants and a stretchy tank top that clung tight against her belly. Her black hair was loose and partially concealed her face. June looked up. Had she crawled out of the TV, like in that horrible Japanese horror movie Tom had forced her to watch?

June's mouth opened and her eyes blurred with the hot swell of tears, and then Derek was looking down at her with Jaxx. The baby's downy orange hair had been washed, and was combed to the side in tiny lines. Derek quietly closed the door. June slid off Percy's back and turned to sit on the step below. Randy lay at the bottom, one leg bent underneath him like he'd been pushed. He was silent but his whole body heaved. It stunned her. Where was the Happy Wanderer? She eased herself down to him.

"Fergus." His voice was cracked pottery.

"I'm sorry."

Randy pulled himself up to a sitting position. A potato bug lumbered past. June wiped her eyes.

"I never met him," he cried into his hand. "I sat in the parking lot when she was in labour. I'd been in the hospital that same day." He held up the hand with the scar — a raised bump the size and texture of a raisin below his knuckle. "I saw her parents wheel her in. All night, I watched people go in and out of the emergency room for hours, and then just before midnight I left because I knew. I knew he'd been born, and that he was mine but not." He wiped his nose on his sleeve. "Remember we bought Derek a star for his ninth birthday?"

June did. They'd gone to the planetarium for his party. She'd put dots on the cupcakes to form the big dipper.

"Remember how frustrated he was because even though it was his star, he knew he'd never be able to touch it or see it from Earth? It was essentially just an expensive piece of paper."

"Yeah," she nodded. "I remember that."

"That's how I felt, June. Estranged, helpless, ashamed. I was so distraught that I crashed into a tree on the way home from the hospital."

June felt lightheaded.

"When I got home, I begged my mother to take me back to see him. She grabbed her coat and purse and told me to get in the car."

June furled her eyebrows. "She drove you back to the hospital?" It did not sound like something Hazel would do. June imagined she was more likely to assault Randy with a Bible.

"She drove out of town and dropped me off at the end of a range road, and she said, *Randall, you are going to walk home, and by the time you get home you will have forgotten this bastard was even born.*"

"She did that?" June touched his leg.

"And then she said, *and if you can't forget, you don't come home.*"

This was the Hazel June knew. "I'm sorry."

"So that was it. I just never talked about him."

"But still, Randy, me. You could have told me." The words squeaked out painfully. Like they were too big for her mouth.

"I . . ." he paused. "I didn't want to go there. Because of your own history."

"My *own* history?" She balked. "I was adopted, that's it. That's my history. It doesn't have to be any more than that."

Randy opened his mouth to speak, but said nothing.

"What?" June said.

"Nothing."

June wished Randy would go back to his happy place. Back to the room of denial he'd built himself, where bastards were forbidden and negative emotions banned. In fact, she wanted to join him there. Emoting was ugly. She saw it in the reflection of Randy's glasses. And in the mangled mess of horse parts and neoprene handles lodged behind her.

"I just want to go to bed." She braced herself between the walls to stand. She imagined Randy sitting in the hospital parking lot. Had her birth father done this too? Had he kept watch? Did he know the moment she was born? And what about her birth mom? What about her?

"What about Percy?"

"He can sleep there for the night," June said. She plugged her ears and ran upstairs.

9

The next morning, sunlight poured in on June's face, offensive and blinding. Randy snored beside her, stretched out like a gingerbread man. She went to the bathroom and washed her face, her eyes bee-stung from the day before, her skin weary. Downstairs, Derek was in the pantry.

"Where's Jaxx?"

Derek peeled open a granola bar. "He's in the cradle."

June rinsed the coffee pot in the sink, where half a dozen bottles were set up like bowling pins. Derek's pants were on backwards.

"He should be up any minute for his next feeding." A bit of wet granola was on his cheek.

"I'll feed him," June offered.

Derek yawned and gave her a thumbs-up. He was shirtless. "Formula's on the counter." He pointed to a shiny tub.

Jaxx was in the cradle Randy built, swaddled in a receiving blanket and wearing a butter-yellow toque. He looked smaller than yesterday. She bent down and inhaled. His scent was sweet but subtle. Biscotti. She kissed his forehead.

"Hey, Derek? Since Jaxx is still asleep, I'm going to run out and get a coffee. I'll feed him when I get back."

"Coffee. Yes, please. Get me an extra-large?"

"What do you take in it?"

"Four and four."

"Four and four? As in four cream and four sugar?"

He stuffed bread in his mouth. "Uh-huh."

"That seems excessive, but okay." She picked up her keys. "I'll be back in a minute."

There was a Tim Hortons not far from the house, but the parking lot was too hard to navigate, so she drove to the one near the airport. She turned off the radio and opened the window, trying to draw in the smells and sounds of spring, and pulled in line behind a pickup truck. Her phone rang.

"Hello?"

"Vanessa wants a cheese bagel toasted with herb and garlic cream cheese and a large coffee with two cream and one-and-a-half sugar."

"One and a half?" June searched for a pen. "That's confusing. Can't she just make it one or two?"

"No," Vanessa shouted in the background. "Thanks, Mom."

"And Tom wants a ham and cheese breakfast sandwich on a biscuit and an iced cappuccino."

"Just wait." June pulled ahead to the order screen.

"And Dad wants a bacon breakfast sandwich and a coffee."

A voice asked June for her order, but she couldn't remember anything but the bacon breakfast sandwich. She stared at the menu pictures, selected things at random, and ordered all the coffees black. When she returned home, everyone was seated at the table except for Randy. Leslie drank tea from a travel mug.

June placed everything on the table. "I couldn't remember the order, so you'll have to sort through for something you like."

Derek looked at the coffees. "Which one is mine?"

"They're all black. You can add your own cream and sugar."

Randy slid through the kitchen in his wool socks the way the kids used to when they were young and agile and didn't say things like *fuck off* or *die bitch*. "Did you get me something with bacon?"

"Yes, that I remembered."

Randy grimaced. "I don't think I can eat it now."

June held up the sandwich. "Why not?"

Vanessa was already halfway through a biscuit.

"Because I just watched a YouTube video of pigs playing together and going down a slide. And," he held his face, "they even know their names."

"Like *Bacon*?" Tom said, peeling back the top of a creamer.

Randy covered his ears with his hands and then dropped them heavily to his sides. "When they're left alone, they're highly social animals."

"Why are you on YouTube?" June sipped.

"They communicate," Randy said. "Just like us."

Vanessa helped herself to a second biscuit. "Are they on Twitter?"

"Vanessa," June cautioned.

"Hamela has favourited your Tweet!"

"Chris P. Bacon is now following you," Tom added.

June didn't know what either of these meant, but she knew it was mean, because the Figg children laughed.

"It's true," Leslie piped in. "Mother pigs sing to their babies while nursing."

Vanessa stopped eating her biscuit. Tom put down his bagel.

"They sing to their babies?" Randy asked.

"Uh-huh." Leslie closed the lid on her mug. "Newborn pigs recognize their mother's voice. I read it in a book about animal emotions. That's why I'm a vegetarian."

"A vegetarian? You should be a vegan," Randy said.

"Dad!"

"I mean, we all should."

From the cradle sitting beside Derek's chair, a fist appeared and then disappeared.

"Can I still feed him now?" June asked.

"I got it." Derek took a long sip of coffee, went to the counter where a bottle was warming, and tested the formula on the inside of his wrist. "Perfect." He picked up Jaxx. "Can someone bring me a burp cloth?"

"I can." Leslie followed Derek to the family room with a cloth.

Randy sat solemnly at the table.

"I think there's a muffin in one of those bags," June pointed.

"You know they play chase, too?" He peeled the liner off a blueberry muffin.

June gathered the empty bags and ferried them to the garbage. Randy slurped his coffee. It was otherwise quiet. A rare lull in the conversation. And then from the family room, Derek began to sing. A theme song? A commercial? The song Vanessa sang to Jerry? She didn't know what it was called, but it was for Jaxx. His nursing baby. Her heart fluttered. A half-speed hummingbird. The way it did at the airport when she watched people reunite with their loved ones. The opening scene of *Love Actually*. And then Jerry starting singing too. June held onto the fridge when there was a knock at the back door. Vanessa got there first, followed by Randy. Standing behind it, with a box of diapers and salt-stained Ugg boots, was Marissa. Derek stopped singing.

10

Vanessa uttered a meek hello. Jerry mimicked.

"Come in," Randy said, reaching for the diapers. "There's some breakfast on the table if you're hungry."

"No thanks, Mr. Figg. I'm just here to see Derek."

Marissa stepped inside and removed her boots. She looked nothing like a new mother. Her jeans made her look anorexic, and she wore a distressed T-shirt that hung off one shoulder, revealing a blue satin bra strap. Her long blond hair was curled into stiff locks. Bartender hair. And her lips looked like they'd been doused with K-Y Jelly. June thought of the early days after Tom was born. She wore nightdresses and industrial strength bras with straps the width of lasagne noodles. She didn't wear lipstick for a year, and because of her five-foot frame, she looked pregnant for months after he was born. June eyed Marissa suspiciously.

Derek got up from the couch and placed Jaxx back in his cradle. Marissa bent over the edge and looked at him. "I think we should change his name to Arrow."

"Arrow?" Derek said. "Why?"

Marissa shrugged. "It's edgy."

"Baby pigs know their names," Randy called, placing the diapers at the foot of his chair. June sat down beside him and kicked his shin.

Marissa arranged her hair so it hung over the shoulder with the exposed bra strap. She looked at Randy, puzzled.

Randy attempted to clarify. "Jaxx probably already knows his name. Like baby pigs do."

"Gotcha," Marissa said. She looked at Derek. "Maybe it could be a nickname."

A nickname? June thought. Why not just call him *kettle* or *skateboard*?

"I kind of like it," Tom offered. June shifted in her chair and kicked him too.

Derek and Marissa disappeared into the living room.

Leslie looked at her watch, a masculine-looking Timex with a large face. "Gotta go," she said. "Have to cost out a job in the south." She took her travel mug, bowed slightly, and kissed Vanessa's hand. June's heart skipped at both the chivalry and delicacy of the gesture. She took comfort that Vanessa did not seem deviant or gross, and also felt guilty because she thought of her daughter's sexuality as deviant and gross, when really it was Derek who had sex like an inmate and Tom who had feelings for Japanese cartoons.

"Love you," Vanessa said.

Leslie blushed and ran her fingers through her hair. She backed out of the house clumsily, her brown work boots scuffing against a planter that June hadn't put away from last summer.

The door closed. "How old is Leslie?" Randy asked.

June looked at Vanessa, awash with emotion, and said, "Who cares?"

Derek walked in from the living room and gathered Marissa's boots and purse.

June picked Jaxx up from the cradle, relieved Marissa hadn't come for him. "I think he needs his diaper changed." She placed him on the family room rug, which had been repurposed from old shirts. Jaxx stretched his arms over his head and toppled to the side. His eyes remained closed.

"You need to put this on his balls." Tom handed her a tube of hospital-issued petroleum jelly.

"And Derek said to use a washcloth."

June searched the area and spotted a package of wipes. She pulled one out. "What's wrong with these?"

"They've got alcohol in them." Vanessa tipped her head back, finished what was left of her coffee, and heaved herself up out of her chair. "I'll get you a washcloth."

Once June had changed Jaxx's diaper, Derek dressed him in a high-waisted baseball uniform.

"Did Marissa go home?" June was tentative, in case she was still in the living room.

"Yeah, she has to work this afternoon. She just wanted to drop off the diapers someone gave her."

June guessed nothing had changed with their arrangement. Marissa would be the weekend parent. The summer parent. Derek would be the stay-at-home dad. She was equal parts reassured and saddened by it. How would Derek work?

"Those pants look ridiculous," Vanessa said. "Let me hold him."

Derek passed her the baby while June got up from the floor. "Doesn't anyone else have to work today?"

Vanessa looked as though she might open her mouth, but before she did, Randy interrupted. He stood on a kitchen stool that June kept in the pantry.

"I have an announcement," he said, finger in the sky.

"Is that why you're standing on a stool?"

"Yes, Vanessa," he replied, annoyed. "I'm standing on this stool because I would like your attention."

"'Cause that stool is only a few inches off the ground."

"Would you like me to stand on a chair instead?"

"Yes," Tom encouraged.

"You're not going to give us one of those speeches about responsibility and living on our own, are you?" Vanessa pretended to shoot herself.

"No," Randy replied.

Tom flipped a water bottle. "Please don't say you're forcing us to go on another road trip."

Randy shook his head. "That's your mother's thing."

"I've never forced anyone to go on a road trip," June said defensively. "I've suggested it a few times, but it's not like any of you ever say yes."

"You suggest it at least once a month." Vanessa blew a pink bubble that snapped in her face.

June was quiet. It was true. Most recently she proposed they drive to an indoor amusement park as a way to reconnect. She'd gotten the idea from one of Oprah's life classes. Now it was the subject of a joke.

Randy dismounted the stool, pulled a chair from the table, and climbed up. He took a deep breath.

June waited. He was going to tell them about Fergus. She observed their children while Randy poised himself to speak, clearing his throat. Derek's eyes were half closed. Tom and Vanessa waited with anticipation for something they could make fun of, but Fergus would be their half-brother. She wondered if they'd want to meet him, and if Fergus would be anything like them. He was older and maybe he had kids and they could have play dates with Jaxx.

Randy clapped his hands together, still trying to find the words.

June speculated whether Randy had ever tried to locate Fergus. It was easy today with social media. Last year one of Tom's friends found his birth parents on Instagram.

"As you may have witnessed yesterday, your mother is bit overwhelmed."

June gave an obligatory nod of support, and then paused. "Wait, what did you say?"

"It's okay, honey," Randy urged.

"Did you just say *I* was overwhelmed?"

"You did try to ride Percy up the stairs," Vanessa offered.

"I was trying get rid of him, and he got stuck on the railing. Have you seen the mess down there?"

Derek rubbed his eyes. "That's not what it looked like."

"You weren't even there."

"Not at the beginning, no, but Tom showed me the video."

"The video?"

"Tom, I warned you about that," Randy said.

June had a hot flash. "Can you come down off that chair now?" She turned to Tom. "Let me see the video."

"I deleted it."

"It's still on YouTube." Vanessa held up her phone.

"YouTube?"

"It's a video-sharing site."

"I know what YouTube is, Vanessa. Tom, is that true?"

"Sorry. I didn't know you were upset. I thought you were just messing around."

"Here," Vanessa said, scrolling with one hand, Jaxx pressed against her shoulder. "It's only got 193 views."

"Give me that." June snatched Vanessa's phone. "Why is it so hot in here?" It felt like the Amazon exhibit at the zoo with its dripping trees and the gorillas that all looked the same. And the bats. Save the bats! She hated the bat propaganda. Had these people never had a bat get caught in their hair? What were they trying to imply with it all? It's not like people were out there culling bats or eating them at parties. She waved her face with a paper plate and pressed play.

The video started with her assaulting Percy with a series of frenetic karate chops, and ended with her straddling him. It froze with her in that position, looking up at the camera. She slid the phone back to Vanessa, traumatized by the parting image of her eyes. They looked deranged. She looked like the poorly restored Jesus painting, or the type of early human who might eat her own baby.

"Get it off there," she said. "And for the record, this isn't about me, and I'm not overwhelmed. I'm disappointed."

"In whom?" Vanessa asked.

"In what?" said Tom.

Derek was asleep with his head on the table in a puddle of drool.

"I'll get that." Randy dismounted the chair like a gymnast and fetched something quilted from the linen drawer. He lifted up Derek's head, and slid it under his face.

Vanessa crossed her arms. "Is this about Leslie?"

"No, this isn't about Leslie."

"Is it because Tom's into elder porn, then?"

Tom elbowed his sister. "I'm not into elder porn."

"There's such thing as elder porn?" Randy asked.

"What is wrong with you people?" June said. "This is not about Leslie or elder porn, which, by the way, I don't want to know anything about."

Randy frowned. "I'd kind of like to know."

Vanessa leaned back in her chair. "Is it because I won't sign up for that boot camp you keep suggesting?"

"No. Though a little exercise would probably not hurt. For either of you. We just think it's time you guys start planning for the future. And I don't mean next week or next month. I mean long term. Where's all that Figg ambition you used to have?"

"Are you seriously going to talk about this again?" Tom looked hurt. "What about you? What happened to that list of retirement goals you made?"

"This isn't about me."

"It's in the junk drawer." Vanessa pointed.

Tom went to the drawer and removed a notepad. It was decorated with roosters. "Learn the ukulele, clean out the basement, plant kale."

"Plant kale?" Vanessa laughed.

"Vanessa, kale is a superfood," Randy said.

"Never mind my list," June sighed. "I haven't had to time to finish it."

"What about Derek?" Vanessa said. "He counts bottles for a living, and you're concerned about me and Tom?"

"Don't be nasty, Vanessa," Randy cautioned. "Earle said Derek's one of the best there."

Vanessa laughed out loud. "You've got to be fucking kidding me."

Tom shook his head. "Maybe he could compete on *Canada's Next Top Recycler.*"

Randy opened his mouth.

"Not a real show," June jumped in.

Vanessa put her feet up on the table. "Are we done now?"

"No," June said. "I'm serious. It's time you start setting some goals. And I want that basement finished."

"And you want us to accomplish all this by going on a fucking road trip? Where was it you suggested last time — the Enchanted Forest?"

"West Edmonton Mall," Tom corrected.

"I haven't said a thing about a road trip."

"Your mom wants to see the sea lions."

June looked at Randy. "What are you talking about? When have I ever said I wanted to see the sea lions?"

"Well, you like the otter exhibit at the zoo."

June fanned her face. "No, actually, I don't. I hate the zoo."

Randy frowned. "You hate the zoo?"

"I only go there because *you* like the zoo. It smells. If I wanted to spend my afternoon looking at tilapia, I'd go to the grocery store."

"There's more to the zoo than tilapia," Randy said.

"Look, I only ever suggested a road trip because that's what we did when you guys were little and I thought it might be a neat way to reconnect."

Vanessa got up from the table and carried Jaxx over to the

cradle. "Don't you get how weird that is? In one breath you're telling us to grow up and move out and in another you want us to go to a theme park that serves Kraft Dinner and has a potato for a mascot."

"We can stay in one of the theme suites," Randy suggested.

"I wanted to stay in a theme suite when I was ten. When it mattered," Vanessa replied. She pulled a neon elastic off her wrist and tied her hair in a messy bun.

"Maybe they'll have a *lack of ambition* suite."

"Tom . . ." Randy said.

"With a hot tub shaped like a dumpster."

"And instead of room service they could offer career counselling," Vanessa added.

"And recyclers stay for free."

June closed her eyes.

"Enough!" Randy yelled, waking Derek. "Show some respect."

Derek rubbed his eyes and yawned. "What's going on? Where's Jaxx?"

"He's fine," June said. "He's in the cradle."

Randy stood back on the chair.

"Oh, fuck, here we go again." Vanessa scowled.

"What's going on?"

"Dad's making an announcement."

"What kind of announcement?" Derek asked.

"That the regularly scheduled puppet show has been moved to the dining room."

"Huh?"

"Listen!" Randy shouted. That was twice in one day he had raised his voice. "I want you to know that before I met your mother, I had a son."

All three children froze.

"You have another kid?"

"Yes." He exhaled as though someone had been sitting on his chest and just got off.

"Is that why Mom wants to go to West Edmonton Mall? Does he work there?" Tom asked.

June yelled, "We're not going on a road trip."

Vanessa rested her elbows on the table. "Is he a carnie? I'm confused."

"He's not a carnie," Randy said. "At least I don't think he is. I never got to meet him."

The sarcasm dissipated, leaving an atmosphere of vulnerability and anxiety June hadn't witnessed since dinnertime conversations about pinworms and strangers.

"Do you know his name?"

"Fergus, I think."

"Was he raised by his mother?" Derek asked.

"He was adopted."

June listened attentively.

Randy dismounted his chair again. "She wanted to pick a couple who liked to travel. His mother loved to travel."

"Hmm," Vanessa shrugged. "Maybe Fergus can come to West Edmonton Mall with us. He can stay in the Bastard Suite." She got up from the table, grabbed her phone, and stomped through the kitchen to the back stairs. The lid of a teapot rattled on the counter as she passed.

"I have to shower," Tom said. He gave his father a mild slap on his shoulder as he left. June didn't know the meaning of the gesture.

Derek had already left the table and was making a bottle

of formula. Jaxx was awake again, crying like he'd been left on an ice floe. Randy trembled and sat down. June got up. "Do you need help, Derek?"

"No, I'm fine."

Formula had spilled on the counter and over Derek's shorts. He wiped the back of his hand on his T-shirt and picked up the baby. "Come here," he whispered. "Let's eat."

June wiped up the spill as Randy sat, staring off into the distance the way her mother did at the nursing home. June always left wondering what her mother saw when she looked at the blank wall. She guessed a silent film. Black and white and perilous. With someone in trouble.

Derek was singing again. A mother pig. June lifted the plates quietly out of the dishwasher so she could listen, when Randy turned to her. "You hate the zoo," he said sullenly.

"So?" she replied. "I'm allowed to hate the zoo."

"But I proposed to you at the zoo."

"You did," she replied. "And I said yes."

11

June collected baby laundry from Derek's room and stopped on the landing on her way downstairs to pick up a forgotten receiving blanket. She stared at the Figgs' family crest, nestled there amongst the kids' school portraits and family pictures of camping trips and vacations. It had gold leaves, a clenched armoured hand, and a simple shield. It looked as though it should be accompanied by the word "kapow!" in pixelated comic book blue, but instead it displayed a row of swallows. Three of them — all plain, all plump, and, mysteriously, all wingless. They pecked at an engrailed line near the bottom of the crest just above the family name, with its fancy F and the Gs. The crest made her sad. Nothing in their family photos suggested they wouldn't grow wings. It had been Popsicles and swinging legs and shooting stars. The crest was tilted, but she carried on downstairs, the laundry on her hip.

She placed the basket in a queue behind another and then grabbed sneakers from the closet. They were turquoise with yellow laces. Too young for June's taste, but Vanessa had mocked her previous all-white walking ones, saying they looked like baby shoes from the sixties.

The sun was bright and June went back for a visor. "I'm going for a walk," she called.

"Wait," Randy replied.

She stood in the doorway, listening to Randy clamber up the stairs.

"Where are you going?"

"Probably the loop through the park. I need to clear my head."

He held up a piece of wood. "I get that." Orange earplugs stuck out from his ears. He kissed her cheek.

Outside, June made herself small, passing between the van and the hedge. Parts of the concrete driveway had crumbled over the winter. She kicked at a small pile, and turned up the street toward the bike path. A magpie pecked at a flattened prairie dog ahead of her, its sapphire feathers flashing like the lining of a fine jacket.

She thought of Marissa's jewel-toned blue bra strap, and how she checked on Jaxx like he was a cake in the oven and never bothered to pick him up and it made everything around her feel wrong. June's toenails felt too long, her visor too tight. She ripped it off. Birte once tried to show her how to tap out her cortices. Something she and Earle did on a regular basis to balance their brains and reduce stress. She walked uphill tapping her forehead. A child on a bike without pedals wobbled by. June thought he looked rather foolish. His parents followed closely behind, riding in tandem and hollering praise.

Despite repeated tapping, June didn't feel any different. Maybe she wasn't tapping hard enough, or in the correct place. Or maybe her cortices were so full she had to tap longer. She should have paid more attention when Birte demonstrated the method. She continued up the hill toward the park, periodically flicking her forehead when negative thoughts crept in, but they stayed there like a gang of renegade protestors. It would take a sledgehammer to release them. June couldn't even get her kids out of the house. Why had she believed she could remove thoughts?

She turned down an embankment toward the green space. A woman with a pair of amber-coloured dachshunds on plaid leashes was sitting on a bench. June knew by the dogs, it was Shirley Knowles.

"June!" She waved. "I heard that Derek's just had a baby."

Why don't you yell that a little louder, Shirley, June thought.

"Yes," June replied. "A boy."

Shirley's son Andy had played soccer with Derek. He was a nice kid. Tall like Derek, but muscular. He played varsity soccer in Montreal. June remembered this because he could have gone to the US, but Shirley wanted him to stay in Canada where there were no Republicans or guns or cheese that came in a spray can.

"I bet you just love being a grandma." Shirley scrunched her nose up, then reached in her pocket and dropped food down to her dogs.

"Sure," she replied. "There's nothing quite like it."

"Our oldest and his wife are expecting at the end of the summer. We can't wait. Of course, they're in Toronto. You're so lucky to have your grandson here in Calgary." June nodded, but she didn't feel lucky.

"How is Derek, anyway? Aside from being a new dad? He still working at the recycling depot?"

June wanted to lie. She wanted to say he'd gone back to school. That he'd changed careers. But she was weary. "Yes," June said. "For now."

"It's an important job," Shirley offered. "Reduce, reuse, recycle!"

June produced a painful smile, and then she did lie. "He's planning on going back to school in the fall."

Shirley dropped another handful of treats onto the ground. "That's wonderful. You and Randy must be over the moon. What's he taking?"

"Accounting."

"You can never go wrong in that field. And what about your other two?"

"Tom runs his own cleaning business, and Vanessa works at Petland."

Shirley nodded. "Are they still at home?"

Shirley was getting into June's cortices. "Yes," she answered.

"How nice." She moved the pair of leashes to her other hand. "Andy's not coming home this summer. He's running soccer camps through July, then going to Asia for a month to see his girlfriend. She's Korean. Very quiet girl. We met her in January on our way to Paris. Sweet little thing, but doesn't look a day over sixteen. She's studying to become a doctor." She tugged the dogs away from a pizza crust under the bench. "Well, please tell Derek we said congratulations."

"I will." June waved and went back from where she came. The magpie was still on the prairie dog. The bike family had discarded their bikes on the side of the path and were having a picnic.

"I'm home," she called out, unlacing her sneakers at the back door.

"We're downstairs," Randy replied.

She hung her visor on a hook and went to him. "Where's Derek?"

"Sleeping. Check it out. Look what Earle dropped off."

Jaxx was asleep in a semi-reclined swing that rocked horizontally. A mobile of obese farm animals dangled overtop.

"They also sent over some diapers and a gift card for The Bay."

"We have to talk to Derek," June said. "He doesn't have a plan."

"He got Jorge to cover his shifts this week."

"But he needs to work."

"Yes, but he also needs to take care of Jaxx. He's only a few days old. Marissa doesn't want him, June. You saw that today, I know you did. And Derek wants him. You heard the way he sang to him. And he times his feedings, and he's ordered a lovely crib online for when Jaxx outgrows the bassinette. It converts into a toddler bed."

"But what if she changes her mind?"

Randy placed his hands on her shoulders. "He already contacted a lawyer."

"Derek contacted a lawyer?"

"Well, I did, but it was Derek's idea."

"Still. What if she changes her mind before anything becomes legal? I mean that stuff takes time."

"She won't change her mind." Derek stood in the hall with an empty laundry basket.

June whipped around. "How do you know that, Derek? This is someone who never bothered to tell you she was even pregnant until she was eight months into it. What makes you think she's not going to decide one day that she wants him back?"

"She told me he was a mistake, Mom." June flashed back to her conversation with Randy about Fergus. Was she also a mistake?

"But that could just be postpartum. Hormones. A lot of women feel that way after birth. They have a hard time connecting, but it's temporary."

"She's not coming back tonight, because she won tickets to see Drake in Edmonton. She didn't even try to hold him today."

"What about her parents? Have you talked to them, Derek? Do they even know about Jaxx?"

"Her parents are divorced."

"So?"

"Her dad works in Fort Mac and is addicted to OxyContin, and her mom lives in BC."

"That's it?"

"They wanted her to have an abortion."

"Well, something's wrong here, Derek, because mothers don't just give up their babies. He's not a rabbit."

Derek dropped the basket on the floor. "Why are you so pissed off? I thought you'd be proud of me for doing the right thing, here."

"You're right. I'm sorry. I'm very proud of you. I just don't see how you're planning on making it work long term. Who's going to look after him when you go back to work?"

Randy raised his hand.

· "You? Yesterday you said you wanted to go on a cruise. What happened to downsizing and selling the house so we could travel?"

"I changed my mind."

Derek opened the dryer. An army of tiny socks tumbled out. "And Vanessa said she'd watch him on her days off."

June sighed. "Vanessa doesn't do anything on her days off."

Derek scooped up the clothes and threw them in the basket unfolded. "And Tom said he'd trade bedrooms so I can fit the crib in my room."

June exhaled. "So, it looks like you've got everything figured out then."

"For now." Derek was defensive.

"We thought you'd be happy," Randy offered.

"Right? All these bullshit lectures on responsibility, and when I finally take some, you complain."

"I'm not complaining, Derek. I'm just worried."

"Well, it's not helpful. Me and Jaxx will be fine." He stormed off, leaving behind a knit hat the size of an orange.

"Derek!"

"Leave him," Randy said. "He has to get ready for work."

"I thought you said Jorge was covering his shifts?"

"Leslie's training him to build and install kitchens. Her business is booming. She needs someone."

"So you guys really have figured everything out then." She was shaking.

"June, what is wrong? Derek's right. All the lectures and talks, and the kids are finally starting to take initiative, and they're being nice to each other, and for the first time in years they're actually making decisions — together — and you're disappointed. It's like you're mad at them for doing what you asked."

"That's not true. Besides, I heard Vanessa say *go fuck yourself* this morning."

Derek was back in the basement with a soother on the end of his finger. "Only because she tripped on a box of wipes in the hallway."

Randy took June's hands. "Tom even offered to do the four a.m. feedings. He'll wake Jaxx when he gets home from work."

"That's great!" June said.

"You're being hostile."

"I'm not being hostile. It just all seems too cavalier for me. Remember when the kids got their first guinea pig? They fought over who was going to feed him, and who got to change his cage, and who got to hold him while his cage was being changed?"

"Yes, what was her name?"

"Tammy. And remember how long it lasted? You were her primary caregiver."

"That's not true."

"It is true! It was you who changed her cage each week and filled her water bottle."

"Vanessa helped."

"Fine, Vanessa did help, but the point is they got over the whole thing quickly."

"But Jaxx isn't a guinea pig."

"No, he's not, which is why this whole situation makes me nervous. He's a child, and right now we don't have the best track record for raising children."

"I find that offensive." Randy balked. "You have a very skewed idea of success. Try, for once, to be positive. Since Jaxx arrived, everyone seems happier except for you. What if he is the change you've been begging for? That trigger that will make the kids want to set goals and work together and move out."

June stopped talking. In many ways he was right. Everyone had come together since Jaxx arrived, in the way natural disasters inspired large-scale cooperation. She had watched footage of post-tsunami Japan, where citizens calmly lined up for food and water, sometimes for hours. The lines were always quiet. They were always straight. No one barked or yelled or struggled or fought. Not externally anyway. Sometimes the camera would catch someone crying, but the tears, the silent tears, were the only clue. She was the one running through the streets looting. With a gun.

"Okay," she agreed. "You're right. I'll try to be more positive. I'm just scared."

"I know you are," Randy said.

"And I hate retirement. The ukulele hurts my fingers. I can only play two chords."

She marched upstairs looking for a distraction. What did she do before Jaxx came? She planned dinner. She fed her family. She worried about them and wished better things for them, but ultimately she fed them. She opened the fridge. The vegetables in the crisper were limp. "I'll make soup."

"What?" Derek asked.

"Nothing." She shook her head. "Talking to myself."

His phone pinged. Every few seconds it pinged.

"What the fuck?" he said.

June let the *fuck* go. She tried to be positive. Derek had embraced fatherhood with a maturity and grace she hadn't seen since kindergarten. She cut the tops off a bundle of carrots.

"Did you tell someone I was going back to school for accounting?"

"Why?"

"Because I just get a text saying, *didn't know u were going back to school. Dude, accounting?*"

June gave Jerry a piece of celery. "That's odd."

"Yes," Derek agreed. "Andy said, *my mom ran into yours at the park, congrats bro.*"

"That's very weird," she said. "I don't recall saying anything of the kind." A hot flash followed. In ten seconds she felt like she was in Calcutta or a dishwasher. She waved at her face with a realtor notepad that had come in the mail.

"Whatever. Are you and Dad free on the weekend?"

June checked the calendar hanging beside the fridge, though she knew their schedule was likely blank. She was cautious. "Why?"

"A friend of mine is hosting a baby shower, and she said to invite you."

She peeled an onion with her eyes half shut. "That's nice. Who is it?"

"My friend Jenny. She used to work at Moxie's. You've met her."

"Was she the girl who went to the prom as a vampire?"

"Yes," Derek confirmed. "Short dark hair, piercings."

"I remember her. That's nice of her to throw you and Jaxx a shower."

"I'm a single dad now."

June filtered this out. She heard it, but she pretended he said something less alarming, like *I like sandwiches.* She guessed this was what Randy did since he seemed to react to nothing. KEEP CALM AND CARRY ON. She saw that phrase everywhere. On the napkins at HomeSense. On people's T-shirts. Keep Calm and Trust God. Keep Calm and Eat Chocolate. Keep Calm and

Hakuna Matata. What did that even mean? How exactly did you Hakuna Matata?

"So I gather you've let your friends know."

"Didn't you see my Facebook announcement?"

"I can't get into my account."

"Again?"

"Never mind."

"Check out my pic. Tom took it."

June pushed the celery to the side, dried her hands on a dishtowel, and sat down at the table. Derek handed her Vanessa's tablet, which was opened to his Facebook page. The cover photo was of him in the turtle sandbox with Jaxx on his chest. A smaller photo showed Derek in his Tap Out shorts.

"Is Jaxx in that one too?" She pointed to his profile.

Derek clicked on the picture. "No, that's just me."

"Derek, is that your pubic hair sticking out?"

He grabbed the tablet and studied the photo. "Maybe a bit." He squinted.

She cringed. "Is Tom still on Facebook?"

"Yeah."

"Let me see his page."

Derek pressed some buttons and then gave June back the tablet. Tom's profile featured a graffiti-covered train and a smaller photo of himself that had been altered as if it were taken with night-vision goggles.

"He only has ten friends?"

Derek looked at the page. "He doesn't really use Facebook."

She closed the screen and rested the tablet on her lap. "What about Vanessa?"

"Her page is full of lesbian stuff."

"What do you mean?"

He took the tablet from his mother's lap and opened Vanessa's Facebook page. "Check it out. How is that for lesbian stuff?"

"What is the Big Gay Prom? Why is Vanessa dressed as a maître d'? Is that Leslie? Is Leslie in the rabbit suit? Is this person a boy or a girl?"

Derek looked at the androgynous character on the right side of the photo wearing a satin shirt and skinny suspenders. He or she was sporting a wrist corsage the size of a Christmas wreath. "Dunno," he said. "I think it's a dude."

There were two others in the photos, girls, wearing suits with lion manes and lime green and turquoise high heels.

"Wow," June whispered. Perhaps this is what they meant by Keep Calm and Hakuna Matata.

12

On Saturday morning, June set up a change station on the coffee table. It was easier on her back than changing Jaxx on the floor. A piece of his belly button fell off. She moved it to the side, while she struggled to feed Jaxx's legs into his pants. Couldn't he just wear a bag?

Randy picked up the shrivelled belly button. "Do we have more of this?"

"That's what's left of the umbilical cord."

Randy wrapped the belly button in a piece of Kleenex like it was a bonbon and placed it in the garbage. The lid slammed down.

Vanessa thumped into the kitchen with Jerry on her shoulder. Her hair was tied back with a juvenile bow, her eyebrows thicker than normal. She was singing to the bird in French.

"Good morning," June said.

"I guess," Vanessa shrugged. "Do you have Jenny's address?"

"You're coming to the shower?" June handed Vanessa the directions.

"Leslie's driving." Vanessa plugged the information into her phone. "I'll see you guys there."

"Mom, can you get him in his car seat?" Derek tossed her a pair of tube socks she thought were finger puppets. "We're going to be late." Derek wore jogging pants with a glob of peanut butter smeared down the front.

"We'll take care of him. Go get ready."

Randy brought Jaxx to June, and she stretched the socks over the baby's slender feet.

"These aren't going to stay on," she said.

"I got it." Randy placed Jaxx in his car seat, pulled the socks up over his knees, and recited a Dennis Lee poem he used to read to Derek. Jaxx fell asleep.

When Derek was ready, he loaded Jaxx into the car. Randy and June took the van.

"What's that?" June pointed at the container near Randy's feet.

"Macaroons. I made them the other night when we went to Earle and Birte's but forgot to bring them in."

"That reminds me. I didn't bring the gift. Shoot." June got out of the car and went back into the house. She'd ordered a highchair online and had intended to put a picture of it in an envelope. It was still sitting on the printer. She sat down at the computer, folded the image, and rifled through the desk drawer for an appropriate envelope.

On the computer screen in the Google search box was the name Fergus. June pulled the chair closer and browsed the search history. The list was extensive: "Fergus," "Fergus 1982," "Fergus 1982 April," "Fergus 1982 April Foothills Hospital," "Calgary Fergus 1982 Adopted," "Calgary Fergus Randy Figg Glenda Mitten 1982."

Glenda Mitten. Fergus's mother. Mentally, June had not ventured there. She hadn't asked Randy who Fergus's mother was or the circumstances of their relationship. A relationship, which bore fruit. A Figg.

"June?" Randy called from the top of the stairs. "Aren't you coming? I thought you said we were going to be late."

"I'm coming." She Xed out of the screen, grabbed an envelope and stuffed the picture inside.

"I'll drive?"

"Yes," she said, "Huntington Hills."

She followed Randy to the van. He was in a particularly good mood. Glenda Mitten. Did June know her? She repeated the name in her head. Glenda Mitten. Glenda Mitten. But she pictured her Great Aunt Glinda Mueller, who collected bells and watched the Weather Network and was obese before it was popular. Glinda in mittens. Glinda with kittens. Glinda and Randy. June started tapping her forehead.

"What are you doing?" Randy backed out of the driveway.

"Nothing," she muttered. *Glenda Mitten,* she said in her head, but again the name turned into something different. A changing cloud. Glenda. Splenda. Glenda and Randy in the hacienda with mittens. Making Fergus. Smitten. Adoption. Bitten. It is Written.

"You're awfully quiet," he commented, placing a hand on her thigh.

June noticed the garnet of Randy's class ring looked nearly black. The stone was not centred on his finger and it bothered her. She attempted to twist the ring into place, but it didn't budge. "Ouch," he said.

"Sorry," she mumbled. "Tell me about Glenda Mitten."

Randy gulped audibly and looked straight out the windshield. He returned his hand to the steering wheel. He gulped a second time, and June watched his Adam's apple rise and fall, and she thought of the red and white floats her father used when they went fishing in Montana.

"That's Fergus's mother."

"I gathered that from the Google search." She brushed her bangs out of her eyes. "Do I know her?"

"You met her once, but you wouldn't remember it. She used to work at Wicker Land."

"By the milkshake place?"

"Uh-huh."

"We never bought anything at Wicker Land."

"Yes, we did. After we first got married. Remember that little patio set we put on the balcony?"

June thought of their first apartment, which was part of a fourplex in the inner city. She remembered the balcony with its wrought iron rails, and the lilac bushes that grew underneath and around as if they were holding the concrete slab in place. The yellow tin ashtray, left behind by the previous tenant, that they held between them when they smoked. And, yes, the patio set tucked in the corner and rarely used. She did not remember Glenda Mitten.

"What did she look like?"

"Long hair. Really long. All the way down to her waist. And glasses. They were kind of greyish."

His description didn't trigger any memories. That patio set was the first and last thing they'd bought from Wicker Land. Still she made up a Glenda Mitten with long hair and grey goose glasses. She put her in a long skirt to match her hair and she pictured Randy getting lost in all of Glenda's long things. She supposed Glenda Mitten no longer worked at Wicker Land.

Randy read her mind. "She works for a dentist now," he said. "She manages a family of them."

This amused her for a minute without good reason. There were all sorts of careers passed down through families. She saw it on TV all the time. Usually cops. A baby-faced police officer telling the camera *my dad was a cop and my uncle was a cop and my grandfather was a cop.* But Glenda, now with piano fingers and narrow sculpted nails, managing the dentists like they were a family of circus performers. She rolled down her window. The air was crisp and clean. A knife blade. She could smell Canmore and Banff. An earthy rock-and-water smell she likened to a terracotta pot. She pulled her sunglasses down from their perch on her head. They rested on the bridge of her nose perfectly, a rare find for her small face, and she decided maybe Vanessa was right when she said they were kid's glasses.

She tried not to think about Glenda Mitten. She never thought about any of Randy's previous girlfriends, because they would have been practically teenagers. It seemed juvenile to wonder about girls who were likely more into popcorn and knee socks than sex, but Glenda was different because of Fergus.

Randy pulled up to a row of square townhouses with beige stucco and rust-coloured doors. "Did they say which unit?"

June couldn't find the directions. "No, but I'm assuming it's the one on the end, with the balloons."

"Makes sense." Randy parked across the street from the unit. A mountain bike was chained to the front railing where three balloons, sans helium, had also been tied. The neighbourhood smelled like Dairy Queen and pot. June knocked. A bearded man with a mesh hat answered the door.

"Hey," he said. "Come on in."

Randy placed his hand on the small of June's back and guided her through the door.

"I'm assuming you're Derek's parents," he said. "I'm Jenny's roommate."

"Yes," Randy said.

The roommate smiled. His teeth were white. A pre-LED light bulb sheen. They followed him down the carpeted hallway. "Grandma and Grandpa are here!"

More than a dozen people were gathered in a room with cat trees and glass end-tables. They drank beer out of silver cans. It was just after eleven a.m. There was a large flat-screen TV mounted to the wall, and a rectangular fish tank in the corner, though June couldn't see any fish. She did not see Derek or Vanessa or Leslie, but she did see Jaxx. He was swaddled in a brown fur blanket and tucked in the arm of a pale-skinned girl with cleavage. Jenny emerged from the kitchen.

"Hi, Mr. and Mrs. Figg. Come on in, have a seat. Can I get you a drink?" Jenny's hair was short and swept to the side like Leslie's, with one side of it shaved. She was holding a pink spatula covered with chocolate icing. She licked it clean. "We've got beer, ginger ale, apple juice, vodka, water . . ."

"I'll have a ginger ale," Randy said.

"Just water for me." June sat on an aluminum folding chair with a shallow seat. The roommate played music through a speaker and ate Bits & Bites by the handful.

"I'm Jolene," said the girl holding Jaxx. "Congratulations."

Jolene had a gap between her teeth, like Johnny Depp's French ex-wife, and her lashes were impossibly long. June blushed.

"I used to work with Derek at the depot," Jolene added.

A collective "Oooh" erupted, and June swung around to look at the TV. A bloodied man with Scottish colouring was sprawled out on a mat. Another man with bare feet and ears that looked like they had been cooked in a crockpot raised his fists in victory. His arms looked too long for his body. He did not wear gloves. This made her think of Glenda Mitten.

"Big fight last night," the roommate explained. "This is just a recap." The Berber carpet reminded June of a short-haired cat. It snagged the bottom of her sport socks.

"Is this UFC?" Randy asked.

"Yep," someone replied. "The finest."

Vanessa came into the living room with a plate of chocolate cupcakes. June felt relieved to see her face, even though Vanessa was wearing a shirt that said *I See Orange People*. Leslie followed behind with dip, and Derek rounded out the line with a bottle of greyish formula. Was this the same colour as Glenda's glasses? June sipped her warm tap water. She hadn't been to a baby shower in a long time, but she didn't remember cage fighting and cleavage and beer. It depressed her. She identified with the fighter sprawled in the ring. The fact that he didn't try to get up. That he looked more and more like a logo stitched into the mat. A two-dimensional loser with shorts that glistened and scrambled ears like his opponent. "May I have a beer?"

"Of course." Jenny snapped open a can and handed it to June. "Okay, everyone, I didn't plan any games."

June could see Randy was disappointed.

"But I do have a prize for the person who can guess how much Jaxx weighed when he was born. If you know, you can't play."

Randy frowned as people started shouting out numbers.

"Seven pounds, three ounces," guessed Jolene.

"Ten pounds!" shouted a guy standing by the fish tank with an e-cigarette hanging from his lip.

"Fourteen pounds, twenty ounces!" This was clearly someone who worked at the depot, June concluded.

The guessing continued. When someone guessed two pounds, June shot her beer. This was why Randy was so adamant about supporting Derek. His friends, though genuine, had the collective intelligence of a potato. Derek had showed such potential growing up. His Grade 1 teacher had said he was gifted. By Grade 3, he had memorized the periodic table. Derek's friend currently sitting across from June wore a hat that said "DUH."

The winning guess went to a girl whose makeup made her look like a virtual assistant. Her prize was a bottle of vodka.

"I think we should let Derek open some presents," Jenny suggested.

"Who wants to feed Jaxx?" Derek asked, holding up the bottle. "He's overdue."

June resisted the desire to shout *yes.* She knew she could feed him any time. The guy who guessed Jaxx weighed two pounds shot his hand up first. "Dylan wins," Derek said. He took the baby from Jolene and handed him to Dylan. June took a cupcake. Did Dylan know Jaxx was a real baby? She choked the cupcake down in three bites and stared at the fish tank. Dylan squirted formula on his tongue like it was a hot dog. "Tastes weird," he said. "Like mushroom soup." Then he stuck the bottle into Jaxx's mouth.

Derek opened presents. A baby bath, bibs, a mat covered in caterpillars for tummy time. Someone from work gave him a playpen and three large boxes of diapers. The gifts were endless. A thermometer. A rubber seat with a tray. A diaper shirt with a barcode across the chest and the slogan *Made in Vagina*. That one was from Dylan.

While Derek thanked his friends, Vanessa consolidated gifts into larger bags and collected stray pieces of tissue paper. Leslie had taken Jaxx, and was now pacing the room patting his back. The doorbell rang and Jenny left to answer it, returning with two of Derek's high school friends. June knew one of them well. Smitty. He had been friends with Derek since preschool.

"Sorry we're late."

Derek greeted them with fist bumps and backslapping hugs.

"Congrats, man," Smitty said. "This is from both of us. Open it."

Smitty thrust forward a crudely wrapped gift that Derek tore open. It was a primary-coloured train being driven by a giraffe. A hippopotamus rode in the caboose, and several other animals with a penchant for rail travel hung off the sides.

"It's for when he gets a little older," Smitty said.

Smitty had shared Derek's love of Hot Wheels. They'd spoken car together, Derek with a lisp. A constant melody of beat-boxed engines and brakes. The sounds of speed and danger a regular soundtrack. June remembered how they'd built ramps out of cheese.

"Mrs. Figg!" Smitty held out his hand.

June stood up from her chair and shook his hand. "Hi, Smitty." She asked after his parents and his older sister, who had been in Vanessa's grade. He accepted a beer from Jenny as she passed, and talked about his trip to Thailand. He called it a pilgrimage.

Behind him, Derek was on his knees, testing the animal train.

"And I just got engaged," Smitty continued. "My fiancée's an artist."

"Are you still in the city?"

"No, we bought a few acres about forty minutes north. That's why I'm late."

June wanted Smitty to go away.

Football replaced the fight highlights, and Randy was gathered in a group watching a countdown of the top ten best field goals. Every minute or so a fat bronze number crossed the screen, and the uniforms changed on the field. An old player or a coach would review the famous play like it happened yesterday. It would be shown several times. In real time. In slow motion. From different angles. One play. June reached down for her purse and then went into the kitchen, which was small and cluttered with baking things. Jenny was loading the dishwasher.

"Thanks for the lovely shower," June said.

"Hey, no prob," Jenny said, standing upright. She held a pair of beaters in her hand. "Derek's a good guy. I know he's going to be an amazing single dad."

June wished people would stop using that term. Couldn't Derek just be a regular amazing dad?

"His room's going to be great too."

"Pardon?"

"His room, downstairs. Charlie still has to move his camping gear out of it, but there's a ton of space for Jaxx's stuff, and we just painted it."

June's heart palpitated.

"You want to see it?" Jenny asked.

June wanted to crawl into a hole, but she nodded, devastation caught in her throat like a brick cracker. Her legs wobbled en route to the basement — a sensation that was becoming too familiar. Sea legs. When they reached the bottom of the stairs, Jenny said, "Close your eyes." When June did, tears sprung out like they'd been rung out of a cloth. Jenny took her hand and led her down a hall. A door creaked.

"Open!" Jenny commanded.

June opened her lids wide and with force, as though she might stop herself from crying. The room was bright for a basement. There were two windows, the size of microwaves, at the back. She could see yellow-green grass through metal bars that had been painted white. The rest of the room was cream. Baseboards had been fitted into place but not yet secured. The Berber carpet, a darker colour than upstairs, looked clean. In the middle of the room was the camping gear Jenny had warned about. A newer-looking Coleman stove, a Styrofoam cooler, a bagged tent, loose sleeping bags.

"That stuff is obviously not staying." She pointed to the gear. Kicked a few tent pegs into a pile. "He just brought it in here to air out."

June nodded. There was a nightstand in the corner with a small table lamp, the cord wrapped around its base.

"I picked that up at a garage sale last night," she said. "Three bucks."

June didn't know if it was the nightstand or the lamp Jenny was referring to, but she knew they were for Jaxx because they were little. She clenched her teeth until her jaw ached.

"Did you see that?" Jenny asked.

June whirled around to the other side of the room. Spread across the wall in the shape of an arc was the name *JAXX*.

The letters were two-feet tall and had been sprayed with a graffiti-type script in shades of blue, outlined in black.

"What do you think?" Jenny folded her hands beneath her chin in anticipation.

June thought the artwork was more suited to a railcar driven by a giraffe or a drug addict. "It's nice," she said flatly.

"I know," she beamed. "Do you think Mr. Figg would want to see?"

"Yes," June replied. "He'd be delighted."

Jenny bounded up the stairs, leaving June behind to break down. A lead skeleton. She felt like she'd been hit by a train. An old one with a boiler, and a plough in front to scrape people off the track.

Randy came up behind her. Jenny had stayed upstairs to see people out. June heard the front door open and close. A cacophony of goodbyes and high fives and hinges. June pointed to the wall.

"JAW," Randy said.

"Jaxx, Randy. It says Jaxx."

Randy read it again. "Jawwwwxx?"

She turned to look at her husband. His hands were on his hips. It wasn't registering. Jenny hadn't explained.

"We're looking at Derek's room. Jaxx and Derek's room."

"What do you mean?"

"According to Jenny, Derek is planning to live here. With Jaxx."

"No," Randy said. "Tom said he'd switch rooms with Derek so there was enough space for the crib. This is a mistake."

"You're right," June nodded. "It must be for another Jaxx."

"But why would he move out? He'd have to pay rent. Did you tell him he had to pay rent? He can't afford rent."

"No, I didn't tell him he'd have to pay rent." She hugged herself.

"Well, I don't get it. We had it all worked out." Randy tugged at his facial hair. "The boys switching rooms, the childcare, the feedings. Are you sure you didn't say anything to him?"

"No. I mean, we've both talked to the kids about taking some responsibility for their lives . . ." June's voice trailed off. Amongst the tent pegs was a pack of rolling papers.

Randy picked up the lamp. There was a sad brown owl on the shade. "Well, June. I guess this is what responsibility looks like."

"I hope you're not implying that this is my fault. Is it my fault? I didn't mean for Derek to move out. Not now. Not with Jaxx."

Randy traced the owl with his finger. He was silent.

June turned to go, but she saw something in the closet. It was Percy. He'd been abducted. She charged over, and pulled him out by the neck.

"Why's Percy here?"

"You said to get rid of him."

"You authorized this?"

Randy's eyes shifted nervously. "Derek just said he knew someone who wanted it."

June grabbed Percy around the torso, crashed up the stairs and out the front door. She slid him into the trunk sideways and climbed in to the front seat. Adrenaline zipped through her like a pinball, and she hit the steering wheel once, twice, sixteen times. Her seatbelt locked, and she thrashed around until it loosened.

Randy's container of macaroons rested on the centre console and nearly toppled when she pulled into traffic. *Stupid coconut assholes.* When she braked for a crosswalk, the container tumbled and the lid popped off. *Ah, you. Stupid.* She grabbed a handful to throw out the window and instead stuffed them into her mouth. She wanted to say terrible things. Use the foulest of language, but even in her rage it was against her sensibilities. Instead, she swallowed another, and yelled out the window the names of things she hated: *zoos, Jenny, cottage cheese, Pierce Brosnan!* She smacked her knuckle on the doorframe and accelerated through the stop sign.

Her phone rang inside her purse. She fished it out. It was Randy. She pressed *decline.* He could get a ride home with Leslie and Vanessa. At the next light, she collected the remaining macaroons between her legs, periodically moving them back into the container, hollering: *bed skirts, cankers, cilantro, sushi, retirement, Glenda.*

13

June pulled into the driveway, turned off the car, and wept into the steering wheel. Chocolate melted between her legs and coloured the seat an ugly brown. Her head throbbed. She closed her eyes, breathed in the smell of coconut, the scent of her family: workshop, pet store, recycling, orange peels, and the faintest hint of newborn. She wiped her eyes on a napkin. In the rear-view mirror, she saw Tom coming up the drive, his work backpack slung over his shoulder, wearing around his neck the kind of complicated headphones she imagined a technician at NASA would use to communicate with someone on a space walk. When he got close, he peered in through the back of the van. She lifted a hand to wave.

He came around to the passenger's side and opened her door. "Whatcha doing out here?"

"Oh, Tom." She motioned for him to sit.

"What's wrong?" He tossed his backpack on the floor and climbed in.

"I've just come from the shower, and there was a room done up in the basement for Derek. It even had Jaxx's name on the wall. Did Derek mention anything to you about moving out?"

"First I've heard of it." Tom pulled a box of doughnuts out of his bag and offered June one. "You don't want him to?"

"Not with Jaxx! At least not until things get settled."

Tom shrugged, biting into a lemon-filled doughnut. "Want me to text him?"

"Would you? Tell him you don't think it's a good idea."

Tom brushed powdered sugar from the seat and told Siri to text Derek.

June tore her doughnut in half. "These are Mom's favourite," she said, swiping some of the lemon filling with her finger.

"That's why I bought them. I dropped in to see her after work."

"Today? How come? Didn't you just take her that puzzle yesterday?" June put down her doughnut. She'd missed her regular visit with her mother because of Jaxx's birth, and now she was too exhausted to feel guilty.

He shrugged. "I wanted to drop something off."

"How was she?"

"Good. I wasn't there very long because some kids' choir was coming in to perform."

"Did she eat the doughnut?"

"She ate *two*."

June smiled. "Of course she did."

A squirrel ran across the backyard and scaled the fence.

"Thanks for doing that."

Tom ate another doughnut, looked down. "Derek says he's not for sure moving out." He scrolled the surface of the phone with his thumb. "Says it depends on Vanessa."

"Depends on Vanessa? Why Vanessa?"

"She and Leslie are looking at a place this afternoon."

"They've only just met."

"Nah. It's been a few months."

"Really? Still. She seems a little too old for Vanessa."

"I don't think that's a bad thing."

"No?"

"When's the last time you heard Vanessa tell someone to go die in a hole?"

June thought. "Christmas?"

"March, but close."

"She does seem a lot happier." June looked at her son, the empty box on his seat, the giant headphones wrapped around his neck. "What about you? Are you happy?"

Tom exhaled. "Kind of thought I'd have a kid before Derek."

"I always believed Derek would be first. I'm just glad it wasn't in high school. I always worried he'd be a teen dad."

"Did you ever worry about me?"

June looked at Tom. "Parents always worry about their kids." She placed a hand on his shoulder. "You okay?"

"I'm okay." He folded the doughnut box in half. It reminded June of the Napoleon hats she made the kids when they were little.

"I hope Dad finds him," Tom said. "Fergus or whatever his name is."

"Yeah?"

"It'd be kind of nice to be the younger brother for once."

A car pulled in the driveway behind the van, casting light into the back so Percy looked demonic. Tom and June both turned around.

"What's he doing here?"

"Never mind," June said. "Can you bring him in for me?"

"I can." He handed June the empty doughnut carton and got out of the van. June followed and watched Randy say goodbye to Vanessa. A hula dancer bobbled on Leslie's dash. She waited for Randy as Tom shut the trunk and took Percy inside.

"Why'd you leave me there?"

"I'm sorry. I saw that room with Jaxx's name on it and I just couldn't be there any longer."

He held up a bottle of rum.

"What's that for?"

"I won a prize."

"What was the contest?"

"Beer chugging."

"Seriously?"

"I'm kidding."

They took their shoes off inside.

"I've got to go check on something in my workshop. I'll be up in a bit to help you with dinner."

Music blared from Tom's headphones. He'd made himself a sandwich and was feeding Jerry bits of lettuce through the bird's cage. Jerry stood on his dowel looking stoical. Beneath the lettuce, half a dozen celery stalks were stacked like timber.

June took an armload of multicoloured potatoes from a drawer and dropped them onto the counter. The purple ones had grown ears. She cleaned them and took out a knife. She thought of Vanessa's bed being replaced by a crib. Would she even take her bed?

"You're cutting those potatoes awfully small."

"What?"

Tom's headphones were dangling around his neck again. He cleared his plate.

June looked down at the cutting board. She'd chopped the potatoes, skin on, ears intact, into miniscule bits. She sighed, pushed them into a pot of water, and made herself a cup of tea.

The enclosed front porch was cool in the afternoon, so she set her tea on a plant stand and wrapped herself in an animal-motif quilt. It had been Vanessa's and still smelled like a little girl's room. The wicker loveseat creaked as June made herself comfortable.

"Knock, knock," Randy said, closing the door behind him. "Thought you were in your workshop?"

"And I thought you were in the kitchen."

"I needed a cup of tea."

"I made you something."

June moved over so Randy could sit down. "What is it?"

Randy held up a wooden creature the size of an apple.

"It looks like an elephant," June said.

"It is."

June didn't ask why the elephant's trunk was so long or why one of its eyes took up eighty percent of its face.

"Elephants are one of the few species that have grandmas."

June held the carving in her hand. The feet were perfect.

"It's lovely," she said.

Randy took the elephant and set it beside her tea. "Now," he took her hand, "dance with me."

"Dance with you? It's three o'clock in the afternoon. I just hacked the potatoes to death and our grandson is probably back at the shower getting his lip pierced."

"Come on, June," he pleaded. "Forget about all that for a minute. Just one dance."

June groaned. "I'm tired. And I didn't visit Mom this week. Tom did, I didn't."

"You can visit her tomorrow." He pulled June up so she was standing in front of him."

"This is stupid." She shook her head. "Dancing is stupid."

"You used to love it when we danced."

"Not in the front porch. People can see."

"Then let them watch," he said, taking her hand and placing the other on the small of her back. "What's that saying? Dance like nobody's watching?"

"I'm not dancing, and I'm especially not dancing because you used that expression. I hate that expression."

"Fine, I have a better one." He stopped swaying side to side, held his finger in the air, and said, "Keep calm and dance like nobody's watching."

"That's even worse."

"You're no fun."

Randy grabbed a hat from the coat tree in the corner of the porch. It was Vanessa's Che Guevara military beret. Was this supposed to double as a top hat?

"How can you say no to this?" He twirled around on one foot.

June could think of a million reasons to say no. First of all, the beret was too small for his hair so it sat on top like a bowl. Second, he'd said *keep calm and dance like nobody's watching*, and third, "There's no music."

"I can fix that," he said. "I'll be right back."

She plunked herself back down on the loveseat, drank her tea, which was already cold as a puddle, and wondered when she became so cynical. Dancing on the front porch — that was something Birte and Earle would do. And though part of her thought the notion of spontaneous dancing was unnecessary and contrived, there was another part of her that longed to be touched by familiar hands.

Randy returned with his workshop CD player covered in a fine layer of sawdust. He blew it away from her and plugged it in. "So, what do you say, my beautiful elephant?"

"Jesus Murphy."

"That came out wrong." He turned on the radio, pulled her back up onto her feet, and held her tighter than he had the first time. They moved in a clunky circle, tripping over the wilted porch carpet, the beret falling of Randy's head onto a cactus.

June was somewhere between laughing hysterically and sobbing. And she was dizzy. She closed her eyes as Randy moved in to kiss her. It was an aggressive kiss. All tongue and stress. A hurricane in a box. But she kissed him back. Out of duty, out of guilt, out of possibility. She was bothered that it felt so unfamiliar. That it had been so long. That skin had wrinkled and paint had peeled since the last time they kissed like that.

June became aware of the music suddenly, in the way she did at a grocery store when someone turned it up a few notches out of the blue. She knew the song from when she was a young mother. When the kids wore overalls and got jam on their cheeks. The whistle, the references to Russia. A song about the fall of the USSR. Of Glasnost and Perestroika. But that was never what it felt like. She did not think of Gorbachev or abandoned Soviet athletic facilities or the expansion of McDonald's into Moscow. She felt love. A Biblical love. Corinthians 13. And she kissed her husband back. Aggressive and hard because he was patient and kind and old and sad. Everything he'd ever done for her rolled off her tongue and back into him. He'd made her a dress on their first anniversary, and he didn't drive too fast, or look at dirty magazines when she didn't want to be touched, and he never complained when she asked *would you mind just going to the store?* He never minded. They kissed and shook like they hadn't seen each other in years.

14

Randy and June didn't talk about the incident on the porch. They finished cooking dinner in a hazy calm that made their kids suspicious. June felt ten years younger.

"Why are you guys acting weird?" Derek put on a shirt and joined the rest of the family at the table.

Randy picked up his fork. "We're not acting weird."

From across the table, Vanessa dragged her spoon across the surface of her stew. "What the fuck is this?"

"It's stew." June took a bite.

Vanessa slouched heavily into her chair, making the seatback bounce. "This is not stew."

"Mmm," Randy said. "Stew is subjective."

"Music is subjective," Vanessa argued. "Stew is supposed to have meat in it. This is pretty much potato paste."

"Fuck off, Vanessa," Derek said. "If you don't like it, don't eat it. You bitch about everything."

"Whoa," Vanessa mocked. "Is the new daddy tired? Were you up all day breastfeeding?"

Randy ate faster.

Derek shook his head. "You know, you can be an ungrateful bitch sometimes."

She leaned forward. "No more than you."

"No." Stew dripped from his spoon. "You live at home, and you never offer to cook, and you're pissed off all the time, and no one knows why. We always have to walk on eggshells around you. *Mind your sister, she's in a mood.*"

"Maybe I'm always in a mood because you're the bloody favourite."

"We don't have a favourite," Randy interrupted.

"No, it's true, I am the favourite," said Derek.

June put down her spoon. "We don't have a favourite."

"Mom, don't bother. We all know it's true." Derek got up from the table, took a roll from the counter, and dipped it in his bowl.

"I object," she said. "We love you all equally."

Vanessa pushed away her bowl. "Tom said you wanted him to move out."

"Only because we thought it would be good for him. Not because we liked him less."

"He also said you leave gym brochures and recreation guides all over the house because you think he's fat."

"Those were for you," June said.

"See?" Vanessa poured herself milk. "You think I'm fat, you want Tom to move out, and Derek's the golden boy. Maybe I should go get knocked up with triplets to improve my status, then my litter and I can take over the entire upstairs."

"Vanessa!" June shouted. "I thought a little exercise might help release some of that anger."

"Oh right, my anger problem. The reason you all have to — what was it, Derek — walk on eggshells? I'm not fucking angry."

"Your mother just wants you to be healthy."

"Well it's Golden Boy you should be worried about. Isn't Marissa the *second* girl you got pregnant?"

Derek threw a bun at Vanessa's forehead. "She had a *miscarriage*."

"Keep telling yourself that, Derek. The clinic on eighth and eighth? It's for abortions."

Vanessa looked at her parents. She was so full of rage June said a quick prayer in case a demon was working through her daughter. "And why, you might ask, did she have an abortion? Because she was *fifteen*."

June plugged her ears, and because her fingers were big, relative to her ear canals, she did not hear the resounding crash when Derek flipped the table. She did see the surprise on Vanessa's face and the clumps of white potato that could have been a cheesecake Blizzard on the chest of her cowl neck sweater. Randy started cleaning up immediately, scraping lumps of potato into his empty bowl and picking up the pepper-shaker, which had rolled to a stop on a floor vent. Upstairs, Jaxx was screaming. Derek said, "Sorry," and punched the wall on his way up the back stairs. Vanessa waited for him to leave, then took the stairs from the living room. "I hate you all," she screamed. June remained frozen in her chair, which seemed odd now that there was no table. She felt like a piece of installation art. Now it was she who wanted to leave, but she didn't know where to go. She just wanted out. She stood up as Randy righted the table.

"I'm going for a drive." She grabbed her keys off the wall.

"I'm coming with you," Randy said.

She held open the door. The air was bitter.

15

June drove to the nature reserve just north of their neighbourhood. It was still light out, and they'd be able to walk the trails if they wished. They stayed in the car, while a fringe station played music from the forties.

"Derek got a fifteen-year-old pregnant," June whispered.

The grass was a monochromatic buff colour. Winter grass. It looked cold.

Randy warmed his hands. "We don't know that for sure."

"Vanessa always knows." June turned to him. "That's one thing we know about her. She knows everything about her brothers."

Randy cocked his head a little to the side in agreement.

"Remember when we caught Tom with that joint?"

He sighed.

"Vanessa said he'd been doing it for years before then. It's why he always took the dog for a walk."

"I thought he was just being responsible."

"He was a pothead."

"Geez. And he took that dog out three times a day. No wonder it died."

June turned off the engine. "Two pregnancies. Why wouldn't Derek be using condoms?"

Randy ran his fingers through his hair. "I don't know. I told them a thousand times. *Don't be a fool, cover your tool.*"

June decided this was better than *keep calm and wear a condom.*

"Clearly Derek never got the message."

"Twice a year we'd have that talk."

"Maybe it's because you presented it in a rhyme. Dr. Seuss."

"Love Dr. Seuss. *Oh the thinks you can think if only you try.*"

"Like thinking about not using a condom." June shook her head. "I thought Derek was the most sensible of the three."

"Because he's your favourite?"

She hit him in the arm. "I don't *have* a favourite. I just never pictured Derek as that careless to have two unplanned pregnancies. Two."

"Carefree," Randy corrected. "You know how he is. He's always been a glass-half-full kind of kid. He doesn't always think of consequences."

Like you, she thought.

"Come on," he urged. "Let's walk. We'll feel better after some fresh air and a little exercise. Like you told Vanessa."

She made a face like she might object, but her hand was already on the door. A silver suv pulled in beside them, loose rock crunching beneath its tractor-like tires. Randy waited by the rear of the car and took June's hand when she approached. They headed in the direction of a large rock, a landmark at the mid-point of the hill. People who looked like they loved nature but probably worked in the oil industry zipped by on mountain bikes and on foot, their all-American dogs named by their children in tow.

As the hill wound to the left, it steepened, and June felt her heart rate increase. Her calves tightened, and she stopped twice before they reached the rock. The area around it was well worn, trampled down by adventurous people with small children and by alcoholics. Remnants of beer bottles cluttered the ground. Someone had written "my bitchez rule this rock" in red graffiti.

Randy climbed up on top. "Join me."

June scanned the rock face. "I can't get up there. I'm too short."

"Oh, come on," he said. "I'll help you. Go around that way and I'll pull you up."

He looked like an oversized four-year old, proud and stupid. But she relented. "Fine."

She found a foothold and heaved herself up. Randy, crouched on one knee, took hold of her wrists and hoisted her to the top. He motioned for her to sit. To the left was the airport and to the right, the downtown core. The highway, a bent line between with a steady flow of traffic. The noise of the city did not carry to the rock. They watched it on mute. Planes landing and taking off, freight trains curving in the distance. Randy spread a cloth napkin on the rock and emptied out a box of chocolate almonds.

"Have one," he encouraged.

She didn't want one. It reminded her of the macaroons and Jaxx's sad little room with the graffiti. *My bitchez rule this bedroom.* "Randy, did you find Fergus?"

Randy looked up from the cloth. He'd arranged the almonds into a circle. "Not yet."

"Did you at least find any leads?"

"There are literally thousands of records. And you have to search by surname. I don't know his surname. I don't even know that they named him Fergus. It was one of a few names they told Glenda they were considering."

"Have you ever talked to Glenda about it?"

"No." He shoved a handful of chocolate in his mouth. "I haven't even seen her since that time in Wicker Land."

"But you said she worked for a family of dentists. That shouldn't be hard to find."

"Maybe." A plane from the north made its descent onto the runway. They watched it land.

"What else do you know about her? Did she ever marry?"

"No idea. I tried looking her up years ago." He had assembled a pile of pea-sized rocks in a depression beside the napkin and began pitching them into the grass below. "She knows sign language."

"You should try to look her up again. If you're serious about finding Fergus. Find out what she knows. Maybe they've already reconnected." Everything seemed logical coming out of her mouth, but once it was out there June wondered if she was making a mistake. What if Glenda liked Dr. Seuss and whistling as much as Randy? Would she find them on the porch one day finishing each other's sentences and eating ice cream with sprinkles?

"I'm scared to meet him," Randy confessed.

"Of course you are. That's completely normal. You're worried he won't like you."

"No, actually." He looked mildly hurt. "I'm likeable."

"Yes, you're likeable." It was true. Randy had a Ned Flanders vibe that people found endearing.

"What if he's . . . you know . . . not successful?"

"Like a loser?" June asked.

"I don't like that word. I mean what if everyone I've spawned didn't quite make it? What if he works at 7-Eleven or is unemployed and makes Minecraft videos for YouTube?"

"Or works at a recycling depot?"

"June!"

"I'm kidding." She watched the brown and yellow tail of a UPS plane disappear into the only pocket of clouds in the sky.

"Or, on the contrary, what if he's really successful? Like a lawyer or a doctor."

"Then he's probably ugly."

He looked at her with pleading eyes, and she came to the horrifying conclusion she was acting like Jim Carrey. "Sorry," she apologized. "Continue."

"I think it would be weird."

She understood, because she thought about it too. She wondered what impact Fergus's perceived success would have on all of them. Would they be inspired and go back to school or give blood? Or would they feel like failures, collect employment insurance, and sell Shakeology? If Fergus was successful, did it mean it was her genes that let Tom, Derek, and Vanessa down? Or if he wasn't, was being an underachiever just simply part of being a Figg? A bird hopped along the grassy path above the rock and pecked at the ground, its body the size of a golf ball. It reminded her of Jaxx. Then she thought of the crest. The birds without wings. A curse.

"Success is subjective," she reminded him.

"Like stew," he replied.

"Like stew." She took one of the stones from his pile and flicked it down the side of the rock. It stopped in a crevasse near the bottom. "Maybe Fergus has been looking for you."

"You think?" He crossed his legs.

"Sure. Lots of adopted kids look for their birth parents."

"Not you."

She shivered. "Yeah, but this isn't about me. I had perfectly good parents. Why look for another pair? And besides, I'm too old. Too old to invite more people into my life. I can't even manage who's already in it."

"Maybe Fergus feels the same way."

June was quiet.

Randy continued. "You think there's a chance he doesn't know he's adopted?"

"Maybe, but he'd be, what, thirty-four, thirty-five now? He probably figured it out by now. That he never really fit in." She looked at Randy, who stared back at her with his mouth hanging open. "What?"

"That's a terrible thing to say."

"I didn't mean anything negative toward you. It's just something you hear adopted people say. That they always felt like a stranger in their own family. You hear it all the time."

"Did you feel that way? I hope he didn't," Randy said. "Makes me sad."

She placed her hand on his bent knee. Once-pink gum was stuck to the bottom of his sneaker. "I used to feel that way, but then I got to a point where it didn't matter. It's hard though. The feelings of isolation. Not being able to connect or make sense of things. Poor Fergus."

"Geez, June. I'm sure his childhood wasn't *that* traumatic.

Glenda said she chose a really wonderful couple. They couldn't have kids of their own and they didn't care if he was a boy or a girl. That says something about them."

"Oh, I know. I didn't mean to imply that Fergus grew up unhappy. I just think if you ever get to meet him, be sensitive to the fact that he may have spent a considerable amount of time feeling like he never fit in. That's all."

"Duly noted." He ate the remaining almonds and carefully folded the napkin into a small triangle. He looked worried.

"What?" she asked.

"Nothing," he said.

She hugged her knees up around her chest. It was an uncomfortable position that drove her sit bones into the rock, but the air had cooled. She wondered if Fergus was somewhere out there, wandering around feeling that he never belonged. Not being able to identify with the shape of his mother's face or her slow metabolism or the way she planned everything so meticulously. Or his father. His six-foot frame and crooked spine. His love of Chaucer and pickled fish and open spaces. June gasped at what her brain had just done. This was not supposed to be about her and her parents. She covered her mouth, as if to keep the thoughts from escaping, and tapped her cortices. It didn't work. Coming to the park had seemed like a good idea, but now it only reminded her how she hated open spaces. Growing up in the country was boring and exhausting. She was always in the fifth percentile for height, and the walk to the bus stop was too far, and sometimes the bus driver would forget to stop and would drive past her house. And she never understood why she had to eat pickled herring when the ocean was nowhere in sight. She remembered her mother with her parallelogram-shaped head and size-ten feet hanging out the back of her kitchen clogs, telling her it was in her blood to like fish. But June disagreed. Other than the battered haddock from their favourite diner, eating fish felt about as natural as eating hamster.

Randy helped June down from the rock and motioned for her to start down the path toward the parking lot, but her legs were unsteady. She moved slowly, turning her hip to the front so that she side-stepped down the steeper portion of the hill. She experienced a wave of adrenaline she couldn't explain. She was not afraid or in danger. No one was lost or injured. It was that she didn't want to be adopted. She didn't want to go there. It was a notion she'd buried, like a seed, deep beneath the floorboards where it was invisible and not privy to the resources it needed to grow. And now it was a tree that crashed through the floor, all trunk and branches. She couldn't get away from it. She needed a chainsaw. All she had was butter knife. David and Goliath.

She concentrated on breathing in through her nose and out through her mouth until they reached the edge of the parking lot. A collie peed on a sign identifying wildlife in the area. She gave her legs a little shake and released an exaggerated sigh of relief. "Poor Fergus," she projected, pointing for Randy to drive home. "Must have been tough."

16

Jaxx was awake and sucking on Derek's hand when they returned from the nature reserve, his eyes the pageant blue of a dress uniform.

"Can I hold him?" June asked.

Derek raised him up and placed him into June's arms. "Sorry I flipped the table."

June concentrated on Jaxx, hoping if she ignored Derek's apology long enough he would go away and she wouldn't have to talk about the baby he aborted or the age of that baby's mother. But Derek persisted.

"It was a miscarriage," he said. "I swear."

"How's my sweet baby boy? You're a hungry boy today. Getting so big drinking all that non-breast milk."

"Mom," Derek said. "Acknowledge me."

"What, Derek? What do you want me to say? Am I supposed to congratulate you because you only have one unplanned baby and not two?"

"I just want you to believe me."

She brushed Jaxx's hair to the side. "Why didn't you ever consider using a condom? How does this happen twice? Vanessa's right, you know. About that clinic."

She passed Derek a receiving blanket and moved Jaxx to her shoulder. Derek didn't respond. He put his head down on the island and looked like he might fall asleep, eyes red and outlined with fatigue.

"Why don't you go to bed?" June said. "I'll look after him."

"I have to work tomorrow." He lifted his head.

"Maybe you should shower first. Jaxx will be fine. Work will be fine."

"Leslie's teaching me how to install kitchens."

"Tomorrow?"

"The depot is giving me another week off."

"Then go get some sleep."

Derek threw his arms around her. She stumbled backward. "Whoa."

"I love you, Mom," he croaked.

"I know you do, Derek."

He pulled back and wiped away tears, his face all blotched from pressing it against the counter. He seemed both bipolar and hormonal. A typical new mother.

"Okay," he said. "I'm going to bed." He patted Jaxx on the head, his hand still immense in comparison, and he disappeared up the stairs, past the hole he'd punched in the wall.

June wondered if Vanessa was home, but suspected she wasn't. Nothing had been slammed in the past twenty minutes. She took Jaxx to the makeshift change station that was still set up on the family room coffee table. When she pulled up his diaper shirt, the remainder of Marissa's umbilical cord fell off. It was an amber-coloured chunk the size of a large raisin. She picked it off and gently cleaned the pool of custard-like pus that had collected in his belly button.

"Grandma's going to get you a new diaper," she cooed, crawling toward a box of Pampers. Jaxx sucked his fist, his eyes slightly crossed.

Derek, looking no different than he had five minutes ago, was back in the kitchen. "I forgot to give him his vitamin D."

"Leave it on the counter, I'll do it."

The cupboard door closed. "One squirt," he said. "And by the way, when Vanessa was in Grade 11, she brought a knife to school."

June fetched the bottle of vitamin D drops. "Impossible, Derek. We would've known about that. There is no way the school wouldn't have contacted us."

"Vanessa paid Tom two hundred bucks to pose as Dad. She was suspended for a day. They never expelled her because it was a first offence, and you and Dad agreed to send her to counselling."

June squeezed the bottle in her hand. "And you knew about this?"

"She gave me fifty bucks not to tell."

"Vanessa brings a knife to school and you decided her safety and perhaps the safety of others was worth fifty dollars?"

"She told me it was just a prop for art class."

"And you believed her?"

He shrugged. "Sort of. Remember that big mural by the gym?"

June vaguely remembered the anti-violence mural. She thought Vanessa had painted the grenade. "So the school believed Tom that it was a misunderstanding?"

"Yes, but only because you and Dad agreed to some investigative counselling just in case."

"Investigative counselling?" Randy said. "What does that mean?" He stood on the top step from the basement in an undershirt and track pants.

"Don't ask," June said. "Derek, go shower and go to bed." She looked at Randy. "I have to give this to Jaxx." She held up the bottle with its built-in dropper.

Jaxx was still comfortably on his back, a second fist now jammed in his mouth. She measured out a dose and moved his hands away from his face. "Good boy."

"So, what does investigative counselling mean?"

June heard the rotational hum of the microwave and wondered what Randy was making. A stack of clean baby-laundry teetered on the arm of the couch. She zipped Jaxx inside a fleece sleeper and thought about Derek's story of Vanessa bringing a knife to school.

Randy hovered in front of the microwave. "Tom pretended to be me?"

June placed Jaxx in the cradle. "Yes."

"Maybe it really was for the mural," he said. "I do remember seeing it when Derek graduated. I'm sure there was a big knife on it. And it was signed. Vanessa's name was in black upper-case letters at the very bottom."

Was it written backwards? June wondered, looking down at Jaxx. Randy removed whatever it was he'd put in the microwave.

June bit her nails. "Think we should talk to her about it?"

"I'm sure it's nothing. And it was years ago. But if it really bothers you . . ." He dug at his teeth with a fork. "Call her and ask."

June dialled Vanessa's number. "Hi, it's Mom. Do you have a minute?"

"A minute, yes," Vanessa belted from the other end of the phone. "I'm just about to go into Starbucks."

"Remember that time you brought a knife to school in Grade 11?"

There was a long pause. "What are you talking about?"

"When you brought the knife to school and you paid your brother to pretend he was Dad when the principal called."

"Did Tom tell you that?"

"Actually, Derek mentioned it."

"Well, tell Derek to fuck off."

June expected her to hang up, but she didn't. She added, "It was for an art project."

"That was the only reason?" June switched to speakerphone so Randy could hear.

"What are you implying, Mom?"

Someone frothed milk in the background.

"I just wanted to make sure that it was for the mural and nothing else."

"Like?" Vanessa asked.

"Like hurting yourself . . . or others," June said.

Randy made a stabbing gesture.

"Randy," June scolded. "Are you still there, Vanessa?"

"No, I'm stabbing someone with a knife. Can I call you back?"

"Vanessa, I needed to check. Two hundred dollars was a lot of money for you back then."

"Yes, but if you found out, you would have grounded me, and it was the same week as the Fall Out Boy concert. And besides, I only ended up paying him fifty."

Randy made a face suggesting this was reasonable. "That was nice of Tom."

June threw a cushion at him.

"You wanna know why I only paid him fifty?"

"No."

"Because I covered for him that time you found weed in the car."

"I don't recall finding weed in the car."

"Because I said it was lettuce."

"Lettuce?"

"Yes, and you were mad because you made that rule about no eating in the car."

"That was weed?"

"You let it go because you were so proud I was eating salad."

June sighed and hung up without saying goodbye. She tossed her phone on the couch.

"I remember thinking that. And I went out and bought a bunch of salad dressings."

"Yes, and they all expired."

June bent over the cradle, traced the outline of Jaxx's mouth, and smoothed down a few pieces of stray hair.

Randy rinsed a plate in the sink. "I'm going to spend some time looking for Fergus."

"I'll join you in a few," June replied. "I told Derek I would look after the baby tonight. I'll bring Jaxx down and put him in the swing."

June sliced an apple and slid pieces into Jerry's cage. The bird was on his trapeze. He was sweet natured, good for Vanessa.

"I see you," June whispered through the metal bars. Jerry bobbed his head and June felt melancholy, knowing Vanessa would take him when she went.

17

Jaxx woke up four times in the night, causing June to question whether she was dying. The fatigue was unbearable. Even though she was still in bed and Derek had taken Jaxx for his morning feeding, she felt like she'd spent the last eight hours doing rigorous exercise with her eyes taped open. She pleaded, "I need to sit down."

"June," Randy said. "You're lying down."

"Yes . . . am I?" She moved her arms through the space around her. Yes, she was still in bed. She could barely lift her head in the direction of her husband, and when she did, she saw his bare, virtually hairless, white bum. It disappeared in a blink beneath a pair of underwear she'd bought him at Marshalls. He was into his reserve underwear — an indication she had not kept up with the laundry. His boxer briefs had a rubbery sheen that made her think of Cher. And they were so tight, despite being labelled extra-large. His crotch resembled a balloon animal.

"I kind of like these." Randy adjusted his package and squatted.

June dropped her head back on the bed. Her thousand-pound head. The pillow puffed up around her.

"Now, I'll be taking Jaxx for a walk this morning," he said matter-of-factly. "And you will be going to the spa."

She lifted her head again. Randy was pointing at her. His hair hadn't been brushed, and it reminded her of the quiet *Joy of Painting* host she used to watch on PBS. She wondered what happened to him. His large hair and soothing voice. His trees that appeared from nothing. She closed her eyes.

"June, did you hear what I said? I said you were going to the spa."

She shook herself out of her stupor. "Yes, I heard you."

He was still at the end of the bed, looking intense in an Inigo Montoya sort of way.

"And I'm so grateful," she added. "Really, I am."

Randy placed his hands on his hips in satisfaction and smiled until she could see the gap from his missing tooth on the upper left side of his mouth.

"And that's not all. Earle and I have arranged for you and Birte to go together. She's picking you up at ten and then you have lunch reservations after."

June smiled, though the thought of Birte driving made her anxious. Birte was a drive-talker. Constantly trying to make eye contact with her passenger instead of looking at the road. And because she drove a Smart Car, with essentially nothing beyond the windshield, June always felt like they were going to hit whatever was in front of them. Randy crawled on the bed, now wearing a pair of awful cinnamon-coloured pants he'd bought on clearance and a black compression-style shirt athletes wore under their gear. He hovered over her, a heavy-breathing bear, and kissed both cheeks. "Have a lovely time." His breath smelled like an old man's bathroom.

June waved him off and remained in bed for another hour, not moving, as though she were having a CAT scan. She imagined her brain would look like a sea cucumber if it were examined right now. As ten o'clock neared, she finally got out of bed and forced herself to do jumping jacks, the way Randy used to when they were first married. Dressed, she ate a croissant at the window, flakes of pastry sailing to the floor like ticker tape.

Birte arrived just after ten and parked on the grass. "Sorry!" she said. "I almost had it and then poof! I'm on the lawn."

"It happens." June buckled her seatbelt.

Birte ate a miniature log of carrot cake, its plastic wrap wedged between her thighs. From the radio, someone was delivering a monologue on a controversial new pipeline.

"So, we're having massages first and then pedicures." Birte looked over at June and then swerved to avoid a plastic bag.

June tensed.

"I haven't had a massage in ages." Birte licked icing off her knuckle. "At least not at a spa. Earle and I take turns giving each other massages at home. We use a timer to keep it fair."

June pictured short Birte straddling Earle's expansive bare back, like a toddler on a horse.

"So, how's little Jaxx doing?" Birte asked.

"He's wonderful," June gushed. "He's alert and growing and sleeping really well. Except for last night. Lord have mercy, he was up every couple of hours."

"And how's Derek coping? Is he doing okay?"

"For the most part. Though he's back to work today."

"At the depot?"

"He's learning to install kitchens with a friend of Vanessa's."

Birte said, "Darn it. I had some bottles to return."

"I think it will be good for him."

Birte pulled into the spa. It was in a strip mall flanked by a Subway and a hemp shop. The reception area was decorated with cat statuary. A Gregorian chant hummed from a speaker fixed to the ceiling.

The receptionist handed them each a clipboard, followed by a robe and a pair of flat flip-flops. Birte sent hers back.

"I have my own," she sang, waving a sandal she pulled from her purse.

June never thought to bring sandals. The receptionist showed them to the women's change room and a second waiting area that looked like the Clue library. There were built-in book-shelves, wing-backed chairs, and fancy water jugs with things floating in them — mint leaves, strawberries, lemons, and cucumbers. Birte filled her glass with the cucumber water and sat in the chair closest to a bowl of wafers.

"Ooh, look." She set a wafer on the arm of her chair. "*The Canterbury Tales.*"

"I hate Chaucer," June said. She placed her mechanical pencil down and took a wafer.

"Didn't your father love Chaucer?"

"Yes," June replied, her mouth full. "And it probably wouldn't have bothered me so much if he didn't always refer to him simply as *Geoffrey*, like he was our neighbour." June circled an area of the lower back on her massage questionnaire.

"My father was never much into literature." Birte used her robe to wipe sweat from her glass. "He read Norwegian science journals."

"You know what else my Dad loved? *America's Funniest Home Videos.* That's all we watched at the hospice. Vanessa would sit on his lap and he'd try to braid her hair. He did a better job than I did."

"I bet you he loved that."

June dropped her pencil. "Birte, what do you think about adoptees searching for their birth parents?"

"Oh, I don't know. I suppose it makes sense for medical reasons."

"Only medical reasons? What about just to know where you came from?"

Birte twisted the tie of her robe around her finger. "I guess it depends on what the person wants to do with the information. Some birth parents don't want to be contacted so if the purpose is to have a relationship with them, it doesn't always work." Birte sipped her water suspiciously. "You're not thinking of searching for your birth parents, are you?"

June put down her questionnaire. "You know I said I would never look for them. But lately . . ."

Birte waited.

"Lately, I've been thinking I might want to." June exhaled. "Birte, I don't really know who I am."

"None of us do." A massage therapist with a sleek ponytail entered the library and asked Birte to follow her down the hall. Birte took another wafer, tightened her robe and placed a hand on June's shoulder. "I'll see you on the other side."

June filled a glass. What if Fergus had no desire to meet his birth father? It would break Randy's heart.

A massage therapist introduced herself and summoned June into a room at the end of the hall. She left June to undress and hide under the covers, taking the clipboard and questionnaire with her. June hated this part, because they always gave her too much time. She was already in a robe. Why did they always think it took eleven minutes to remove the robe and climb under the sheet? Did she look older than she was? Decrepit?

With each passing second she became more aware of her nakedness. The spreading of her body across the table, like batter in a pan. And the longer she lay there, the creepier she felt. What the heck was the massage therapist doing out there? Eating a ham sandwich? Spying on her through a crack in the wall? She stared at the ground through the face hole. Somewhere there was a speaker on the floor and the monks were chanting about meatballs. The massage therapist knocked.

"I'm ready." June was impatient.

Heather, the therapist, applied light pressure to June's upper back. "Let me know if anything feels uncomfortable."

But everything was uncomfortable. Her hips and cheekbones felt like arrowheads against the table and she was annoyed with Birte for acting like *medical concerns* were the only legitimate reason for an adoptee to seek out her birth family.

"How's that feel?"

The room smelled like lemongrass.

"It's fine," June said, but it wasn't. Heather was sort of pinching the back of her neck the way one might pretend to pull off a child's nose. She clenched her teeth and focused on the hotel-like carpet below.

"You're quite tense," Heather said.

June thought Heather's voice was too soft. Melted ice cream. She wanted to plug her ears, but she was instructed to roll over onto her back. Heather tried to help by lifting June's legs like she was newly paralyzed and in rehab. On a shelf of neatly rolled towels was a decorative gold cat with one paw up like it was waving. June wanted to break its arm. Heather pressed down on her shins. June jumped.

"Too much pressure?" Heather withdrew her hands.

"Sorry," June said. "They're really sore."

"I didn't see that on your questionnaire," Heather said. "They weren't circled."

She moved behind June and cupped the back of her neck, pulling her head away from her body. Decapitation. It was the first part of the massage that actually felt good, and June closed her eyes. She thought of ET, his long neck and phono-graph-shaped head, and she wanted to go home. Instead, Heather gave June a finishing shoulder squeeze and sent her back to the library. Birte was sprawled out on a chair, balancing a glass on her stomach.

"I could fall asleep," she sang through a yawn. "That was so relaxing."

June loosened her robe and sat across from her. "Randy has another son."

Birte, who had closed both eyes, opened one of them and sat upright. She waited for more details.

"He's older than Tom," June added. "He was given up for adoption."

"Well," Birte stammered, "that's news to me."

June looked at her friend. Her cheeks were petal pink, her blond hair a sweaty mess. Birte ate a wafer out of discomfort.

"You already knew, didn't you?" June slumped in her wing-back chair.

"Yes," Birte confessed. "But I only found out yesterday, and it was by accident."

"Randy told you?"

"Earle did. Randy had asked him the name of our dentist."

"Why, who's your dentist?"

"We go to twin brothers. Harold and Herman. Randy asked if there was someone named Glenda that worked there. Do you know that they were born almost two hours apart? Herman's older. I don't like him as much. He's allergic to latex and uses these funny-tasting gloves, plus he drives a BMW, which makes me think I'm getting ripped off."

"Glenda was his son's birth mother."

"Randy mentioned that. He said that you suggested he search for her in order to find him. What was his name?"

"Fergus," June said. "At least that's what they think."

A pair of aestheticians arrived and escorted them to a white room. Blue water gurgled from the footbaths at the base of the chairs. They were ushered to a panel of polish and told to select a colour. June chose beige and climbed onto her assigned seat. "I worry Fergus will reject him," she said.

Birte held up a bottle of coral polish. "It can happen. Remember Ruby from water aerobics? She spent ten years looking for her birth parents. Unfortunately, her mother had died of cancer, and when she finally tracked down her father, he refused to meet her. Said he was dying of cancer too and didn't need any more trouble."

That was another thing that kept June from acknowledging her beginnings. Her adoption, like Ruby's, would have occurred at a time when such arrangements were secret and dirty and sacrilegious. Like prohibition. "That's sad." June said, conflicted by the pleasure she felt of having her heels buffed.

By the time the pedicures were finished, June didn't want lunch. She'd eaten a dozen wafers. She shuffled to the reception desk in her disposable flip-flops. Birte, out of breath, treaded behind, her feet rolling over the edges of her leather sandals.

Twenty minutes later, they were spread out on either side of a booth designed for parties of six. June pointed at a quesadilla on the menu. Birte ordered a cheeseburger.

"Isn't young love wonderful?" Birte's earrings dangled while she raved. Tiny chandeliers.

"Sure," June agreed, but she wasn't picturing young love. She imagined Birte straddling Earle for a back massage, the egg timer from Birte's kitchen, with the googly eyes and feet, watching from their bedside.

"Sweet. Innocent," Birte mused, stirring her water like it was a fine cocktail.

The only young love June was aware of was dirty and raw and full of disappointment. Derek slip-sliding on the counting table. Vanessa doing lesbian things, which she knew little about but assumed were damp and involved rubber toys in video game colours. And God only knew what Tom did. Young *perversion,* she thought. Not love. And when she did consider love, she thought not of herself and Randy, young and clean under the covers, but of Glenda and Randy, who were younger and had more hair to get lost beneath.

Birte's hamburger arrived lopsided and wet. She immediately cut it in half and took a bite.

"There they go again," she said.

June turned around to see what Birte was talking about. She expected a train of Chili's workers to emerge from the kitchen to wish someone a happy birthday. Instead she saw

Marissa nestled under the arm of a man with biceps the size of coconuts and a T-shirt so tight that, even from a distance, June could see his pierced nipples. He picked up his napkin and wiped his mouth like he'd just eaten someone for dinner. *Maybe it's not Marissa*, June thought, but resting on a sports bag beneath the table on feet crossed at the ankles were the same black Converse sneakers with neon orange laces June had seen under Marissa's bed at the hospital. That was a week ago. One week? Nine days? She suddenly couldn't remember. Why couldn't she remember? Was she having a mini-stroke, or was this the beginning of dementia? Her quesadilla was now on the table, and she had no idea how long it had been sitting there, or who served it. The guacamole was missing. Had she already asked for it? Should she ask again?

"Is there corn in that?" Birte stabbed a mushroom with her fork.

"I hope not," June said, but a niblet did appear to be clinging to the edge of the tortilla. She cut the corn away with her knife. She was terrified of dementia. The way it progressed from *where did I put my glasses* to *who are you* in a matter of months. Her mother. She smoothed her napkin over her lap and turned around again. Marissa removed a chip from a stack of nachos and picked it apart. The man opened his mouth, and she playfully placed a chip on the tip of his tongue, which he waved from side to side. When Marissa went to add a second chip he closed his mouth around her finger like a flytrap and sucked it back to her knuckle. June gasped. "There's corn in my quesadilla!"

Birte and an impish man eating soup at a neighbouring table stared. A server en route to another table stopped and asked if he could help.

"Corn," she repeated, "there's corn in my sandwich."

"It's a quesadilla," Birte corrected.

"You ordered the Santa Fe quesadilla," the server said. "It comes with corn."

"Blame it on me," June said.

"That's what you ordered, ma'am."

"It is what you ordered, June," Birte whispered. "I heard you."

"Fine." She threw up her hands. "I ordered the corn, I'll eat the corn." She cut the end off one of her triangles and swallowed without chewing.

"Is this about Derek?" Birte asked.

"Derek? Why would this be about Derek?"

"I know you're kind of stressed about the whole him becoming a father thing and the new job."

"Derek's fine."

"Is it Randy then? Is it about his . . . *illegitimate* child?"

June was agitated. "Why do you insist this is about something?"

"Because you're crying." Birte fake-smiled at the people around them.

June wasn't really aware she'd been crying until she touched her face. "I hate corn."

Birte handed her a napkin. "I don't like corn either." She dipped a fry in a paper tub of chipotle mayo, leaned across the table, and whispered. "Is it your mom, then?"

June stared.

"Sorry, trying to help."

"You know that couple behind us? The *young love* you were going on about."

"I don't know if I was going *on* about them." Birte avoided eye contact.

"That girl is Marissa. Jaxx's mother."

Birte's eyes blew up. "She doesn't look like a mother."

"Exactly. Right now Randy is at home being his mother and she is getting her fingers sucked by Homo erectus."

"Shame on her!" Birte said. "She should be taking care of that baby."

"Thank you," said June.

"And it's Derek who should be sucking her fingers!"

The server placed the bill between them on the table.

"Sorry," Birte offered. "That sounded weird."

Not as weird as it looked, June thought, taking the bill. She placed her Visa on top of the leather envelope and apologized. "I wasn't great company today."

Birte waved her hand like it was nothing and scrambled to eat the remaining fries before the server took her plate away. They left the restaurant in time to see Marissa sitting in the passenger seat of a black car that was low to the ground and jerked like a crab-walking child. Birte reversed out of her parking spot and gently tapped June on the knee. "It's all going to be okay," she said. "It will all work out." She dragged out her *alls* which emphasized the sheer number of things that needed to be worked out. Then she bumped off the curb and made a hard left into traffic. Two cars honked, but Birte's expression remained fixed. "Some drivers," she mumbled.

June looked out her window at an elderly man jogging. Both of his knees were wrapped, and he wore runners' shorts that caught the wind like a kite. He didn't use his arms. He didn't have headphones. She wondered what he thought of.

Did he have grandkids he wanted to spoil with airplane rides and developmental toys? A divorced daughter who needed help buying a Toyota and picking deck materials from Lowe's? Or was he running to make himself forget?

18

When Birte pulled up to the house, Randy was raking leaves from last winter, and Jaxx was asleep in a vibrating pod. He stood in front of the baby, she assumed, in case Birte was planning on driving onto the lawn and through the front door.

"How was the spa?"

"It was nice, thank you."

Leaves were assembled in piles throughout the yard.

"It's a work in progress." Randy leaned on the rake and pointed at Jaxx. "He only just fell asleep."

"But, you had a good day though?" June sat on the front step next to a travel mug.

"We did," Randy said. "We fed the birds, and went for a walk and dropped in on the Dekkers." He bent down, nearly toppling over, and took a sip from the travel mug. "And, I got a custom order for a table. Client wants it before the end of next week. Jaxx and I already picked up the wood."

June interrupted. "I saw Marissa at Chili's."

"Our Marissa?" Randy pulled an orange yard bag out of his vest pocket.

"Marissa, Marissa," she said. "She was feeding chips to some steroids man."

"Why would she do that?" Randy scooped up handfuls of leaves. "Maybe they're just friends."

"Not likely." June took the garbage bag from Randy and followed him around the yard. He smelled like rum.

Randy picked up more leaves. "What did Birte have to say?"

"Nothing. Are you drinking?" She stared at the travel mug.

"It's the rum from the baby shower." He burped. "Tastes a bit like candy. And hot sauce."

"Should you be drinking when you're looking after Jaxx?"

"I've only had one glass."

Was he drinking it straight? "Birte mentioned you told them about Fergus."

He raised his hand as if asking permission to speak. "I did, but only because I remembered they went to a dental office run by brothers." He tripped over a rake. "Not the right one though. No Glenda working there." Randy stopped stuffing leaves and lifted Jaxx out of his pod and onto his shoulder.

"Let me take him," June said. "Have you heard from Derek?"

"He checked in a couple of times."

Randy handed her the baby. They went inside, and June placed Jaxx on a blanket inside the turtle sandbox.

Randy touched his stomach. "I need to eat."

Why don't you have some rum cake, she thought. They both went to the kitchen, where Vanessa was at the table eating a bowl of cereal, still in her pyjamas. Milk dripped down her chin.

"Good morning," June said, though it was afternoon.

Vanessa raised her eyebrows in acknowledgement. A silver laptop sat open beside her. "Check it out," she said, turning the screen toward Randy, who was eating a white bun. "Found an Aaron Frevola born January 18, 1982, at Foothills Hospital searching for his birth parents, and a Mark Joseph Harnish born February 14, 1982."

"No," Randy shook his head. "Fergus was born on April 11."

June glanced around the kitchen for the rum. They didn't have a designated liquor cabinet. Most of the alcohol in the house belonged to the kids and it was usually beer, stored in the fridge.

Vanessa typed something on the keyboard and then added a spoonful of sugar to her cereal. "There's a Judith Pond looking for a daughter she gave up in 1974 and a Nicole Lester born April 11, 1989, looking for her birth father."

Randy finished his bun and frowned.

June took a package of drumsticks out of the freezer and set them on the counter. "Would Leslie like to come for dinner?"

"I'll text her," Vanessa replied. "We're supposed to check out a townhouse, but the realtor hasn't confirmed yet."

June coughed. "So it's true?"

"Is what true?"

"You and Leslie are moving in together?"

Vanessa shrugged. "If we find the right place."

Randy opened a cupboard. "I wonder if Fergus likes white buns or whole wheat ones."

June knew better than to bring up Leslie's age. "But don't you think it's a little soon? I mean at least rent first. Or go on a vacation. Have you and Leslie even gone to a movie together?"

"We've already shared a toothbrush."

June put on an apron.

"Me and Glenda used to share a toothbrush," Randy said,

sitting down at the table.

June grimaced. First came love, then came toothbrush, and then came Fergus. "Ask Leslie how things are going with Derek."

Vanessa moved her bowl and texted furiously.

"Can I see this for a second?" Randy slid the laptop toward him.

"Fuck, Dad, you smell like the bottle depot. Since when did you start drinking in the day?" Vanessa continued texting.

"I drank a tiny bit of the rum I won at the shower."

From the island, June could see Randy scrolling through rows of birthdates. She returned to the freezer in search of green beans.

"Leslie'll come for dinner. We're seeing the townhouse tomorrow morning instead. Derek's fine. She says he's good."

"I found a Fergus." Randy pushed back from the laptop.

"Where?" Vanessa set down her phone.

"See?" Randy pointed. "Fergus Daniel Littleton. Looking for his birth father."

"Fergus Daniel Littleton," Vanessa read out loud, "born April 1982, no date given . . ."

Randy clasped his hands together in anticipation.

There were no green beans.

Vanessa continued. "In Swift Current, Saskatchewan."

"Saskatchewan? Where does it say that?" Randy leaned back in.

"You have to look down here." She gestured.

Tom appeared at the back door, wiping his shoes on the mat.

"Hi, honey," June said.

"'Sup?"

"I'm about to make something for your father. You hungry?"

"No, I grabbed a sandwich on the way home." He pulled a toque off his head. His hair looked like a crop circle.

"Here's another one," Vanessa said. "Born April 11 or 12 at Foothills Hospital."

Tom poured himself a beer. "What are you guys doing?"

Vanessa put her hand in the cereal box and pulled out a handful of flakes. "Searching for Dad's love child."

June's heart dive-bombed into her pelvis. *Love child?* Was that what Fergus was? She wanted to correct Vanessa and say, *you mean his bastard, he's looking for his bastard* or *he's looking for half of his DNA*. Anything but *love child*. Love child was too sweet. Like that terrible Stevia sweetener Birte once forced June to try in her tea. *Love child* implied love. Naked hippie maypole dancing love. Was love the reason Randy never talked about Glenda? Because he talked about Marta the skier with the big nose, and Evelyn who now grew organic potatoes in Prince Edward Island with her much younger husband.

Vanessa read, "Jason Huckabee, year of birth, 1984."

"Randall Figg, in the case of thirty-two-year-old Jason Huckabee, you are *not* the father," Tom said.

June noticed the rum sidled up beside the toaster. It was a small bottle, but it was still half gone. She hid it in the breadbox.

"This shit's depressing." Vanessa scrolled down the track pad of her Mac. "Listen to this one. Looking for my birth mother. I was born at the Royal Alexandra Hospital in Edmonton on December 15, 1991. My mother was fourteen and went by the nickname Dee-Dee. I need a bone-marrow transplant and am searching for a compatible blood relative donor. Please help."

"That's awful." Randy held his face. "What if Fergus needs

a kidney or something?"

"Then I'm sure he'd be on here," Tom said. "You know, we could always take a picture of you holding a sign with all of Fergus's adoption details on it and post it on Facebook."

June poured herself a small glass of Pepsi. It burned going down her throat. "Birte said the only reason someone should look for his birth family is for medical reasons." No one listened.

"Check out this one. Looking for a son I gave up for adoption in 1976. He was born in Grande Prairie, Alberta on November 6 and adopted by Bob and Marion Seber. Given name unknown. Had a red birthmark on the back of his leg that looked like a map of Newfoundland. May have moved to the Valleyview area or Spirit River."

"Someone must know who that is," Randy said, hopeful.

Tom topped up his glass. "Read that one," he pointed to the screen between sips. "The pathetic one all in caps."

Vanessa read aloud, "ARE YOU MY DAUGHTER? Gave up my baby girl when I was fifteen years old. She was born at the Grace Hospital in Calgary just before midnight. Adopted by a really nice couple originally from the Maritimes somewhere (New Glasgow? New Waterford? New Brunswick?). She was a tiny little thing the size of a football and had hair the colour of cheddar."

"Does it actually say cheddar?" Tom asked.

"Yes, but I'm not done," Vanessa said. She backhanded him in the gut. "You made me lose my place."

June screwed the lid back on the pop. She hoped Derek was indeed doing well at his new job, and that Leslie wasn't just being nice.

"Okay, here," Vanessa said, repeating the cheddar line

under her breath. "I believe the wife's name was Margaret, but I don't remember his name. They didn't have any other kids."

Margaret was June's mother's name. It was the name June whispered in her mother's ear when she visited her at the home because the word *mom* meant nothing to her anymore. It was like any other three letter word. Cat. Pin. Toe. It had no significance.

Vanessa continued to read. "Hurry up," June interrupted. "I want to clean the table."

"Before handing my baby over to the nurse I took her hand-print on my nightie with an inkpad I took from the front desk. I would have named you Wanda, but . . ." Vanessa stopped reading. "I should . . . I should text Leslie and see when they're going to be done. I want to get some hair dye before dinner."

"And can you ask your brother to pick up some rice on the way home?"

"Sure." Vanessa was quiet.

June rung out a dishcloth in the sink, pleased Vanessa expressed a rare moment of niceness.

"What kind of rice? Derek wants to know."

"The regular kind." She picked up the laptop and wiped beneath it. "I actually enjoyed that Pepsi." She tossed the dish-cloth into the sink and sat down. Vanessa and Tom had cleared out of the room.

June looked at Randy. "Maybe you should register your name on here. Say you're looking for your son. Or," she straight-ened the laptop, "there's a DNA bank you can sign up with. You do a throat swab, they enter your information into a database and contact you if there's a DNA match."

She squinted at the screen. "'I would have named you

Wanda,'" she read, "'but they called you June.'" She paused. "Huh," she considered. "Like me." She raised her brows playfully toward Randy and then looked down at the keyboard. "How do you work this thing?" She fiddled with the track pad and landed on a date: June 29, 1959. Then her hand ceased moving. It stopped flat on the pad, fingers flared, angled slightly to the left, perfect for tracing or making a handprint. For bracing her collapse onto the floor upon realization her hair colour was good on tacos and her real name rhymed with Honda.

19

June lost all sense of time. She'd watched a show once about people who experienced the phenomenon of missing time. Someone would pull over to the side of the road to open his Thermos, and then six hours later he was still there but his soup was cold and his toenails were gone. Hypnosis would later reveal encounters with black-eyed needle-wielding aliens. She had no idea how long she'd been on the floor with her legs splayed and knees lazily slumped against the linoleum. Randy was behind her, holding her up by her armpits, like she was in labour. She breathed like she was in labour. Rapid and random, unlike how she'd been coached. It was all a coincidence. Her name, her birthdate. The connection to the Maritimes. Their love of fish. Her Cracker Barrel hair. Margaret, her mother's name. Her real mother. The one who let her feed the barn cats and drink tea at a young age. No siblings. None of it proof. Not even the hospital. The proof was in the handprint. In the bedside story her father always told about *the girl with the one blue hand*. It was a magical story, her favourite. About a baby who arrived on the curl of a wave.

One hand in the sea and one on the land,
'tis the tale of the girl with the one blue hand.
A man missing the sea and tending his grass
witnessed a wave like a Turkish man's 'stache.
Riding the wave, on the back of a pearl,
was an even more magical nymph of a girl.
Then his wife ran out and she saw it too,
the nymph of a girl with one hand that was blue.
Five painted fingers she saw as a sign:
this child, she declared, she's meant to be mine.
The wave soon vanished into the late June air,
leaving the babe with the sun-red hair.
And that one tiny palm, a mark of the sea,
made the once lonesome couple a family of three.

June peeled herself out of Randy's arms and sat on her knees. "The tale of the girl with the one blue hand," she said. "It was my adoption story. How could I have not recognized it before?"

"You didn't know about the handprint." He held up his hand.

"No. That part never made sense."

June mused over the two accounts of her birth. Her father's version, lyrical and sentimental, and her birth mother's sad Cheez Whiz version. She all of a sudden identified with her father. Maybe Chaucer, fishcakes, and open spaces weren't so bad when the alternative might've been low-income housing and tater-tots. What bedtime story would her mother have told? Quiz results from *Teen* magazine? Yet there was also something endearing about the stolen handprint.

"Am I her daughter?" June looked at her hand.

"Maybe," Randy replied.

"I only asked my father about my adoption once. Before he died."

"And what did he say?"

"He told me the tale of the girl with the one blue hand."

"You could try asking your mom?" Randy climbed onto one knee and fixed his glasses, which were twisted on his face like he'd been in a fight. "She might be able to tell you something."

"I don't know. She gave me that book when I was seven, and that was it. We didn't talk about it."

Tom was back in the kitchen rooting through his backpack. He pulled out an iPhone charger. "So, you think she's your mom?" He was cautious.

"It's a definite possibility." Randy tousled the back of June's hair. It was damp with massage oil.

"Does that mean I have one of those really young grandmas who still wears red nails and shows cleavage?"

"Tom," Randy slurred. "What kind of comment is that?"

"What?" Tom shrugged. "I meant that in a good way."

June pulled herself up on the island. "I better put these in the microwave." She held up the package of drumsticks. "Or they'll never thaw in time."

Tom plugged his phone in on the counter. "I hear the baby. I'll get him."

June turned to Randy. "You think she's my mother, don't you?"

"I do."

"It's the handprint." She looked at her reflection in the microwave. *Who am I?* "You think I should respond?"

"You know what I think." Randy touched her shoulder and then withdrew, clenching his hands into excited fists.

June felt nauseous. "I don't think I'm ready."

"Not ready?" He felt around the toaster.

"Once I respond, there's no going back. What if I change my mind?" She trembled.

Randy pointed to the laptop. "If I thought for one second that Fergus was on the other end of that ad, I'd have already contacted him." He hiccupped. "But if you don't think there's any rush, then I guess you wait until you're ready."

Was there a rush? What if she was dying? Or moving out of the country? "I don't know if there's a rush. Can you just look in the fridge for some broccoli?"

Randy fished out two heads, one of which was slightly yellowed. He set them on the counter. "Listen, I should work on that table if I'm going to finish it by the end of next week. You and Tom okay to watch Jaxx?"

"I hope you're not cutting anything," June said.

Randy slid a pencil behind his ear. "The girl with the one blue hand, or not, remember you're still the same person. You're still June. June who won't respond to her mother." He went to the basement, slipping down the bottom third of the staircase. She heard the blip of rejected radio stations before he settled on a baseball talk show. Batting averages were soon drowned out by one of his machines.

"I think he needs a bottle." Tom appeared from the living room with Jaxx, who was crying like he'd been left in the woods to die. June went to the baking cupboard, which Derek had been using to store formula. She pulled out the container and read the label three times, because she absorbed nothing from it. She kept thinking about Randy's comment. *You're still June.* "My birth mother was going to call me Wanda. Do I look like a Wanda?"

Tom shrugged. He'd stuck the end of his finger in Jaxx's mouth, to stop him from crying.

June scooped powder into a bottle she took from a row marked "sterilized" with masking tape, and added water from the kettle. "Wanda," she said. "Wanda, Wanda, Wanda."

"You could always hyphenate it?" Tom suggested. "We can start calling you Wanda-June. Or June-Wanda."

June paced the kitchen shaking the bottle with excessive force. Tom arranged stacks of pillows on the family room couch and propped Jaxx up between them.

"Pass me the bottle." He sat next to the small fort he'd constructed, fed Jaxx with one hand, and with the other turned on the TV. The volume was low enough that June could hear Jaxx's guttural swallow, rhythmic and relieved. He'd not been left in the woods to die.

She took the chicken out of the microwave, cut open the plastic cover, and hacked the meat clubs out of the tray. Why the heck were they still frozen? Was it wrong to not want to contact the woman behind ARE YOU MY DAUGHTER?

"Tom, go downstairs and check on your father. He's probably sawed his arm off down there."

"Yeah, is Dad drunk?"

"He was drinking. I don't know what the hell he was thinking."

June picked up a drumstick and locked her hand tight around it. Mucus-coloured pockmarked skin, fat bits and pink flesh the shade of her lips oozed between her fingers. The bulbous knob at the base of the bone jutted beneath her grip. She pitched it at the fridge with the finesse and force of a knife thrower. Barnum & Bailey. June & Wanda.

Tom returned to the kitchen from the basement to see the second drumstick hit a magnet about chocolate.

"Are you throwing chicken?" He wiped formula from Jaxx's chin with his thumb.

June picked up another drumstick, a fat one with skin hanging off it like melted wax. She drew her arm back. Jerry bobbed up and down in his cage and squawked.

"Stop!" Tom shouted. "Don't throw it!"

He moved Jaxx to the rug on the floor and vaulted over a barstool with an urgency that surprised June. It wasn't like she had a gun.

"Mom." He was calm. "Put down the dinner."

She wanted to put it down. Half of it was still frozen and made her hand cold and the longer she stood there holding it, the more she felt like an idiot. June had always been in control. Control was her thing. It was why she was always asked to chair the meetings, lead the committees, and organize the parties. But now control was leaching out of her like minerals from overused soil. Bit by bit, leaving her exposed and childish. Was she responsible for her own loss of control? Maybe she'd accidentally tapped it out. Or perhaps she was becoming Wanda, daughter of whom? She was considering this when Tom lunged toward her and wrestled the poultry out of her hand, disarming her. He tossed the chicken in the sink, and it made a pleasing clink against the stainless steel.

"Mom, that was whack."

"It was, wasn't it? I don't know what came over me."

"I'm guessing, stress? Probably the same reason Dad's half in the bag down there." Tom picked the drumsticks off the floor with a napkin and added them to the sink.

"I'm the girl with the one blue hand," June said.

"I don't know what that means. You're more like the mom with the bird flu." He pumped soap on her hands. "Why don't you go burp Jaxx and I'll start the barbecue. Vanessa and Derek are on their way home. They're going to walk in that door any minute expecting dinner, and Leslie will be here too."

"You're right." She washed her hands vigorously and scooped up Jaxx, tapping his back. His pit-sized heart pulsed below her collarbone. He spit up on her shoulder.

Tom returned with the barbecue lighter. "You good?"

"I'm sorry you had to see that."

"I've seen worse. Remember that time I took Grandpa for x-rays and he put the gown on backwards so it opened in the front?"

June managed a smile and put Jaxx in his cradle. "I wasn't expecting any of this."

"None of us were. I now have a nephew, a half-brother, and a grandma who's young enough to pick up sailors." He counted these things on his hand.

"Thomas Figg."

"Listen June-Wanda, the key to life is to lower your expectations. Better yet, get rid of your expectations completely."

"That's a terrible way to live."

"It's the only way to live."

June frowned. "It doesn't have to be. You're still young. You still have time to do things. I can't even learn to play the ukulele."

Tom shrugged.

"Look at your brother. He's trapped." There was quiet, and then June said, "Don't tell anyone I threw the chicken."

Tom made a peace sign. "Want me to cut this?" He held up the broccoli.

"Please. Your father still alive down there?"

"I didn't see any blood."

June and Tom worked side by side to the soundtrack of Randy's belt sander. It was after four. The sun faded in the curtains over the kitchen sink.

"Vanessa mentioned you signed up for Tinder. Wanna tell me about it?"

But Tom replied, "Another time," and went outside with a pair of tongs.

The words resounded in her mind. *Another time.* That's when she was adopted. When underwear was mostly white and people had dress-coats and nice handwriting. And she was certain that babies from *another time* were conceived out of something akin to love and not out of some knuckle-sucking lust-driven Kardashian-waxed porn. Most of the stories she heard of were of lovers who simply made a baby at the wrong time. If she had to be adopted, she hoped that love was at least the catalyst to conception. Slow dancing, Buddy Holly, summer-fair picnic-blanket love. But what if it hadn't been? What if she was conceived in a barn or behind an outhouse? What if her birth father drank whiskey and dined on canned meat?

20

Derek, Vanessa, and Leslie crashed through the door. Derek plunked a box of rice on the counter.

"How was work?" June asked.

"It was awesome," Derek said with the enthusiasm of a six-year-old at an amusement park. "I actually love wood-working."

Randy tripped up the top step. "You love woodworking?" He beamed.

"Well, this cabinet stuff," he elaborated. "It's cool how every-thing has to be exact." He put his hands together to form a right angle.

"Good," June said, turning on the oven.

"I can't wait for tomorrow."

"You're going back tomorrow?"

Leslie nodded. "I have an infinite amount of work," she said. "And Derek's a quick study."

Vanessa had removed Jerry from his cage and was petting the back of his neck. The bird made a low purring sound.

"What about the depot?" Randy asked. "Are you going to leave them high and dry?" He took off his safety goggles.

"I'm sure they can replace me." Derek peeled the sticker off an apple and stuck it to the sink.

"But who are they going to get to close?"

"Lawrence can close. So can Claudia."

"You should think about this first." Randy wiped his hands on the back of his work jeans. They were covered in stain.

Derek ignored his father and bent over the cradle. "How did my little man make out today?"

"Good," June replied. "Is he asleep?"

"He is." Derek adjusted Jaxx's blanket.

"Anyone want a beer?" Tom held up a case of Coors Light.

"Derek, give me your apple core," Vanessa said.

Derek passed it to Vanessa, who fed it to Jerry. She whistled as the bird pecked.

"I'll take a beer," Leslie said.

Tom handed her one. "Let's sit outside."

Vanessa placed Jerry back in his cage and followed the others to the back deck, where smoke billowed from the barbecue. She sat on Leslie's lap.

June turned to Randy. "What the hell was that all about?"

"What?"

"Geez, Derek," she mocked, "maybe you should think about it first."

"But he loves his job at the depot, and he hates woodworking. Remember the time we tried to build a birdhouse together? He put the roof on upside down."

"He was five."

"Eight."

"Counting bottles isn't a real job; building kitchens is."

"So what about the time I tried to help him build a display

for his science fair project, huh? Hinges on *backwards*." He brushed sawdust from his hair into the sink.

"Don't do that," June scolded. "It clogs the drain."

"I think he's making a mistake," Randy said. "Derek doesn't like woodworking."

June stirred the rice, steaming her face in the process. "Randy, he just walked in and said he *couldn't wait until tomorrow*. When's the last time he said that about something other than *The Walking Dead* or Pancake Tuesday?"

"I'd like a beer," he said. "Since that's what it seems everyone is doing now. Drinking beer and installing kitchens."

"Sure, have a beer, and while you're at it, why not have some scotch too?"

"You're overreacting." Randy opened a beer and leaned against the island, perpendicular to June. He was pensive.

"What?" June finally asked.

"I spent my entire life trying to get our kids interested in carpentry. Once I even bribed Derek with a Big Mac if he'd just watch me build some shelves, and you know what he did?"

"Ate it and left?" June guessed, straining the broccoli.

"He said, *boring*, and then shot me with a Nerf dart."

June tried not to laugh. "It's all timing," she said, fanning her face with an oven mitt. "He just needed some incentive."

"Yeah, Leslie," he whispered, beer dripping down his chin.

"I meant Jaxx," June said. "He has a baby to support. You should be grateful Leslie gave him the opportunity. And besides, maybe he specifically likes installing kitchens as opposed to making furniture and finishings."

Randy considered this, and seemed comforted by the suggestion. "Maybe I'll see if he wants to help me build that table."

"Good luck." June cringed, and opened a bottle of Riesling. She over-poured, splashing wine on the counter, and followed Randy outside.

Tom held up a pair of tongs. "I just turned them," he said, the wind whipping around his afro.

"Good. Then we're about ten minutes away from dinner." June sat down. "So tell us about the condo you're seeing tomorrow."

Leslie attempted to sit upright in the chair, forcing Vanessa off her lap. "It's a two bedroom with a loft, on-street parking, main floor laundry . . ."

"And a hot tub," Vanessa blurted. She sat on a planter.

"What's the big deal with hot tubs?" Tom snapped the tongs. "It's like taking a bath in someone's GI tract."

"Frig off," Vanessa said.

"For real. I know someone who got Legionnaires' disease from a hot tub," Derek said, not looking up from his iPhone.

"Hot tubs are lovely," Randy said. "Derek, how would you like to build a table with me?"

"You want me to build a table?"

"I would love you to."

"Like now?"

"I have a custom order."

"Fuck, no." He slid his phone back in his pocket despite the chirp of an incoming text message. "Sorry. I'm tired, Dad. I worked all day and Jaxx is going to be up soon. I just want to eat supper and chill."

Randy looked at Tom. "What about you, son? Would you like to build a table with me?"

"Did you just call me son?" Tom laughed.

"What's wrong with calling you son?"

"Oh, nothing, Pa, just sounded a little 1965."

"I don't get it," Randy said.

"Never mind, Randy," June said. "He's making fun of you."

Tom peeled the label off his beer. "I might have been interested if you hadn't asked your favourite first."

"Derek's not my favourite!" Randy said. "He's your mother's."

June backhanded her husband's shoulder. "We've been through this before. I do *not* have a favourite."

"And I only asked Derek because he's taken an interest in woodworking."

"Cabinets," Derek corrected. "Kitchens."

"Maybe Fergus likes woodworking," Tom offered, rolling the label into a long cylindrical tube between his fingers.

Randy looked sad.

"I'll make a table with you," Leslie said. "What kind of wood are we working with?"

"Thank you." Randy scrambled out of his chair. "Walnut for the top, gum for the legs."

"I like a good walnut table," Leslie replied. She made eyes at Vanessa and followed Randy into the house.

"Why couldn't one of you just do it? Now she's going to be down there all night." Vanessa slouched into Leslie's vacated chair.

"Not our fault your girlfriend's nice," Derek said.

Girlfriend, June repeated in her head as she stood up. Leslie the Girlfriend like Garfield the Cat or Jack the Giant Slayer. June didn't think of Leslie when she heard the word *girlfriend*. She thought of Marissa. Love Pink Marissa. Chive On Marissa. Smoke continued to roll up from the barbecue.

Half of the drumsticks were burnt. "Tom, did you put sauce on these?"

"Shit, only on one side," he said. "I forgot." He grabbed the barbecue sauce.

"I'll get a plate."

Inside, Jaxx was awake. He had blanket creases across one cheek. He whimpered while June washed her hands. The doorbell and the buzzer on the stove went off.

"Derek!" June hollered through the open window. "Jaxx!"

June pulled the broccoli off the stove and turned off the timer before hurrying to the front of the house. Through the porch she could see the silhouette of a wide-shouldered male in a hat. A friend of Derek's? She slipped on a magazine and nearly fell on the floor. The man stepped back.

"Sorry." June opened the door. "I almost gave myself a heart attack." She kicked the magazine under the loveseat and stared at the vaguely familiar person in front of her. Was it someone from Derek's shower? The guy who guessed that Jaxx weighed two pounds? Lawrence from the depot?

"Hi," he said.

Once June had seen Val Kilmer at a magazine kiosk in the airport and she tried to hug him, thinking he was a former classmate. June strained to figure out how she knew the stranger at the door. She found herself focusing on his hat, which was red and had a logo she didn't recognize, as if it might tell her the answer. Then it occurred to her that he looked like Randy. Had Fergus come for dinner?

"Fergus?" June blurted. "Is that you?"

Randy, who had unknowingly landed behind her with a piece of walnut and a bloody finger, started crying. "Fergus?"

He dropped the wood. "My son!"

It was such a dramatic reaction, all June could think of was the Cowardly Lion from the *Wizard of Oz*. She patted her husband on the back, hoping it would somehow quiet his moaning, but it only seemed to make him wail louder.

"What's going on?" Derek stepped into the front porch with Jaxx tucked in his arm. "What's wrong with Dad? Why is he crying?"

"Derek," June said in a solemn tone, "this is Fergus."

"Who, Damon?" Derek asked, pointing to the door.

"*Fergus*," June said, like Derek wasn't listening.

"No, it's actually Damon," Damon said, lifting his hand and producing an awkward finger wave.

Randy was bent over with his hands on his knees, blood dripping on the Lebanese porch rug. He stopped crying and looked up. "You're not Fergus?"

"No, I'm Damon. I didn't have a chance to say anything before . . . that . . . happened."

"They renamed you Damon?" He looked at June hopefully. "That's why I couldn't find him! I was looking for *Fergus*."

"My parents were going to name me Fergus?"

"No," Derek interrupted. "Dad, Damon isn't your son."

"You know my parents?" Damon looked bewildered.

Things were sliding out of control. June tried to intervene. "My husband thought he knew your adopted parents."

"I'm adopted?" Damon stabilized his trembling hand on the doorknob. June noticed tattoos along his knuckles. Letters or roman numerals. Symbols?

"I am your father," Randy said, taking a step forward. He moved like Darth Vader.

"You are?" Damon asked.

"No," Derek interjected. "He's not your father. He's confused. He thought you were the son he'd given up for adoption."

Damon released a long sigh. *Of relief?*

"Damn," he said. "You really had me going for a second."

"Damon used to work at the depot," Derek explained.

That's where I know him from, June thought, but then she noticed his over-developed shoulder muscles and nipple rings poking through his Hollister T-shirt. Beyond him, the low-riding black car shaped like an arrowhead was parked along the curb. The same car Marissa had been swallowed by after they'd left Chili's this afternoon.

Damon scratched the back of his head.

"'Sup?" Derek asked, nudging Jaxx's green soother back into his mouth.

"Marissa and I were hoping to take Jaxx for a ride."

A ride? June pondered. *Why? So he could eat him?*

"Nah, he just got up," Derek said. "I got to feed him and make him lie on his stomach, or his head will get all fucked up and he'll have to wear a helmet."

Damon winced.

"Tell Marissa maybe tomorrow," Derek said. "He's got a doctor's appointment at four. Maybe sometime after that."

"Cool, bro," Damon said. The two bumped fists and nodded.

June closed the door as Damon cut across the front lawn to his car.

"We don't know for certain that he's not my son."

"Yes, we do, Dad. You've met his father. The long-haired guy that drives a Harley and works in the Safeway floral department."

"That guy? I've always liked him. He always lets me pick out extra ribbon."

"Yes, that's his dad. Damon looks just like him except for his short hair."

Randy slumped down on the wicker loveseat, looking dejected. June had no words. Part of her was brimming with pride. Derek had made Jaxx a doctor's appointment, and he seemed to understand the importance of tummy time, but on the other hand, Damon wanted to take Jaxx on a joy ride in his Batmobile and Derek didn't seem phased. Why hadn't Marissa come to the door? Had Damon eaten her?

"Isn't it odd that Marissa didn't come to the door?"

"Nah, she hurt her ankle," Derek said, switching Jaxx to his other arm. The baby stared up at Derek lovingly, as if he was his mother, as if he had just been saved from being eaten. His eyes, under the porch light, the grey-blue of ocean at dusk. He had tiny Braille-like bumps along his chin. Infant pimples. He was an exceptionally contented baby. He reminded June of Derek. She smiled, and then frowned.

"Are Damon and Marissa together?"

Derek shrugged. "They could be, I guess."

"Does that bother you?"

"Not really," he said. "Marissa and I aren't together. We never really were, except for, well, a few times."

June held up her hand. "Stop there," she said. June squeezed her eyes shut. She had a new flashback of Derek speed-thrusting on top of Marissa with his teeth clenched as though they were wired shut from jaw surgery. Like there'd been a coach lurking in the darkness with a stopwatch telling him to go as fast as he could for ten seconds.

"You all right, Mom?" Derek asked. "You look sick."

She blamed it on a hot flash and pushed and pulled on the door, swinging it forward and back to create a draft.

"I'm going to go change his diaper," Derek said. He touched his father's shoulder on the way out. "Sorry, Dad," he said. "I hope you find Fergus someday."

"Come on," June urged. "Supper's getting cold."

21

The kitchen was quiet. Vanessa sulked, presumably because Leslie had volunteered to help Randy. She got up from the table and returned with Jerry.

"Vanessa," June said, "Jerry isn't allowed at the table. Please put him back in his cage."

"What?" she argued, moving her hair out of the way so Jerry could side-step the length of her shoulder without obstacle. "It's not like he can do anything from up here."

"It's gross," Derek said. "He's probably covered in bacteria."

"He's not covered in bacteria."

"Vanessa, just put Jerry away," Randy said.

June watched Randy struggle to cut the meat off his drumstick. "Just use your hands."

"I can't!" He held up his bloodstained finger. "So, Leslie," he said, "when did you know you were a lesbian?"

"Dad!" Vanessa dropped her knife and fork.

"What? What's wrong? Is that wrong to ask?"

"Did you ask Marissa when she knew she was straight?"

"No, but then I only met her at the hospital."

"So, if Derek had brought her home to dinner, would you have asked her then?"

Randy considered this. "No, Vanessa, I think you're right." He severed a spear of overcooked broccoli with his fork. "You know, I do wish I asked her when she knew she wanted to be a singer. For me, it was five." He smiled and ate his broccoli.

Vanessa rolled her eyes.

"It was five for me too." Leslie politely pushed her empty plate to the side. "When I knew I was a lesbian," she clarified, folding her hands under her chin. She wore a green leather bracelet the width of an old tennis wristband wrapped around her left arm, complimenting her pink lipstick, which was girlie and gum-like. Her head had been freshly shaved on both sides, revealing a finger-length scar the size and texture of a caterpillar.

"Really? That young?"

Randy's amazement embarrassed June.

"Yep. As soon as I understood it wasn't really normal for girls to marry girls, I wanted to marry one."

Vanessa smiled at the admission and then immediately frowned to maintain appearances.

"My mom used to make figure skating costumes. One of her former customers was getting married and asked my mom to design her dress." Leslie paused as Jerry climbed onto her shoulder. "After a fitting, I snuck into my mom's sewing room and wrapped myself in her gown. I had spent hours holed up in that closet imagining my lesbian wedding when I realized I'd somehow knocked out a bunch of pins." Jerry bobbed his head. "I knew my mom would be furious, so I picked them all up and hid them in my room."

"Did you get in trouble?" Randy asked.

"My mom actually thought it was the boy she babysat from across the street. Until one afternoon, when I thought the coast was clear, I left the playroom and went to get in the dress, and my mother was hiding in the closet."

"And that's when you told her?" June asked, also charmed by Leslie's tale.

Leslie laughed. "I lied and said I really wanted to make dresses. My mom was thrilled, because up until then I only showed an interest in game shows and fixing things with my dad."

June remembered helping her mother make raspberry jam, not because she was a lesbian or enjoyed being in the kitchen, but to avoid trips to the hardware store where her father spent hours mulling over nails.

"And you never had any doubt?" Randy asked.

"Dad." Vanessa added butter to broccoli, which didn't have time to melt before she shoved it in her mouth.

June noticed Leslie place a reassuring hand on her daughter's knee.

"It's okay," Leslie said. "I don't mind talking about it." She looked at Randy. "No doubts," she said. "It felt as normal to me to like girls as it did to breathe. Not that it wasn't difficult — I just had no doubt."

"I guess I just find it fascinating because Vanessa only found out as a teenager that she was a lesbian."

Vanessa covered her eyes.

"I think she figured it out before then, Dad," Derek said, pushing his plate away.

Randy looked to Vanessa for confirmation.

"Do we have to discuss this at the dinner table?" Her face

was red and blotchy. "Why don't you ask Tom when he discovered he liked elder porn?"

June pretended not to hear this. "Would anyone like dessert? I have some little brownies."

Tom and Derek both raised their hands. June excused herself from the table and retrieved a tub from the cupboard. She arranged the brownies on a plate and added dollops of Cool Whip on top of each.

"So when are you moving out?" Leslie asked Derek. "Vanessa said something about it at your shower."

Derek paused, unaware that his mother and father had seen the basement suite. June caught herself eating a spoonful of whipped cream while she thought of the graffiti in the room.

"It's not for certain," he stumbled. "Just a friend offered me a place if I needed."

Randy took a brownie from the plate, which had replaced the napkin holder at the centre of the table.

"Jenny." Tom took three brownies and lined them up in front of him, single file.

"Jenny."

"Why would you want to live with Jenny?" June sipped her wine.

Derek shrugged. "What's wrong with Jenny?"

"Yes," Randy agreed. "What's wrong with Jenny? We met her at the shower and she seemed lovely."

June kicked him under the table. He mouthed, "*What?*"

Tom said, "Jenny's in love with Derek."

"Well, that's nice," Randy said.

"She wants to adopt Jaxx," Vanessa added.

"No, she doesn't," Derek spat. "She just wants to help out."

"Didn't she offer to take drugs so she could breastfeed?"

June nearly choked. It was better than Marissa's choice to feed him milk that looked like pork gravy, but all she could think of was that terrible *Hand That Rocks the Cradle* movie.

"I didn't commit to anything. She just said she had room if I needed it."

June relaxed slightly.

"Can you actually take drugs to make yourself lactate?" Randy asked. He seemed unaware that he'd pinched his nipples before helping himself to a sixth brownie.

Leslie nodded. "I have friends who just had their first baby, and both mothers are breastfeeding."

"I think that's wonderful," Randy replied. "Isn't technology grand?"

June pictured a robot breastfeeding. A hot flash started. She left the table and went down to the basement where it was cooler. She sat at the computer and fanned herself with an energy bill Randy had marked PAID. She considered the possibility of Vanessa having kids someday, and how it would work. Her daughter was so good with animals, it only seemed natural she would be good with kids. Jaxx calmed her. Leslie, too. Both seemed to diffuse her in a way June had been trying to accomplish for years. Would Vanessa carry the baby? She was certainly younger than Leslie and the obvious candidate. Would they adopt? Where would they get the sperm? Wouldn't the baby get confused if it was getting breast milk from two sources? June googled *breastfeeding adopted child*. She scanned over the first article that appeared, which confirmed the possibility of inducing lactation in non-birth mothers. She felt pleased until she read:

Adoption universally involves loss. Babies recognize their mothers at birth and at delivery, healthy babies placed on the abdomen of their mother will crawl up onto her chest and, locating the nipple via its familiar smell, will attach to her breast and suckle. Newborn infants desire to remain with their mother and if removed from skin-to-skin contact with her will give a specific "separation distress cry/call" as an appeal for reunion. Maternal separation is stressful for infants, and all adopted children have experienced the loss of their birth mother (Gribble, 2006).

Profound sadness befell her. This was not how adoption was presented. Public service announcements portrayed it as a win-win situation, where love and a capable set of parents with traditional jobs and expensive strollers were all you needed. Was it all propaganda? Where were the campaigns showing babies being ripped off their birth mother's chests, their separation calls the last thing you heard when the screen went blank and it switched to a commercial for Tide? Had she screamed when she was taken from her birth mother, where nature intended her to be? Was her distress call like that of a Cessna losing altitude or a bleating sheep? A missing firefighter or a fawn? Or did it resemble the agonizing low-pitched wail she was expelling now? How dare her birth mother give her up? Why was it her birth mother decided she was better off with educated Maritimers who liked Christmas than with whatever she was? She did not feel like the girl with the one blue hand. She felt like the girl with the single black heart. She felt adopted.

22

June got ready for bed in silence. She didn't bother to read, because she forgot what had happened in the last chapter of her book. She stared at the ceiling tiles and tried to forget the vignette she'd created surrounding the separation from her birth mother. She knew the details were all wrong. Since in old pictures she looked like any red-headed baby, she made herself three and more recognizable when the nurse, an older lady with perfect skin wearing a dress and bonnet circa 1919, grabbed her by the ankles and pulled her away from her birth mother with one stockinged foot braced against the metal hospital cot. June grasped desperately for something to hold on to as she slid down her mother's body — the gaps between her ribs, her hips, which were hard to negotiate under the guise of her massive gelatine post-partum belly, and eventually her mother's ankles, which she imagined were delicate but still too thick for June to get a good grip. She pictured her birth mother sobbing while this took place, covering her eyes with her iv-pricked hands, head rolling side to side against her stark white pillow. But she also considered the unimaginable — her mother kicking away her tiny dough hands during her final attempt to stay united.

Every time she managed to go minutes without replaying the story, Randy's restless leg syndrome would act up.

"Stop moving," she said, as he rolled from one side to his other, legs flutter-kicking and bending in two-minute intervals.

"I can't help it," he whined. "I have to move them."

"Well, don't put your feet on me." She gave his legs a nudge.

Randy groaned and tried to get comfortable by curling his body into the shape of a shrimp. "Now I can't sleep," he said.

June adjusted her pillow. "I guess there's no chance of selling the house and getting a place in Phoenix now."

"I can't give up my workshop."

"I didn't think so."

"Still wouldn't mind that cruise though."

"What about a river cruise? On the Mediterranean."

"I'd like to go to Alaska."

"Alaska? What on earth for?"

"I've always wanted to see a polar bear, and they're dying."

"You can see those at the zoo."

"You hate the zoo."

She rolled to face him. "Derek didn't seem set on moving in with Jenny, did he?"

"Not really." Randy wiggled his legs.

"If Vanessa moves out, her room would be a good size for Jaxx."

Randy rolled over again. June did too, and then Randy rammed his pelvis into her side. A shark bump.

"What are you doing?" She hoped it was RLS.

"I want to be close to you."

She didn't say anything, because she wanted to be close to him too. She wanted him to be there when she lost grip of her mother's ankles and was removed from the hospital room. How small and far away that room seemed when she left it, the ward, the building. How extreme the loss when she could no longer smell her mother.

Randy mounted her carefully. She picked up the scent of wood glue, the Scope in their toothpaste. He brushed her bangs to the side with one hand, temporarily transferring more of his body weight onto her small frame. She wanted to tell him about the trauma she'd experienced when she'd been taken from her mother. The same trauma Fergus endured when he was removed from Glenda. That no adopted babies were exempt. The loss was all-inclusive. There was no opting out.

He lowered himself on top of her, with the slow and deliberate rhythm of a boom lift, his older abdominal fat pressing into her. It was suffocating and lovely. He slid two fingers between the buttons of her shirt, catching her nipple between his fingertips. She imagined the same fingers slipping inside her. It surprised her how quickly she got aroused. She reached for the Astroglide, even though the name always made her think of the Japanese robot cartoon reruns Tom had watched obsessively as a child during breakfast. She pictured Astro Boy's red boots, Munster hair, and glossy tear-drop eyes. His self-titled theme song. Tom's chin dripping with rainbow-tainted milk from his Lucky Charms.

She grabbed Randy's huge penis to make the thoughts go away. She imagined Randy when he had a Knight Rider moustache and wore tall socks and played driveway basketball with his shirt off. She remembered the suit he wore when he emceed his brother's wedding. She lifted her hips into him and he thrust deeper inside her. The ceiling tiles became Chinook clouds, the blankets capes, the entire room a golden palace. June orgasmed like she was twenty-one.

When it was over, Randy's legs settled. He slept, June cried. Hormonal tears. Astro tears. Like her soul had plummeted off the top of a fifty-storey building and just when she felt it had been returned, she heard Jaxx crying. Like he'd been yanked away from his mother. She pulled off the covers, climbed out of bed, and made her way to Derek's room to tell him it was going to be okay. Sort of.

23

When she reached Derek's room, Jaxx was still crying and Derek looked forty-eight. Bleary-eyed and arthritic. He was standing by his bed as though a fire alarm had gone off and he'd forgotten the part about evacuating.

"Does he need a bottle?" She reached into the crib to pick Jaxx up.

"I'll get one ready," Derek yawned.

June looked around the room for somewhere to sit. Derek's computer chair was part of their old dinette set. "You need a rocking chair." She held Jaxx differently now. As though he was adopted. Because his mother was not present and Derek had not been there during the pregnancy to make Jaxx aware of his scent, his voice, his existence. Trauma by association, or lack thereof. He was part of her club. A dirty assembly of adoptees, which also included Fergus. She and Jaxx and Fergus.

Derek returned with a bottle. "Here."

June sat on the end of the bed and tipped the bottle into the baby's mouth.

"Is Marissa going to see Jaxx tomorrow?" she asked. "After his appointment?"

"Maybe." He crawled back under the covers on his bed that was too small.

"She needs to see him, Derek."

"I can't force her to see him." He folded his pillow. "If she doesn't want to, she doesn't want to."

"You know the only thing a newborn knows is his mother. He pines for her."

"Jaxx?"

"All babies. It makes them feel safe."

"He knows me," he said. "I keep him safe."

"I know. But he still needs a mother."

Derek gave her a troubled look. "What about mothers who die in childbirth? What about their babies? They survive. They learn to adapt and love the one they're with."

June didn't have an answer. Partially because Derek was not part of the club and wouldn't understand, and secondly because she was thinking of the song "Love the One You're With" and trying to remember who was who in Crosby, Stills & Nash. She knew the song was about lovers, not adopted people. It was about settling, and it made her angry, because she believed people shouldn't settle, and she decided Crosby, Stills & Nash were probably secretly singing about adoption. *Hey you, infant down there! You're not my real baby, but I suppose we can pretend.*

"Besides, if she's not going to be a part of his life, wouldn't seeing her make it worse?"

"Huh?" June replied.

"If all Jaxx thinks about is his mother, wouldn't seeing her only once in a while be almost worse? Like a tease?"

June hadn't considered this. Was some mother better than

no mother? Derek's reasoning seemed plausible. Jaxx certainly didn't *seem* traumatized.

"Well?" Derek asked, leaning on his elbow.

"I don't know," she admitted. Why had she said anything? Jaxx seemed like a well-adjusted baby. Why hadn't she read the whole article about adoption? Maybe the next paragraph said something wonderful about adoption. *The trauma of adoption dissolves within weeks after separation, with the adopted child's brain developing faster and more completely than his non-adopted counterpart. Adoption trauma can be cured with bottles of formula and a big family. It's cool to be adopted. Dads can be moms too.* Jaxx finished his bottle before June reminded herself that Jaxx wasn't actually adopted.

"Forget what I said." June balanced the empty bottle on Derek's bed. "You're doing a great job. All you can do is meet his needs with as much love as you can give." She rambled encouragement for five minutes. *Establish a bond! Give him skin-to-skin contact!* The skin-to-skin part made her shudder, because she thought of skinned animals dangling in a butcher shop. Jaxx burped. She told him he was a good baby.

"You know, Derek," she said, transferring to the floor where she could change Jaxx's diaper. "I'm proud of you. It didn't seem to cross your mind not to assume full responsibility for Jaxx."

"I didn't exactly have a lot of time to consider my options."

"True." June rolled up the used diaper. "But still."

"I knew I'd have the support," he said. "From you and Dad. To do the right thing."

June knew this was meant to be a compliment, and she was grateful Derek felt supported, but doing the *right thing* implied the alternatives were the *wrong things*. Like adoption.

She zipped Jaxx into his pyjamas and swaddled him in a receiving blanket dotted with ice cream cones, humming quietly while he sucked on his hand. Derek started snoring, so she took Jaxx out to the hall and paced back and forth until she got tired and retreated to the landing. The family crest was still off centre, but she couldn't adjust it with the baby in her arms. She'd fix it after.

She sat and waited for Jaxx to close his eyes, running her bare feet over the carpeted stairs below her, displacing crumbs and dust. She wondered if her birth mother had the same elongated second toe. Bony and crooked like a walking stick. Her adoptive mother's feet were wide, her arches high. Shoes were always a problem — never enough support, and on the rare occasion too much, which made her feet ache. Margaret was the only person in the nursing home who wore running sneakers to breakfast in her wheelchair. The yellow Adidas shoes were the last practical gift June had given her. Anything wrapped she waved away. Anything she couldn't pet, she rejected. The last time June visited, she walked in on her mother spoon feeding a teddy bear wearing plastic headphones.

June carried Jaxx back to his room. Derek was facedown on his bed with one arm dangling off the side, snoring intermittently. She lowered Jaxx into the crib and went back to her room. Randy was on her side of the bed. She'd forgotten to straighten the crest. She grew up with things having to be exact. When she pulled sheets down to make a bed, the fold had to be a consistent width from one side to the other. Ingredients were always levelled in their tin cups and spoons. Pinches were measured using a handwritten formula her mother had designed and taped to the inside of the baking cupboard.

A pinch of salt was a quarter of a teaspoon, cinnamon an eighth. June pulled the covers up around her neck, suspecting her birth mother only ordered takeout.

24

On Mother's Day, June and Randy drove to her mother's nursing home — a four-storey wood and brick building that looked like student housing. In between the two walkways that connected the east and west parking lots to the main entrance were a fountain and several benches that had been supplied by the families of deceased residents. The fountain was not working today, as it hadn't been on either of her last two visits. Randy strayed from the walkway to look inside. He felt for the drain. "It's probably clogged," he called to June, who was waiting outside the front doors.

They were greeted by June's favourite nurse — a Caribbean woman in her twenties who appreciated Margaret's love for the sea. Yulu wore fuchsia lipstick and made rum cake for the residents at Christmas. For special occasions she played the steel pan, which made all the residents happy. It was all for show. Outside the home, Yulu was into heavy metal. Vanessa saw her at concerts.

"Well, hello there," she said, adjusting the tie of her white cardigan. "Your mom just finished her breakfast."

Randy signed in at the desk and helped himself to an After Eight from a fish bowl. June followed the nurse down the hall. Yulu was pear-shaped and walked with a slight limp.

"She was a little forgetful today," Yulu said, stopping to wait for Randy to catch up. "She insisted she had already eaten breakfast and then asked why she wasn't being seated with her husband when I took her down to the dining room. But we did have a good chat about the ocean." Yulu whispered outside June's mother's room, "And she still doesn't know I hate swimming." She put her finger to her lips and smiled as she pushed open the door. "Margaret," she said, almost singing. "Your daughter's here to see you. Happy Mother's Day!" She patted Margaret's shoulders affectionately, and then turned her wheelchair around from the window to face June.

Margaret reached absently into the air.

Yulu stopped. "Oh, you want your Paro?"

Margaret seemed to nod.

"Okay, honey, let me get Paro."

June and Randy wondered what Paro was. A fancy new medical device? A nutritional supplement? Randy took both of his mother-in-law's hands and kissed them while they waited. "Hi, Mom," he said.

Yulu returned a minute later with a stuffed baby seal perched on a cheap gold novelty pillow. She placed it on Margaret's lap. June saw an immediate change in her mother's disposition. Her shoulders relaxed and she radiated a soft glow, like a tea light. And though she still looked lost, she didn't seem alone. When her mother stroked the seal's head, it moved its face in response and blinked. Its eyelashes were long and black. The animal seemed to inch forward on the pillow and yawn.

"Is it real?" Randy asked, mesmerized. He reached his hand out to touch it.

"Randy," June said, sitting on the bed. She nudged him with her elbow. The commotion caused Paro to blink and turn its head.

"It looks real," he said, stroking the pup under the chin.

Paro reacted by nuzzling Randy's hand the way a cat might. June thought she could hear purring. Her mother became protective and pulled Paro closer to her.

Randy continued to act like the seal was real. "Can I have a turn?" he asked.

Yulu, still standing at the door with hands resting on curvy hips, laughed. "She's not much for sharing when it comes to Paro."

Randy pulled his hand away. "Where did it come from?"

"They're made in Japan," she said. "Didn't Tom show you before he gave it to her?" Her voice went all high-pitched with surprise.

"No." Randy was disappointed.

June was embarrassed.

"He brought it in a few days ago." Yulu pointed in Paro's direction. "That thing costs thousands of dollars, and I'm telling you right now, he's worth every penny."

"Thousands of dollars?" June repeated. She lost her balance though she was sitting down. "For a stuffed animal?"

"That's not a stuffed animal," Yulu corrected. "He's a therapeutic robot. And I wish we had a hundred more just like him. I got to keep him under lock and key." She held up a key attached by a chain to a wooden block. PARO had been written on the wood in thick red marker.

"I've never seen your mother happier," she said. "I'll be back in a bit." Yulu turned to leave. "But watch out, though. He might bite." She laughed her way out the door.

June sat in shock while her mother continued to cuddle the robot. She was both offended and overjoyed. Part of her wanted to throw Paro across the room and curl up on the gold pillow in its place. She wanted her mother to stroke her hair. She wanted to be responsible for making her mother happier than ever. She felt selfish and childish. *I'm the girl with the one blue hand. Your only child and it's Mother's Day, not Paro's Day.* But the glow projecting from her mother was undeniable. It actually seemed to raise the temperature in the room by two degrees, where most visits June found it too cold to take her coat off. And the room felt small and cozy, the way it should. Over the previous year, the growing disconnect in her mother's brain made her small square room seem like an impossibly long hallway with high ceilings and dollhouse furniture. A hallway that grew longer and darker with each visit, her mother at one end and June at the other. Today was different, and she found herself whispering *"Thank you"* into Paro's fluffy ear.

"Did you just talk to Paro?" Randy asked.

"Shut up," she said. "I can't believe Tom did this."

"I can." Randy was proud. "He's a good son."

"Yes," she agreed.

"Remember on his sixth birthday, he asked for donations for the food bank instead of gifts?"

She nodded, remembering that he specifically requested cereal because he'd learned it was the most important meal of the day.

"And he was probably closer to your mom than any of the other kids."

Margaret scratched the top of Paro's head. June moved her purse to the floor. Her mother had given Tom money to buy his first industrial vacuum and paid to have five thousand flyers designed and printed. June didn't know the details of their arrangement. Whether the money had been a gift or a loan. In fact, she only found out about it a year into his business. She wondered now if Paro was some form of repayment. She felt proud and equally guilty for badgering Tom about his debt and still living at home. Had his down payment gone to Paro? She hadn't realized that his love for things Japanese extended beyond anime and sushi.

"How are you, Mom?" Randy asked, placing his hand on Margaret's knee. But Margaret didn't reply. She and Paro were on their own little ice floe in the arctic. It made June think of Vanessa's stuffed animal collection. How she was lost to the real world when they were in her grasp. June felt antsy. She wanted to bring up her adoption, and Paro was getting a back massage. The more her mother withdrew, the more she wanted to club Paro over the head.

"Mom," June said. "Tell me about my adoption."

Randy gasped. "June, do you really think this is the time?"

"Yes," she argued, like her mother wasn't there. "I need to know. I need to hear it from her. Mom?" June touched her mother's arm.

Her mother put her finger to her lip the way Yulu had and made a barely comprehensible *shhh* sound while pointing down at Paro's head.

"Yes, Paro is lovely," June replied.

"I think she means Paro's sleeping," Randy whispered.

June could feel the buzz of anxiety in her head.

"Paro's a robot! I'm the one who's alive." She said this to Randy though it was directed at her mother. "What if I never have another chance to ask?"

"Just play along, June," Randy whispered.

She exhaled deeply and asked her mother if she should get Paro a blanket. Her mother did not reply, but looked pleased when June laid a small quilt over Paro's back. She whispered into her mother's ear. "Can you tell me anything about my birth mother?"

"Baby's sleeping," her mother replied.

June was agitated. Disappointed that her mother would not discuss her adoption. Horrified that she felt disappointed.

Randy tried to console her. "I just don't think she understands, June. She's too far away."

It was that disconnect that frustrated June. Her lips had grazed the opening of her mother's ear canal, yet her words fell into an abyss.

Randy took her hand. "If you want to know more, you'll have to go through your birth mother. Reply to the ad."

Margaret motioned again for Randy and June to be quiet. Randy started to sing "Farewell to Nova Scotia," as he used to when Margaret was still aware and capable. June slipped out of her chair and went to the front lobby. Yulu was in the back office with a clipboard tucked under her arm. She was eating an apple. Its flesh showed the colour of her lipstick.

"You're all done today, Mrs. Figg?" Yulu asked.

"Soon," she replied weakly. "I was just going for a walk."

"And how's your mom doing?"

"Not great," she admitted. "Though she seems quite happy with that seal."

"Paro's the talk of the home," she said, tossing her core in a wastebasket. "We're trying to raise money for a communal one."

June smiled. It seemed both ridiculous and sad. The raising of funds for a robotic asshole that sent your parent on a one-way trip to Siberia.

"Give me a shout when you're ready to leave, and I'll lock him back up."

"Thanks." June ducked into the washroom beside the office and splashed a handful of cool water on her face. She looked haggard. Her hair dry and coarse, the skin around her cheekbones heavy. She washed her hands and stopped at the empty front desk, helping herself to an After Eight. On the desk, she noticed an open stamp pad beside the computer. A date stamp and a half-eaten Caramilk bar lay dormant next to it. June bent over the desk and placed her hand on the stamp pad with CPR pressure. She made sure the ink covered her entire hand, the blue-black colour migrating into the hairline creases. The receptionist, an ordinary-looking woman with eighties spiral hair, appeared from the back office. June quickly removed her stamped hand, placed it behind her back and held up the empty After Eight wrapper.

"I'll take that, Mrs. Figg." The receptionist smiled.

June returned the smile and hurried down the hall toward her mother's room. Randy was sitting on the end of her bed with Paro. Her mother still looked content, and she wondered how Randy had convinced Margaret to give him a turn. June kept her hand behind her back, her heart thrashing around in her chest like a flank-strapped rodeo horse. Randy stared at her curiously.

Her hand shook as it bent outward from her elbow. She held it there, fingers splayed like a catcher's mitt, and waited.

"Why is your hand black?" Randy asked.

"It's blue," she corrected.

"Are you wearing a glove?"

"No, I'm not wearing a glove. My hand is blue." She decreased her volume by a few notches. "I'm the girl with the one blue hand."

"Well, it looks black from here."

June returned her focus to her mother, who slowly raised her own arm into the air and waved her hand like one of the gold cats at the spa. June dropped her hand to her side, took a few strides forward and came to her knees at the base of her mom's wheelchair. "It's me, Mom. The girl with the one blue hand. You adopted me."

Margaret's hand was still in the air, waving. Randy got up and took hold of her wrist and gently folded her arm back down to her lap. He kissed her on the cheek and then extended his arm toward his wife.

"I'm not done." June was insistent.

Randy looked at her with pity.

"She was going to name me Wanda. My birth mother. Mom? Remember?"

"June, I don't even know if she knows who you are right now. You're going to confuse her. Enough." He signalled for her to stop.

"I'm going to confuse *her*? What about me? *I'm* confused. Isn't my confusion worth something?" June cried.

"You've had your whole life to ask questions, and you chose not to. It's too late." Spit flew from his mouth. "You're too late."

Randy returned to the bed, his hands in fists, picked up Paro, and frantically stroked him.

June continued to probe. "My birth mother, do you remember her? Did you know her name? Did she have red hair like me?" June grabbed a chunk of her hair as a means of demonstration.

"Geez, June. Come on." Randy shook his head and looked out the window.

June opened her blue palm on her mother's lap. "You're my mother," she said. "You'll always be."

Margaret's back straightened, like she'd been stung by a wasp. She said, *"One hand in the sea and one on the land, 'tis the tale of the girl with the one blue hand."*

It was a painful recitation. Margaret slurred her words like she was speaking for the first time after life-altering brain surgery. The physicality of making sounds come out of her mouth seemed exhausting and strained. Verbal asthma. And one side of her face seemed less enthusiastic, as though she'd suffered a stroke. June rested her head on her mother's lap until she stopped crying. Then she used her mother's wheelchair to pull herself on to her feet. She felt dizzy. "Thanks, Mom," she said. "I'll always be your daughter." June looked into her mother's eyes wanting more, but her mother's eyes seemed vacant again. All of her seemed vacant. A home slated for demolition, empty of its contents and stripped down to its studs. There was nothing left. Not even the nail above the mantle.

"I love you, Mom," June said. And then as she was about to leave, she saw her mother. Her pre-dementia one. The one who measured things and kept the house smelling like lemons. The one who had wanted her.

"Mom?" June said, as though that single moment of recognition had been imagined. Margaret became weak again. Her muscles relaxed and what little colour her skin had faded to a dull grey. She looked frazzled and bushed the way mediums on TV looked after a séance. Then she simply closed her eyes and nodded off to sleep.

25

June drove home like Birte — accelerating through yellow lights and driving too close to the lines.

"Maybe I should drive," Randy suggested.

"I have to go through those boxes," June said, ignoring Randy, who had one hand braced against the glove compartment and the other on the window. "Somewhere in those papers there has to be something. A name or an address."

"Yes," Randy replied. "But there are boxes of your mother's papers. That could take weeks. Why don't you just respond to the bloody ad?" His shoulders tensed. "Now there's no flashing left up here anymore, so be careful."

June continued not to listen. When the next light turned solid green, she made a quick left and was nearly hit by an F-150.

"June!" Randy hollered. "Concentrate on the road."

"Sorry," she said, but she couldn't stop thinking about the boxes of papers and whether her birth mother's name was inside them amongst the tax files and recipes for fishcakes. She would dump the contents of the boxes on the floor and read every page. June couldn't drive fast enough. There was too much traffic. She pulled into the strip mall.

"Are we going to Pelican Pier?" Randy asked hopefully, but June didn't respond. She got out of the van and started running up the street. Her legs cycled in perfect harmony. She turned back only for a second. Randy was standing outside the passenger door with his hands up, looking for an explanation.

"Home," she called. She tried to think of every movie she had ever seen to conjure images of people running, but *Forrest Gump* was the only one she could remember. So she thought of Cathy Freeman, Usain Bolt. The little boy from India who ran marathons. She hurdled cracks and puddles. A random sneaker on the middle of the sidewalk. She swung her arms excessively. She'd be home in minutes. She would go through every page. Pull apart recipe cards and empty envelopes. When Randy pulled up beside her, she ran faster and waved him on, but he crept along beside her like a pace vehicle. She stopped at the end of the driveway to catch her breath. Her lungs felt swollen, but fresh as a fat baby bird. Anxious and alive. Randy parked and got out of the van.

"What are you doing?" he said.

"I had to get home. I have to see if she's out there."

"The van would've been faster."

"It didn't feel like it," she said, panting. "What if she's dying right now, and I only have seconds to find her?"

He placed his arm behind her narrow back so that his hand wrapped around to her stomach and helped her into the house like she'd just crossed the English Channel. She took comfort in his support. She felt hope like never before. The kind she saw in pictures of crowds who fought for rights and won. Fields of a thousand flowers. Videos of kids with special needs scoring touchdowns or netting three-pointers or generally being remarkable. She was one flight of stairs away from finding her mother. She pushed open the door and stumbled into the kitchen. She kicked off her shoes like they were on fire, and then froze. Bent over the island, Derek was shirtless and sobbing. It took her several seconds to shift gears. To throw her birth mother back in her trailer and consider Derek.

"What's wrong?"

"She took him."

"What do you mean?"

"Jaxx."

"Marissa took Jaxx?"

"She was supposed to just take him for a walk because it was Mother's Day and she wanted to see him, but that was three hours ago and she won't answer her phone."

June wanted to vomit.

"Did you text her?" Randy asked. "Maybe her ringer's off."

"Yes, I told her he was supposed to be back by noon."

"Lie and tell her he needs his medication," June said. "Where were they going? Did she take him in the stroller?"

"Yes."

This brought June some relief. How far could Marissa go with a stroller? Then she thought of Damon and his ugly black insect of a car. Was it a getaway car? Had he parked it down the street for Jaxx's abduction? Would either of them know how to install a car seat? Would there be enough room in the trunk for the stroller beside his Creatine supplements? Was he even able to move his neck to check his blind spot?

Vanessa appeared in the kitchen wearing ripped flannel pants and knee-high slippers with pom-pom ties dangling from the back. "Why is everyone being so loud?" She rubbed crust out of her eyes.

"Jaxx has been abducted," Randy said.

Vanessa stopped rubbing and looked at Derek for an explanation. "What does he mean, *abducted*?"

"Marissa took him for a walk and hasn't come back."

"That's not really abduction, is it? I mean, she is his mother."

"But she was to bring him back at noon," Randy argued. "It's after one."

"That makes her an asshole, but I still don't think it qualifies as abduction. You can't abduct your own kid. Unless you take them to Mexico and change their name."

Randy grabbed the cordless off its cradle by the fridge. "What are you doing?" June asked.

"Calling 911," he said, staring at the phone, confused as though the numbers had been replaced with Mahjong tiles.

"Don't do that," June said. "Vanessa's right. She is his mother. She's entitled to take him for a walk." She looked at Derek's bare torso, chest heaving, freckles faded like camper-van curtains. "Did you try the medicine thing yet?"

"No," he said. "What do I say?"

"Give me your phone," June ordered. Derek handed it to her. She found the messages icon by herself. Marissa, with no last name, was stacked atop the list of Derek's conversations. June clicked on her name and began typing. *Jaxx is overdue for his medication. Bring him back ASAP.* She hit send and passed the phone back to Derek.

"Now what?" Derek said.

"Give her a chance to respond and if she doesn't, we'll go look for them."

Vanessa leaned over Derek's shoulder. She held a Pop-Tart and reread the message. "Don't think she's going to answer." She brushed crumbs off her cheek.

"Give it some time," June said. "It's only been thirty seconds."

Vanessa read aloud. *"Jazz is overdue for his meditation. Bring him back ASAP."*

"Let me see that," June said, getting hot. She snatched the phone and reread the message, which did in fact suggest that Jazz needed to meditate. "Why did it do that?" She raised her voice. "I typed in J-A-X-X."

"Autocorrect." Derek rubbed his eyes.

June's heart raced. "I think we should go look for them."

"All of us?" Vanessa asked.

"Derek, go wake up Tom and tell him to stay here in case she comes back. I'll be in the van."

"I think I should drive," Randy said.

June hesitated. She wanted to drive, but at the same time she felt almost inebriated with fear. "Fine," she agreed. "You drive."

Vanessa kicked off her slippers and put on her boots, which were stained and hardened from overuse. Derek pulled on a hoodie and grabbed the diaper bag. He went upstairs.

"We'll be in the car," June hollered after him. "Make sure Tom is *up* up and not just pretending to be up."

Vanessa rushed past her mother to claim the front passenger seat. "I'd be a better help up front."

"Help?" June said. "Do you understand the definition of help?"

"You're asking me if I know what help means?" Vanessa extended her neck and bulged her eyes, because she knew it made her mother scared. "You just told Marissa to bring back a musical style so it could perform yoga."

June slid open the van door and took a seat in the back. She motioned for Derek to go to the other side as he approached.

"Which way should I go?" Randy waited for Derek to fasten his seatbelt.

"We should probably follow the bike path to the playground."

"Which playground?" June asked.

"Not the one with the swings," Derek said. "The one with the really wide slide."

"The fuck park?" Vanessa asked.

Derek nodded.

"The *fuck* park?" June asked. "What on God's green earth is the *fuck* park?"

"Honestly, Mom." Vanessa shook her head. "What do you think it is?"

"I don't know, Vanessa, because the last time I went to a park it was designed for children to explore and dogs to play catch in. Maybe a place for a nice family to have a picnic."

"A family picnic," Vanessa repeated. "That's hilarious."

Derek laughed.

June whacked his arm. "What's so funny about that?"

"People don't have picnics anymore."

"What do you mean people don't have picnics anymore? Your father and I had one just the other day."

"That's because you guys are old."

"Having a picnic is not an *old* thing to do."

"Excuse me," Randy interrupted. "Going back to the fuck park. Is it one of those parks where people dress up as animals and mingle around?"

The car was silent. Both of the children were too stunned to respond. Finally Vanessa asked, "How did you get that out of *fuck park*?"

"Because sometimes they engage in contact."

Vanessa burst.

June pictured the Calgary Flames mascot, Harvey the Hound, roaming the park on his knees. When he was joined by the Stampeders mascot, Ralph the Dog, she rapidly tried to tap out her cortices.

"No, it's true. I saw it on TV. It's a subculture. People dress up as mascots and have get-togethers with other people who like to dress up as mascots. Ask Tom."

June's heart sank. She didn't want to ask Tom. If Tom had an elephant costume in his closet she did not want to know about it.

"They're called Furries," Randy added.

June changed the subject. "We're supposed to be looking for Marissa. Does anyone see anything?" She looked out the back window for someone with a stroller, but the bike path was empty with the exception of a serious-looking cyclist in an aerodynamic helmet. She tried to focus on the helmet and not the field of pubic hair the Furries had aroused in her mind.

"I don't get it," Derek said. "You say people dress up in animal costumes and get on each other?"

"Derek," June said. "Don't be crude."

"Dad's the one who brought it up. I'm just trying to make sense of it."

"It's not always sexual," Randy explained. "Just sometimes they engage in *yiffing*."

"What the fuck is *yiffing*?" Vanessa asked.

"Don't answer that!" June cautioned. "I don't want to talk about Furries anymore."

"Is it related to sniffing?" Derek asked.

"It's when two Furries dry hump in their costumes," Randy explained.

"Fuck," said Vanessa.

"What's wrong with this family? Jaxx is missing and you're talking about people who dress up as animals?" June bit her nails and shook her head. Angry she would never view Halloween the same way again, like the way pictures of Vanessa's big gay prom made her think all high school dances were characterized by shiny suspenders and unicorn paraphernalia.

"I bet Furries have picnics," Vanessa said. "A Milk Bone for you and one for you . . ."

June was glad Tom was at home, because he would feed off this, and he and Vanessa would go back and forth to see who could be more offensive.

"Is that Marissa?" Randy pulled over near the entrance to a playground.

"No," Derek said, straining to look over his dad's shoulder. "She was wearing bright blue leggings."

"Has she responded to any of your texts? Why don't you try to call her again?" June suggested.

He looked at his phone. "Nothing."

"This is the wrong park," Vanessa said. "You want to go to the one closer to the cemetery."

"Oh," Randy said, pulling back onto the road. "I know which one you're talking about."

June looked over at Derek. He looked pensive and calm, though his eyes still reflected the fact he'd been crying. She tried to make sense of the change in disposition and tapped him affectionately on the knee. He responded as though he knew what she was thinking.

"I keep thinking about what you said," he sighed. "That the only things newborns know are their mothers. That they yearn for them."

"Well, yes," June said guiltily. "But they also need structure and routine and responsible parents who don't take them on three-hour joyrides in their strollers."

"Marissa wouldn't do anything stupid," Derek said. "She made it clear she didn't want to be a mother."

June couldn't help think of her birth mother. She wondered if she made it clear she didn't want to be a mother or whether she just lacked the means to be one. Things went silent as they rounded the block and drove to the next playground. She wondered if it made sense to even be searching playgrounds. It wasn't like Jaxx was old enough to go down the slide or cross the monkey bars.

"I have to know her name," June blurted. "My birth mother."

"Weren't all adoptions in your day sealed?" Vanessa asked.

Vanessa always had a way of making June feel old. *Your day* to her was like the time of Black Death, when doctors wore bird masks and carried batons. She also didn't know how to answer the question. What if Vanessa was right? What if she found the papers, but her birth mother's name was blocked out?

"I don't think they were all sealed," she rationalized.

"Pretty sure they were. I think it was illegal for the adoptive parents to know the identity of the birth mothers."

"There are always ways to find out," Randy offered. "Administrative errors, someone knowing through the grapevine.

Or nowadays by going online and searching through forums."
He added, "And replying to them," in a loud voice.

"I know, I know," June said. "I plan to reply. I was just hoping
to find some hard evidence before I did."

"Remember Karen Fredericks? She used to go to the same
doctor as her birth mother. One time, they sat directly across
from each other in the waiting room. The doctor knew all
along they were related. He did all of her mother's prenatal
care and then took Karen on as a patient with her adoptive
parents." Vanessa pulled down the vanity mirror and examined her jawline.

Randy pulled into the gravel lot of the fuck park. There
was no sign of Marissa or Jaxx. A lone duck waddled past the
playground equipment and down the bank toward the river.

"I don't see any Furries." Vanessa flipped the vanity mirror
closed.

"He's home!" Derek announced, leaning forward in his
seat, eyes fixed to the screen of his iPhone. "Tom just texted."

"Where did she take him?" June asked.

"He didn't say. Only *Marissa just brought Jaxx.*"

June told Randy to drive. No one expected Marissa to still
be there when they returned to the house, but she and Tom
were sitting on the back deck with Jaxx between them, facing
the sun in his bouncy chair. It took several seconds for the Figgs
to make like things were cool and casual, and not as though
they'd returned from a failed neighbourhood search. Marissa
ate blue ice cream from a waffle cone.

"Hey," Marissa said, between licks. "Sorry, my phone died."
She held up the black screen of her Samsung. "I didn't think
we'd be gone so long, but I had a craving for ice cream."

June twitched upon noticing that Jaxx appeared to have been given a taste. She fiddled with her shoe so she could continue to eavesdrop, but Randy nudged her to go in the house. Derek picked up Jaxx from his chair and held him close before taking a seat across from Marissa. June had wanted to do the same thing. She wanted to pick him up and hide him in the closet where she could keep tabs on him, but instead she took Randy's outstretched hand and followed him into the house. Vanessa went to her room.

"I wanted to hear what she had to say," June said, safely behind closed doors.

"What's there to hear?" Randy opened the fridge. "They went for ice cream."

"But what if that was a lie? What if she had planned to abduct him and it didn't work out. Like it was a practice run." She thought of the 9/11 terrorists. "Did you know James Woods was on a test-flight with some of the hijackers a month before the 9/11 attacks?"

"Who's James Woods?"

"A famous actor."

"How did he know they were terrorists?"

"Because they were acting weird on the flight."

"But Marissa isn't acting weird or suspicious."

"Not to us, maybe, but we don't know her very well." June put a tea biscuit in the microwave.

"Make me one too," Randy said. "I think you're overreacting. Maybe we need to trust Derek on this one. She doesn't seem at all like she wants to be a mother. Derek showed more interest in caring for his Sea-Monkeys than Marissa does for Jaxx."

June watched the pair of tea biscuits go around in the microwave.

"Do you want help?" Randy asked. "Getting the boxes?"

"Yes, please." June removed the tea biscuits and carried them to the basement.

Randy hauled one of Margaret's boxes down from a stack and set it at June's feet.

"I don't even know what I'm looking for." She kneeled on the floor in front of the box and removed the lid.

"What are you doing?" Vanessa asked. She stood at the bottom of the stairs with a lollipop jammed in her mouth.

"I'm going through your grandma's stuff." June pulled out a stack of bank statements. "See if I can find any information on my adoption."

Vanessa twisted the stick of the lollipop and sat cross-legged on the floor in front of the second box Randy had retrieved.

"That good for now?" Randy put a hand on June's shoulder.

"Yup," she said, without looking up, the stack of bank statements sliding off her lap.

Randy finished his tea biscuit. "You okay if I go work on the table?"

"Sure."

He patted her shoulder again. "Let me know if you find something."

Tom arrived minutes later with a load of laundry.

"Is Marissa still up there?" June asked.

"No, she left." He stuffed an armful of jeans into the washing machine and looked at the boxes lined up on the floor. "Are those Grandma's?"

"They are," June replied.

Tom bent over a box and pulled out a tiny copper bell. "I used to love this bell!"

Vanessa took the sucker out of her mouth. "What in the hell for?"

"Grandma used to ring it every time I cleaned up without her asking."

"I don't remember that." Vanessa pulled out a bag of coupons.

June rifled through more bank papers. "Why does that not surprise me?"

Tom took the lid off the remaining box. "What exactly are we looking for?"

"Mom's adoption papers."

"What do they look like?"

"I'm not sure, so you have go through every item piece by piece."

Tom removed a pile. "These are mostly greeting cards," he said, leafing through.

"Doesn't matter." June flipped through a cookbook. "Open every one of them just in case."

June returned her focus to the pile mounting on either side of her knees. So far she had turned up nothing official or important. An hour passed, and her neck ached from leaning forward. Vanessa had finished her box and gone upstairs, leaving the contents on the floor. June found sealed envelopes twice, but the first contained pressed flowers, and the second produced a handful of flattened one- and two-dollar bills.

Tom held up a glossy travel brochure with the Great.Wall on the cover. "I never knew Grandma went to China."

"She didn't."

He flipped through the first few pages, which were marked with asterisks and handwritten notes. "Why not?"

"Grandpa died." June held up a tiny lamb figurine. Both of the ears were chipped.

Tom heaved himself up from the floor. "No adoption papers in this one," he said, nudging a box with his toe. "What do you want me to do with all of this stuff?"

"Just throw it back in," June waved, reaching for another stack of papers.

Tom set a few items aside and refilled the box. "I'm outta here."

"Thanks for your help," she replied without looking up.

Toward the bottom of the box, June pulled out a leather-bound book. It had belonged to her father. It was full of sketches of fences and floor plans. Lines and arrows and measurements all labelled with tiny perfect numbers in black ink. About a third of the way through, between the blueprints of a doghouse and a tree house, there was another envelope. Manila, unsealed. The papers. Her birthdate, her name. Her place of birth. Hereby, thereby, whereby. So many words and lines. Everything punctuated, official, stamped. Everything but her mother's name. It was blacked out. Blindfolded.

"Of course," she sighed. "This is how it would play out." She exhaled with frustration. With sorrow. And then she folded the paper, once, and then twice. It was during that second fold. Her father's same perfect handwriting appeared on the reverse side of her adoption record. Her mother's name. Two words. They were upside down. In block letters, fixed at a slight angle as though they'd been blown to the right. DORIS CHANEY.

26

"Randy!" June scrambled to her feet and raced to the computer. The heavy monitor creaked when she banged into the desk. "What was the name of the site that had my birth mom on it?"

Randy appeared at his workshop door with safety goggles strapped tight to his face. "I'm not sure," he said. "The kids were searching on Vanessa's laptop. Did you find something?"

"Doris Chaney," she replied. She was breathing heavily the way she did when she swam in deep water. *Doris Chaney.* She repeated the name several times in her head.

"Just type in *Doris Chaney* and see what happens."

June entered her birth mother's name slowly and methodically as though she were entering the numbers of a Lotto 649 ticket. A number of *Doris Chaneys* responded. LinkedIn counted twelve of them. Facebook another thirteen. A row of *Doris Chaney* images also spread across the screen like a filmstrip. All of them looked between sixty and seventy.

"Click on her!" Randy said, behind her shoulder.

June brought up all of the Google images of Doris Chaney. "This is confusing," she commented. "There's no information."

"There's not supposed to be. Google images are just that — images. But maybe you'll see someone who looks like you."

She considered the possibility of someone other than Derek looking like her. She remembered the anticipation of meeting new relatives. Would there be a ginger among them? A waif? Someone with short arms? Heart-shaped ears? Pronounced kneecaps? She had one aunt who was fair and freckled and thin like she was, but June later learned she had a digestive disorder. She scrolled down the images. There was a Sears portrait-style picture of a nice-looking woman in her sixties, wearing a satiny green blouse and pearl earrings. A stone cottage with a broken wheelbarrow on the front walk. A mug shot in front of a Virginia Beach prison. Someone in her thirties jumping off a dock with her nose plugged. A family photo of a couple and four girls, with no indication of which one was Doris. A promotional photo of Annette Funicello. A picture of Reese's Peanut Butter Cups. A black and white of a hairy-faced man-creature fondling a bow and arrow. A clown. "I don't get this," June said, frustrated. "I don't see a single picture of my mom."

"You don't know that for certain," Randy said. "Maybe you got your red hair from your dad." He scrolled further down the page, passing a number of headshots. "Maybe that's her," he said, singling out a picture of a woman holding an apple, which was still attached to a tree. "Or her." He smiled.

June stared at the image of the clown. She had an elongated forehead, exaggerated pink eyebrows, and a yellow wig with heavy fringe that reminded June of Betsey Johnson. She was making a sad face, presumably because the balloon she was holding on a stick had popped. Or maybe she was sad because she was channelling June's disappointment that her mother appeared to be a wheelbarrow or a convict. She sat back in her chair, deflated.

"Why don't you put in Fergus?" she suggested.

"I've done it before," Randy said. "Wasn't helpful." He entered *Fergus images* into the search box and sat back for June to view the results. The collection was similarly random. A cartoon train with teeth, a model in a beige unitard with an orange afro covering her face, a plate of sweet potato fries, a map of an Ontario town, a middle-aged Asian woman holding a trombone.

"I think we need to go back to the adoption sites." June's enthusiasm had burst like the clown's balloon. She thought of Birte and Earle becoming increasingly unified by their shared goal of owning property in Phoenix. She could see them scrunched up on their couch reviewing properties on Earle's laptop, squealing and high-fiving at the prospect of a ground-level suite with a toaster oven and side-by-side laundry because Birte was too short for a stackable pair. June was envious. She and Randy were becoming closer in an AA sort of way. Bonding over weekly adoption meetings with store-bought tea biscuits in the basement. And when they weren't searching for their birth families, they were searching for others. Marissa and Jaxx, or signs of pre-lesbian Vanessa. June often found herself thinking about pre-lesbian Vanessa, which seemed ridiculous because outwardly there were very few changes. It wasn't like Vanessa had transitioned and was living as Vaughn Figg or Vincent Figg. In fact, lesbian Vanessa seemed nicer and less angry than pre-lesbian Vanessa. The letters LGBT popped out of newspapers and resounded from the radio. LGBT, KGB, BLT.

Randy pulled up an adoption site.

"Put in Doris Chaney," June said.

"It's my turn." Randy entered the name Fergus. "I haven't tried this site before."

June thought of retirement ads on TV, in which couples her age took turns zip-lining or flying small planes, while she and Randy took turns searching for ghost mothers and sons. She felt like the old man who picked through the garbage bins at Tim Hortons for refundable bottles.

"They probably didn't name him Fergus," June said flatly.

"Then how can I find him?"

"You're better off searching his birthdate and hospital."

Randy's shoulders slumped forward as though his entire body was pouting. "I've put the date in a million times. Nothing comes up."

June considered the possibility that Fergus did not know he was adopted. Maybe he'd been placed with a family that looked like him or shared some of his tendencies. Or maybe the family had moved to Argentina or Boston, and there was just no way of searching. Randy went back to the top of the forum and entered June's birth year. A hefty list of names and cities came up but nothing matching her summer birthdate.

"Let me do it," she said. "We need to find the ARE YOU MY DAUGHTER? ad." June typed the question into a yahoo search engine but it garnered a list of daughter quotes and no adoption records. "Why can't I find it?"

"Beats me," Randy said. "There are a hundred adoption sites. You're better off going through each one and checking that way." Randy pulled out a black science lab notebook from the desk drawer. Inside he'd created a log of websites he'd searched, the information he'd entered and the date. There were notes written in the margin with green felt pen. Most of them ended with question marks. He placed the book on June's lap and excused himself. "I have to go work on the table."

She touched his hand as he passed and then moved her chair forward so she could get closer to the screen. She ignored the book on her lap and typed in DORIS CHANEY but every Doris she clicked on lived in North Dakota or High River. They were the wrong age, wrong race, wrong look. Randy turned his workshop radio on low. She could hear the sound of wood being stacked, the same clapping sound she heard when the older neighbourhood trees blew into each other during a storm. It did not feel like Mother's Day. She felt childish and weak and nothing like the mother of three adult children. She put Randy's adoption logbook back in the drawer and pulled out a Ziploc bag of stale brazil nuts, which she ate anyway.

The computer went into sleep mode. June closed her eyes and leaned back in her chair. She tried to visualize the website. *ARE YOU MY DAUGHTER?* It was written in white block letters, the background blue. Something .net. She leaned forward and struck the keys on the keyboard, waking the computer. She typed in *"find my adopted daughter Grace Hospital June."* The phrase ARE YOU MY DAUGHTER? popped up in the body of the second site listed in the search results. June clicked on it six times. A blue screen appeared. It was the correct site. She scrolled madly up and down the page. Where was ARE YOU MY DAUGHTER? She plugged in her birthdate.

Randy started cutting wood in the workshop. The sounds were awful. Screeching and grinding. Slaughterhouse pigs. Dental work. She thought she might have a heart attack. She stared at the screen until the block letters appeared. ARE YOU MY DAUGHTER?

June clicked on the word DAUGHTER. She scanned the paragraph — football, cheddar, blue hand, Wanda. She clicked on the reply button but a window opened instructing her to register. She lifted herself off her chair and dropped back down again. *Why do I need to register, you idiot?* She couldn't remember her email.

"Randy, what's our email address?" she hollered, though she knew her question fell on covered ears. She went to their Gmail account. If she entered the correct letter the address and password should show up. Was it RANDYJUNE or JUNERANDY? Was there a number in there somewhere? An asterisk? When she typed "R", Gmail completed the email. RANDYJUNE82. What was the significance of the 82? Random, or Fergus's birth year? One new message. June saw the sender before she read the subject line. Glenda Mitten. June nearly swallowed her tongue.

Glenda Mitten. Glenda the long-haired child-maker Mitten. Randy's machines continued to chomp and smash in the background. Was he cutting metal? Crashing cars? She yelled, "Shut up!" even though she couldn't hear the words leave her mouth. Subject line: CHARLES FERGUS ZACHARELLIS. She said it aloud. "Charles Fergus Zacharellis." Charles. Charlie. Charles Zacharellis. She thought of Chaplin and Darwin and Machiavelli. Macaroni. Marconi. She cried with glee. It was not only Mother's Day. It was Father's Day. "Randy!" she hollered. "You *are* the father!" She laughed with holy hysteria the way they did in Texan Pentecostal churches. She wiped tears of joy from her face, the laughter reduced to a few elongated *ha has*. The sounds from the workshop remained obnoxious and productive as she opened the email. There was nothing in the body, just an attachment. *Would he look like him?* she wondered. *Maybe he'll look like Derek or Tom. Jaxx!* She opened the attachment. Fergus's obituary took up the entire page.

27

The noise in Randy's workshop ceased, with the exception of his radio, which was playing something quiet. She could make out a harmonica. She tried to close the screen in front of her, but her hands fumbled as though the mouse was electrically charged. In a panic she pulled off her sweatshirt and draped it over the monitor like a drop cloth. She placed her elbows on the desk, her hands together, poised for prayer. "What do I do?" she whispered. She got up from her chair and walked down the hall, hands braced against the wood panelling for support. Randy was bent over a can of nails, one finger fishing through it. Table legs were scattered on the floor below. He did not see her. He picked out several nails and sang bits of Paul Simon's "Graceland," while the radio issued an extreme weather warning for communities south of Calgary. Hail in May. She backed out of the room undetected, knees buckling, arms over her head like the sky was falling and returned to the computer. She lifted her sweatshirt off the screen, scrunched it into a ball, and hit a few random keys. The obituary resurfaced.

ZACHARELLIS, CHARLES FERGUS: The family of Charles Fergus Zacharellis, 22, of Red Deer announces his sad and sudden passing on July 13, 2004, as the result of a motor vehicle accident. "Charlie" was born April 11, 1982, in Calgary, Alberta. He was the loving son of Frank and Laura Zacharellis. Charlie was an all-star pitcher for the Red Deer Riggers and garnered national attention for pitching both a perfect game and a no-hitter in one season. When he was not on the pitcher's mound, Charlie could be found playing with his border collie, Bruce, hanging out with friends, or building things in the garage. A graduate from Lindsay Thurber High School, Charlie was enrolled in the forestry program at Red Deer College; he wanted to become a forest technician in Alberta's north. He was known for his unwavering optimism and million-dollar smile. He was a kind and compassionate young man who loved working with his hands and helping others. He is survived by his parents, Frank and Laura Zacharellis (Luntz), maternal grandmother, Dorothy Luntz, and many aunts, uncles, cousins, and friends. He was predeceased by his paternal grandparents, Frank and Libby Zacharellis, and maternal grandfather, Eugene Luntz. In lieu of flowers, donations can be made to the Red Deer Minor Baseball CHARLES ZACHARELLIS Memorial Scholarship Fund or the SPCA. Viewing will be held Friday, July 16 at 7pm at Parkland Funeral Home. Burial will be held at 1pm Saturday at the Red Deer Cemetery.

More than a decade ago. June stared at the accompanying photo of Charlie and reread the obituary. He did not look like Derek or Tom or Jaxx or Vanessa. Maybe a bit like Tom, because he was dark and broad-shouldered, but he definitely looked like Randy. His hair, which was mostly hidden under a baseball cap, curled out from the sides, and his smile was bright and endearing. A million-dollar smile, as the obituary claimed. In the image, he was resting a bat behind his shoulders. A dog, June assumed this was Bruce, sat in front of him with one paw raised and his head tilted as though someone had said something the moment before the photo was snapped. Charlie looked young and fresh and alive, yet he was dead. Her heart palpitated. She covered and uncovered her eyes. Rereading, un-reading, staring until the words blurred. She touched the screen and said his name. "Charlie. Fergus." Loving son of Frank and Laura, and also of Randy and Glenda. Half-brother to Tom and Vanessa and Derek. Uncle to Jaxx. Something to June. Love child. Young man. Dead man. She felt sick. Her emotions were physical. They pulled at her teeth, stood on her shoulders, stomped on her chest. Then she heard footsteps. She turned off the monitor swiftly. The screen went black.

"What are you doing?" Vanessa asked from behind her, slurping from a straw.

"Just looking for a recipe," June stammered.

"Are you done?"

June whirled around in her seat, clinging to the backrest. She must have looked disturbed or ill or traumatized, because Vanessa's expression weakened, making everything hard on her face — brows, lips, studs — look benign.

"Um . . ." she mumbled, lost for words. "Maybe I'll come back?"

"No," June said. "Stay."

Vanessa halted, stirring the chunks of ice that remained in her Starbucks cup. She surveyed the room. "What do you want me to do?"

"It's Mother's Day," June said. "Just stay here."

Vanessa continued to look around, confused. "Is something wrong? Do you want me to get Dad?"

"No!" June said, extending both arms out as if stopping traffic. "Do *not* get your father."

Vanessa shifted her weight. It took a moment for June to notice that Vanessa was not wearing all black. Her jeans were a pretty coral that made June think of Barbados. Randy came down the hall with a plank of wood tucked under his arm. June leaned back in the chair to block the computer.

"Hello, Vanessa." Randy was cheerful. "See any more condos lately?"

Vanessa looked at her mother. "We put an offer on one. Should hear back this afternoon."

"Fingers crossed." He smiled and looked at his wife. June tried to look normal. She strained her forehead.

"Can you give me a hand?" he asked.

"Why don't I give you a hand?" Vanessa offered.

"You?" He was unable to contain both the surprise and excitement.

Vanessa shrugged and placed her empty cup on the edge of the ping-pong table. "That would be lovely," Randy said. "It won't take a minute." He nodded at June in a *did you hear that?* way and turned down the hall.

Vanessa followed behind. Before stepping into the workshop, she looked back at her mother. June put her hand up. *Five minutes*, she mouthed, holding her hand up to demonstrate. *Give me five.* Vanessa rolled her eyes the way she always did and disappeared into a haze of dust.

June spun around in the chair and turned on the monitor. She closed the obituary, closed Glenda's email. The adoption-connect forum resurfaced, the window still open, instructing her to register. She typed in her name and email address, answered the questions. When she completed the forum, a new screen appeared. It said REGISTRATION SUCCESS! She clicked on the post, ARE YOU MY DAUGHTER?, and wrote.

I may be your daughter. I'm the girl with the one blue hand. I was born on June 29, 1959, at the Grace Hospital in Calgary. My mother's name is Margaret. I have red hair. My name is June Figg.

She did not reread or overthink her response as she'd expected she would. It was her first contact. She'd imagined there would be exclamation marks and capital letters and questions. Overused punctuation. She was blunt and lifeless like Fergus. Her hand was still blue from the morning.

She got up from the computer and checked the laundry in the dryer. It was still damp. She folded a pile of clean towels that someone had removed earlier and left in a heap. The swishing sound of the washer was therapeutic.

June decided she should be the one to tell Randy about Fergus. She'd go into the workshop, tell him they *needed to talk*. She'd take his hands and say *he's gone*. June would stand with her feet wide, one in front of the other, to brace his fall, the way she was instructed in First Aid training when someone

235

was choking. She practised. Left foot forward, then right. Right foot forward was stronger.

"You're welcome," Vanessa said from down the hall, making June jump.

Randy and Vanessa entered the room. His hands rested on top of his daughter's shoulders. He rubbed them affectionately, a jubilant smile on his face. "Vanessa's really good," he said proudly. "She has a perfect eye."

Vanessa made an ugly face, but a smile curled up from her mouth.

"Thank you again, Vanessa." Randy said.

"You're welcome," she repeated flatly. "I'm going to go now." She glanced at her mom as if searching for permission.

"Yes," June said.

Vanessa looked relieved as she sauntered down the hall, the white and pink flesh of her arms swaying as she moved. The stairs creaked beneath her weight, and then ceased. There was nothing between June and Randy except space and knowledge. Approximately six feet. Six feet and one death notice. His smile remained fixed for some time. The pleasure of sharing his workshop, his passion for wood, with his daughter. Having experienced little in common with her own parents, June never quite understood Randy's disappointment in his children's lack of interest in carpentry. Not sharing interests with her children meant moments of reprieve, periods of peace and quiet. Times, particularly when the kids were young, she yearned for.

"Hi," Randy said breaking the silence between them.

"Hi," she replied.

"I'm almost finished the table."

"Good," she said, exhaling through pursed lips to control her breath, which was breaking into a stampede. Head-Smashed-In-Buffalo-Jump. Composure tumbling off a cliff. She forgot how she planned to reveal the news. She looked back at the washer, waiting for some sort of trigger. *Fergus is dead. We have to talk about Fergus. It's about Fergus.* When she turned back around, Randy had closed the space between them. He reached his arms around, and she felt his fingers link together at the small of her back. It felt like a restraining device. A locked seatbelt. There was six inches now. Six inches and one secret. The scent of wood glue and old nails. His breath was calm. A still lake. She was about to drive all over it with a neon jet ski and no lifejacket. "Randy," she said quietly, "Fergus is dead."

He kept his arms in place, locked behind her back, but they doubled in weight. An elephant on her tailbone. Grief. She stepped one foot back. She remembered this part. The choking, but he did not fall. They staggered, drunk-like, a few steps down the hall until they came to rest against the wall, knocking the light switch to the off position.

"How do you know?" he whispered. He tilted his chin. His eyeballs strained upward as if trying to climb out of the tears welling beneath. He blinked.

"Glenda sent his obituary."

"He already has an obituary?"

"He died in 2004."

He leaned his head against the wall. Heavy. It would leave a mark. She placed her hands on his shoulders, the way he had placed his on Vanessa's. She was going to tell him *it's okay*, but it wasn't okay and maybe it never would be okay, because he would never meet his son. He would never have closure.

Instead she told him, "He liked to work with his hands." Randy pulled away slightly, rolling his forehead against the wall. He wept and then turned around so his back was against it and slid down to the floor. She followed, placing one knee down at a time. "There's a gravesite," she told him. "We can go visit." Somewhere in the house, Jaxx was crying. His voice carried through the vents. She wondered why someone hadn't picked him up. What were they all doing up there? The crying continued. Downstairs it was guttural, nearly silent. Upstairs it was shrill and angry. She wanted to tell Jaxx to shut up. She pulled herself to her feet and went upstairs, leaving Randy slumped against the wall like a homeless person on the sidewalk. She looked out the kitchen window to the backyard. Tom and Vanessa were on the back deck. Was Tom smoking? Both were looking at their phones. She climbed to the second floor of the house, stopping on the landing to pick up a receiving blanket. The family crest had fallen off the wall. It was face down on the step, its nail missing, leaving behind a black hole and bits of drywall dust. She set it upright and put the nail in her pocket. The screams were coming from the bathroom. June knocked. "Can I come in?"

"Can you get me a towel?" Derek called out.

June took a bath sheet from the linen closet, opened the bathroom door, and flicked on the fan, hoping some of the humidity would dissipate.

Derek was bent over the side of the tub, his jeans soaked, spine uncomfortably bent. "He's freaking out because I washed his hair." He turned back to face Jaxx and mumbled, "Fuck."

Jaxx's mouth was open so wide June could see his uvula vibrate, and his legs were extended stick straight. His belly had become full and round like the bulbous end of a butternut squash. It made her smile. "Maybe you got shampoo in his eyes."

"I didn't," Derek argued. "I think he just hates water."

June reached over and ran her fingers through Jaxx's fine wet hair. "I think you got it all out," she concluded. "Give him to me."

Derek struggled to get onto one foot and banged his knee against the tub. He lifted Jaxx out and handed him to June, who waited with the oversized towel draped across her arms. Derek placed him inside and June wrapped him up. He stopped crying. "I'll take him for a bit," June offered. Derek looked relieved, his wet jeans drooping. He quickly left the bathroom as though his mother might change her mind.

June carried Jaxx into Derek's room and laid him on the bed, the towel lumped around him in heaps. He rolled to land on his side and put his hand in his mouth. She took a diaper from Derek's nightstand. "Someone doesn't like baths," she said. "What's wrong with a cozy bath? Your daddy used to love having baths." Jaxx looked at her suspiciously. "You don't believe me?" she asked. He continued to suckle his hand while she searched the small dresser Derek had found at a garage sale. She picked pyjamas because they were the easiest to put on. She thought it was silly to dress a baby in jeans. "Let's get you dressed."

She tried not to think of Randy in bits two floors below. If only she could solve his problem with a pair of pyjamas and the soothing voice of a grandma. When Jaxx was dressed, she wrapped him in a blanket and carried him downstairs. When she reached the basement, Randy was sitting at the computer. The obituary was on the screen. He whipped around when he heard her approach, his face full of awe.

"He looks like me!"

Looked, June thought. "Yes, I know. A bit of Tom in him too."

"And he was an athlete! Do you know how hard it is to pitch a perfect game?"

June didn't know. She hated baseball after her father died. The seventh inning organs made her think of his funeral. And the hot dogs were too big. But she supposed doing anything *perfect* was impressive.

"And a no-hitter," she added.

"I think he had a good life, June," Randy said. He started to cry again. "But he was so young. He was only just getting started."

"Here," June said, passing him Jaxx. "It's like Paro, but he's real." Randy pulled his grandson into his chest and turned back to look at Fergus on the screen.

"I'm going to look for something to take out for dinner."

"Don't do that," Randy said. "It's Mother's Day."

She shrugged.

"We'll go out."

"It'll have to be early," June said. "We'll never get in anywhere after five o'clock."

28

The Figgs arrived for dinner at 4:30 p.m. June picked Vietnamese because it was cheap and offered big portions, but the neighbouring KFC made her crave salty coleslaw and original recipe drumsticks.

"Six plus a baby," Randy told the owner as they filed into the restaurant.

He showed them to a long table in the centre of the room. "Mother's Day?"

"Yes." June smiled. The place was largely vacant except for a trio of FedEx employees all eating pho, and a booth of tradespeople in beat-up Carhartt coveralls. The host returned a minute later with a table-sized pot of jasmine tea and a pink carnation.

June sat beside Vanessa. She'd noticed that Vanessa and Leslie had held hands on the way in and were still linked under the table. She wondered if they did this often. What people thought. What they said. She wanted to suggest they not hold hands in public, to protect them from homophobic slurs. Or maybe she didn't want them to hold hands because someone she knew might see them and they would forever view her daughter as Vanessa the lesbian and herself as June the mother of a lesbian. But this was not Vanessa's style. Attention was positive. In a perverse way, negative attention was more positive. June grabbed Randy's hand under the table and held onto it in a show of solidarity for her daughter, even though her gesture would go unnoticed. They ordered meals by checking off their selections on a printed piece of paper that accompanied the laminated menus.

Randy clinked the teapot with a chopstick. "Can I have your attention?"

"Here we go," Vanessa mumbled. Leslie hushed her and refilled her tiny cup with jasmine tea. Her nails were painted turquoise.

"As you know," Randy said, trying to make eye contact with his sons sitting across from him, "today is Mother's Day." He paused. "Tom, put your phone away."

Tom moved his phone to the side, flipping it face down. He crossed his arms. "You're not going to give one of your speeches, are you?"

"Would you let me speak?" he said, but June, too, was hoping he would not. He was too fragile for speeches, especially in public. Randy took a deep breath. "We are gathered here today to celebrate your mother."

Vanessa jumped all over this. "Sounds like a eulogy."

"Let me finish," Randy sighed. June observed the fish in the tank plastered against the back wall. She felt like climbing inside and drowning herself.

"What I mean, is that today is Mother's Day and we are here to celebrate that."

"Yes, Dad," Derek said, "we all know it's Mother's Day."

"Here, Mom," Tom said, pulling a card from a pocket inside his leather jacket. June ran her finger over the embossed *Carlton Cards* above the envelope's seal and then ripped it open with a chopstick. The card was covered in sunflowers. It was blank inside but for Tom's message. *No matter where you came from, I'm happy that I came from you.*

"What a lovely card, Tom," she said.

Vanessa promptly produced her own. "The gift is from all of us," she said, passing a flat box wrapped in crepe paper. June untied the raffia bow and opened the box as a server set down plates of spring rolls. June waited until everyone had taken a spring roll before pulling out *The Complete Idiot's Guide to Playing the Ukelele: Everything You Need to Start Strumming and Picking Today.*

"Wow, this is really thoughtful." June flipped through the book. "Take Me Out to the Ball Game." She closed it.

"Isn't it?" Randy nodded. "There's a CD in the back, too. Over a hundred songs."

He picked up his chopstick and clinked the teapot for a second time.

Derek looked irritated.

"I have something I need to share with the family," Randy said.

Derek swallowed a spring roll in two bites and took another off the table.

"I found Fergus," he said.

Vanessa picked up the teapot. "Your love child?"

"Yes," Randy said, swallowing hard.

June pretended not to hear *love child*. Instead, she looked through the index of her new book.

Derek wiped his chin. "Well, what's he like?"

"Yeah," Tom added. "Have you talked to him?"

Randy closed his eyes. Everyone sat in silence, waiting for him to open them again, but his lids remained clenched. June's children looked to her for an explanation.

"Is there something wrong with him?" Vanessa was cautious. "Does he not want to meet you or something?"

A server with advanced acne set a tray next to the table and delivered their food. She did not seem phased that Randy appeared to be sleeping.

"Mom?" Derek said, looking at June. He raised his eyebrows toward his father. "Will we get to meet him?"

"No," Randy bellowed, shaking his head with his eyes closed. "He's dead."

"Whoa," Tom said, pushing back from the table. "Did not see that one coming."

"For real?" Vanessa tossed down her chopsticks in favour of a fork. "How did he die?"

"In a car accident," June said quietly. "Several years ago."

"Sorry, Dad," Derek said. "I know you were looking forward to meeting him."

"Thank you, Derek," Randy said. "I'm sure he would have loved having a little brother."

Derek reached across the table and gave his father's shoulder a squeeze.

Randy sniffed. "I'm sorry," he said. "This was supposed to be for your mother."

June scraped lemongrass off her chicken and mixed it in with her rice. "I'm fine," she said. "Don't worry about it."

Tom stirred his soup aggressively, causing it to spill over

the bowl. "Where is Fergus?"

"I believe he's in heaven," Randy said.

"I meant physically," Tom replied.

June spread a paper napkin across her lap. "He's in Red Deer. That's where he grew up."

"He grew up in Red Deer?" Vanessa was nearly finished her meal.

"Fergus is actually his middle name," Randy said. "His first name was Charles."

The kids digested the information. The restaurant got busier. Parties of two, of five, of nine, were shown to tables and given tea.

"I have a brother named Charles," Leslie said. She'd taken off her sweater and was wearing a cowl neck shirt that gathered in heaps at her collarbone.

"Does he live here in Calgary?" Randy asked.

She shook her head. "He works for the Department of Fisheries and Oceans. In Newfoundland."

Vanessa finished eating and filled a plastic tumbler with the remains of her can of Pepsi. "We should go visit him."

"My brother?" Leslie asked.

"Fergus," Vanessa said.

"Your father and I were planning a trip to the cemetery." This was not true. Or at least she and Randy hadn't discussed it, but it seemed logical, necessary.

"You'd want to come?" Randy said.

Vanessa shrugged so she didn't appear too enthusiastic or thoughtful. "I guess," she said. "He's kind of our half-brother."

"Oh, it would be wonderful." Randy dropped his fork.

June worried he would cry. "We could have our road trip."

She hoped to inject some optimism into the conversation. It worked for Randy. He clasped his hands together in agreement. The kids, however, were less enthusiastic.

"I can't go on a road trip," Vanessa said. "Leslie and I are still house hunting."

"And I need to work," Derek said.

The table looked at Tom. "I can go to Red Deer," he shrugged, "but it would have to be a day trip. I'd need to be back for work."

Derek and Vanessa looked annoyed at Tom.

"Fine," June said. "Not an overnight trip, just a day trip. We'll go first thing in the morning, spend the day in Red Deer, and get back before Tom has to work."

"But what about *my* work?" Derek said.

"It's okay," Leslie assured. "We can push the Arbour Lake job to Saturday if we need to."

Derek wiped his face with a napkin and leaned back in his chair. "Okay," he said. "Guess we're going to Red Deer." Randy looked poised to make another speech, but was distracted by a boy standing on a chair sucking on a towel at the next table. Hoards of people were pooling into the restaurant.

"We should go," June suggested. "Give someone else our table."

"That would be the right thing to do." Randy took his slip to the front cash, while everyone else stood up and pushed their chairs in. June led the exodus through the narrow entryway and out onto the sidewalk to wait. Two Asian men were smoking and talking at a fast pace. June waved the smoke away and held her purse in front of her. Leslie's phone rang. She walked past June and stood in front of a chiropractic office, which was closed and quiet. Vanessa joined her. June wondered what the deal was. She counted the orange vertebrae decals on the window. Leslie paced while she talked. Tom and Derek stood on her other side, both scrolling.

"We got it!" Leslie said.

"We got it?" Vanessa asked. Their arms were linked, hand to forearm, their faces a foot apart.

"It's ours," Leslie said.

Vanessa shrieked and jumped up and down. "You're sure?"

"One hundred percent."

Vanessa squealed again. One hundred percent. Those had been the words Derek used to assert his paternity. Vanessa turned to her mother. "They accepted our offer," she said, beaming. "We got the house." She ran her fingers through her hair and set a strand free into the wind. She was little-girl happy. Giddy and feminine. Leslie, too. They didn't look like feminists or lawyers or lesbians. They looked like the girls at the mall who got good deals at Victoria's Secret. They looked like Marissa.

"What's going on?" Randy said, sticking his wallet back into his pocket. "What did I miss?"

"We got the house," Vanessa said, more composed. "The condo by the Safeway. The one we wanted."

"That's wonderful!" Randy said. He walked over to Vanessa and Leslie and awkwardly hugged them together. "You see this, June? Happiness. Love. Love doesn't discriminate between gay or straight. Adopted, or un-adopted."

"I think you mean the condo owner doesn't," Tom said.

"We had the highest bid," Leslie explained.

"Yes, but when we have love in our lives, it can overcome all sorts of things," Randy mused.

"Like when you connect two unrelated events and make them seem related?" Derek asked.

June made eyes at her son.

"What?" he said.

June turned her attention to Leslie. "When do you close?'"

"June 1."

"June 1?" Randy said. "That's in a couple of weeks."

June felt a pang of anxiety zip through her body like lightning. It was not how she imagined her daughter moving out. With a partner old enough to start worrying about bone density. How would they decorate? Did Vanessa even know how to pay bills or operate a vacuum? Would she know to lock the door at night? Shovel the front step? Leslie would. June was sure.

She climbed into the van and watched Leslie and Vanessa get into Leslie's vehicle, where they shared a quick kiss. Curt, but sweet. She thought of the place in the mall that sold extravagant candy apples. Then Leslie's hand wrapped around the gearshift, the muscles in her forearm engaged like she was about to operate a crane. She put the car in reverse and looked behind her to make sure the parking lot was clear. All the while, Vanessa smiled, long and hard like she had when she was little, feeding goats at the petting zoo, wrapping Christmas presents, rearranging her room. June watched until the car turned and all she saw was the back of Vanessa's head.

29

Randy filled a Mason jar with water, cut the end off the pink carnation, and placed the flower inside. "That was a nice dinner," he said, patting his stomach. "Would you like a cup of tea? To take out to the porch? The boys went to pick up more diapers. I thought I'd clean up a little."

But June didn't want tea. She had drunk four cups at the restaurant. She was thinking about Glenda. About Fergus the love child. About whether things would have been different if they'd been allowed to keep him. Would they still be lovers? Was she still long-haired and nearly blind? Would they be shopping around for condos in Phoenix like Birte and Earle? Would Fergus still be alive?

"Have you spoken with Glenda?" June immediately regretted asking because for the moment, Randy's emotions were in check.

"Only briefly," he replied. "Over email."

She twirled the Mason jar and observed the tiny pink leaves, crimped and delicate yet hearty, like a cabbage. "Did she ever get to meet him?"

Randy shook his head. "She only found him a few years ago."

"How?" June rested her elbows on the island.

"Through a patient that knew his parents."

"But I thought the adoption was all closed and secret?"

"It was, sort of. Her name hadn't been blacked out on one of the papers. A clerical error. His adoptive parents always knew her name."

"Well, how did the patient know?"

"The patient was Fergus's aunt. Laura Zacharellis's sister."

"How does that happen? What did she say? *Hey, my tooth hurts. I'm your son's aunt.*"

Randy shrugged. "Something like that. I don't know the details, but it was his aunt that sent Glenda the obituary."

"Has she been to his grave?"

"Yes." He went to the cupboard above the fridge and took out the Advil. "I have a terrible headache."

"Why don't you lie down for a bit?"

"No." He opened a bottle of water. "If you don't need me to tidy up or anything, I'm going to work on the table. I need to get it done if we're going to Red Deer tomorrow."

June was sorry she'd suggested the road trip so soon. She was exhausted, but then she remembered the email. *I may be your daughter. I am the girl with the one blue hand.* She pushed past Randy who was still trying to get the second Advil down. He'd almost finished the bottle of water but was gagging between sips. She braced herself on the handrail and thumped down the stairs, her legs heavy as wet towels, to the computer. Her normally sweat-slicked menopausal hair blew away from her face. She went to her email. Two new messages. A Groupon for laser hair removal and a message from Doris Nickerson. Doris Nickerson? Was this Doris Chaney? Was Doris Nickerson at some point Doris Chaney? She opened the message.

Dear June,

I prayed this day would come and now I can barely even type (my hands are shaking too much). So here goes. Let's start from the beginning. (Your beginning, not mine — mine is actually quite boring). Your father and I were fifteen when we got pregnant. His name is Russell. His father worked for a commercial bakery and every Sunday he would give us a pound cake. Russell and I would walk down to the Bow River after church and have what we called our weekly "pound cake picnic." Russell was a ginger. Freckles all up his arms, but he had blue eyes, which was rare (nowadays you see blue-eyed redheads all the time — they use coloured contacts).

June stopped reading. She wanted to slap the screen. Coloured contacts? Pound cake? Where were the pictures?

Russell and I liked each other quite a bit. We had a lot in common. We both had pet hamsters and we liked bike riding and building things out of snow. That's where you were conceived — in a fort we carved out of a snowbank. It had three separate rooms and an old muffler for a smokestack. Anyway. We didn't tell anyone for a long time about the pregnancy. As soon as we did, our parents said we couldn't keep you. But that was our first plan. To have you. To keep you. To bring you along on our pound cake picnics, to take you on bike rides. To show you all the things you could make out of snow.

I never had any more kids because I had a hysterectomy when I was nineteen. Neither did Russell. We just have hamsters.

Doris (Mom)

We just have hamsters? Did that mean that Russell and Doris were still together? Had she found her mother *and* her father? Were the hamsters her half-siblings? She felt confused and intrigued. Her mom said nothing about enjoying the ukelele or tea. Her parents didn't have kids or grandkids. How could they relate? And they liked snow. She hated the snow! Maybe because she was conceived in it. She was cold from conception. But she was wanted. They'd wanted to take her on picnics and bike rides. June hurriedly typed. *Can you send a picture?* Within a minute, a reply.

Scanner quit, but Russell went to Shoppers Drug Mart to put some pictures on a flash drive. I'll email you as soon as he gets back.

She was there. Alive and on the other side of the screen. She'd just sent an email in real time. Real time, which felt false and stalled. Unbelievable, but true. Her other mother, sitting behind a computer monitor, petting her half-siblings while her father — her father! — was scanning pictures at Shoppers Drug Mart. She tried to imagine what they looked like. If she got her red hair from her father, then maybe Doris was blond. But maybe she was dark. Was she on a laptop in her kitchen? Did her kitchen have a nook? A toaster oven? A lazy Susan? Roosters?

"Randy!"

Randy came out of his workshop, looking worried. "Is everything okay?"

"I found her!"

"You're yelling," Randy said.

"I know!" June yelled as if she had to talk over a jet-propelled aircraft engine. "I can't control it!"

He winced at her volume and knelt by her side. "Do you have a picture?"

She shook her head. "They have hamsters."

"Who's they?"

"My parents."

"They're together?"

"Yes!" she laugh-cried. "Can you believe it? They like making things out of snow."

"I don't get it," Randy said.

"I don't really either," she said. "But that's what they like doing. I was conceived in the snow!"

"You hate the snow."

"I know!" She wiped away tears. She exhaled and laughed, and then she thought of her real mother, who was alone with a seal in a home, and she wanted to hug her desperately. She wanted to apologize to her. She squeezed Randy.

"Where do they live?" Randy adjusted his glasses, which June had somehow managed to knock off.

"I don't know, but they wanted me. They wanted to take me on a picnic."

"They're taking you on a picnic?" He looked bright and snapped his fingers. "I told the kids people still had picnics."

"It's true," she said. "Well, they used to."

Vanessa walked into the room. "If you think I'm going on a picnic tomorrow, you're dead wrong."

"No," Randy said. "We're not going on a picnic. Your mother just found her birth parents."

"Her birth parents are going on a picnic?" Vanessa dropped the armload of laundry she was carrying. "Do you have a picture?"

"No!" June yelled, as though the plane was about to take off. "But he's at Shoppers Drug Mart right now scanning pictures onto a flash drive. And my mom," she pointed to the screen, "is sitting on the other side, right now, as we speak."

She raised both of her arms in the air. She wanted high fives. No one knew what she was doing, so Randy and Vanessa stared.

"High fives," she said. Randy raised his hands. She slapped them. "High fives!" She was hysterical. "I feel sick."

"Why don't you tell her about yourself?" Randy encouraged. "While you wait for the pictures."

June faced the screen. "I do feel sick though. I don't think I can type."

Vanessa told her to move and took a seat in front of the computer. "What do you want to tell her?"

"Tell her about me." Randy said.

Vanessa typed. *I'm married and have three children. My husband's name is Randy. I have two sons — Tom and Derek (Derek is the favourite) and a daughter, Vanessa. She's a dyke. I also have a grandson, Jaxx.*

"Vanessa!" June read back the words. "Don't say *dyke*. And don't say Derek is my favourite."

"Tell her I'm romantic and build tables." Randy was serious.

Derek came down with laundry in an empty Pampers box. He stepped over Vanessa's discarded heap and made a beeline for the washer.

"Wait!" Vanessa called after him. "I was about to put in a load."

"Sorry," he said, jamming small things into the hole of the machine. "Jaxx shit all over everything." He leaned against the washer as it filled with water and kicked the empty diaper box to the side. "Why are you all gathered around the computer?"

"Your mother found her birth parents. They have hamsters," Randy said.

"Is there a picture?" Derek asked.

"That's what we're waiting for." Vanessa straightened the keyboard. "Go get Tom."

Derek sent Tom a text. Seconds later, June could hear Tom's heavy feet mobilizing. He plunked down the stairs with a beer in his hand. "You found your birth parents?"

June took the beer out of his hands and drank the neck. "Sorry," she said. "I'm thirsty. Vanessa is just sending them a message."

Vanessa wrote: *I'm married and have three children. My husband's name is Randy. He is romantic and builds tables. He's an optimist and is great at giving speeches. I have two sons — Tom and Derek, and a daughter, Vanessa. Tom runs his own cleaning company and likes older Asian women. Derek, the favourite, is a single dad. He used to work at a recycling depot. Vanessa recently bought her first home. In the fall, she's going to art college. She is the most normal of the children.*

"*You're* the most normal?" Tom scoffed. "*Vanessa's a lesbian who tells inanimate objects to fuck off.*"

"*Tom likes elder porn,*" Vanessa retorted.

"Don't forget he has a foot fetish," Derek added.

Vanessa typed. *Tom likes elder porn and has a foot fetish.*

"Stop it!" June said.

"I don't have a foot fetish."

"Write that I'm an amateur woodcarver and enjoy tennis," Randy said.

June frowned. "When's the last time you played tennis?"

"I said I enjoyed it. I didn't say I played it."

"Who's your favourite player?" Derek asked.

"That British guy with the ears."

"As opposed to the earless Swiss guy?" Vanessa said.

June interrupted. "Did you say you're going to art college?"

"In September," Vanessa said. "I got accepted last week."

"Why didn't you say something?" June opened her arms for a hug.

"That's great, Vanessa," Randy said. "Now tell them my macaroons are famous."

"The baby's awake." Tom pointed at the ceiling. "I can hear him."

Everyone strained to listen. "Fuck, I just put him down." Derek rubbed his eyes.

"Maybe he's still hungry," June offered. "He's probably having a growth spurt." Derek sighed and took the stairs two, three at a time. He returned minutes later with Jaxx tucked in his elbow. The baby was wide awake and sucking his fingers like they were covered in butter.

"He didn't want to miss the party," Derek said, looking content to have him there.

"Tell them I won a squash tournament once."

"This isn't about you," June said. "It's supposed to be about *me*. I'm their daughter."

Vanessa waited, her pork chop hands on the keyboard.

"Tell them I have three lovely children and a grandson, whom I love dearly. That Randy and I have been married for almost thirty years. That I like to read mysteries and don't mind cooking. I don't like fish or the cold, but am willing to learn about all the things that can be made out of snow."

Vanessa deleted the previous message and typed June's words. Her fingers were covered in rings, all of them square and angular. Fuck off rings, June thought. She reread Vanessa's email and told her to send it.

Doris's reply was almost instant: *Can you send a picture?*

"I don't have a picture." June's voice was loud. "We haven't done a family portrait in years."

"Just take one now." Tom gestured to the small black hole at the top of the computer monitor.

"Look at me," June reacted. "I'm a mess!"

"You look normal," Vanessa said.

June smoothed out her hair, and then tousled it a bit. She felt her shirt to figure out what she was wearing. "I didn't even know that was a camera."

Vanessa got up from the chair. "You should be in the middle."

June lowered herself into the chair and fixed her hair again.

"Should I take off my glasses?" Randy asked.

"Why would you take off your glasses? You can't see without them."

"Yes, I can." He removed them and stuffed them in his shirt pocket.

"How do we get it to take the picture?"

Tom leaned in, pressed some buttons, and opened a window. Red numbers started counting down from three and the kids crowded in close to their parents. There was a flash, a long pause, and then the picture appeared on the screen.

Randy said, "Cheese."

"Dad, the picture's already on the screen." Derek pulled Jaxx's socks up to his knees. "Why don't they make socks that stay on babies' feet?"

June stared at the picture. It was weird to see her whole family gathered into one box. She looked small in the middle, her head in particular. Why hadn't she lengthened her neck?

"What am I looking at?" Randy asked, confused.

"Not the camera," Tom replied.

Randy pointed to an icon on the screen. "Isn't that where I was supposed to look?"

"No," the kids said in unison.

"Send it," Derek said. "I have to go change him again." He whisked Jaxx away and climbed the stairs to the second floor.

"Let me do it," Vanessa said, nudging June out of the way. "You'll take an hour."

June complained, but stood up to let Vanessa sit down. It was true. Attachments took several attempts. Doris didn't respond right away.

"Okay, this is boring," Vanessa announced. "I'm going to pack."

"Me too," Tom said.

"What for?" June said. "We're only going for the day."

"I'm moving in a few weeks!" Vanessa called without turning around.

"I work tonight," Tom said.

Doris replied. *You look just like your father! What a lovely bunch you are. Tell me about them!*

Randy excused himself back to his workshop. June wrote, *Derek is a single dad and is learning a new trade — kitchen installation. Vanessa just bought her first house with her partner and is attending art college in the fall. Tom owns his own cleaning business.*

Doris replied. *Sounds like you've raised three successful children.*

June read her comment three times. One, she supposed, for each child. *Raised three successful children.* Had she? The phone rang beside her. "Hello?"

"Hi," said Birte. "Am I interrupting your Mother's Day?"

"Not at all."

"Then Earle and I are on our way over."

"Now?"

"Uh-huh. We're heading to the airport."

"You bought a condo?"

"We did!" she squealed.

"We did!" Earle echoed in the background.

"Yes, come over then. We can celebrate."

She hung up the phone when Doris's email appeared with attachments. The first one was a picture from when they were young. They were both crouching on the bank of the Bow River. It took a minute for June to see there was a duck between them. Her mother had mousy hair and a full-skirt dress with polka dots. Her arms were scrawny. She held the pound cake in her hands. Her father was ugly. His freckles were the size of dimes and his pants were too short. She laughed out loud, because she also looked like him. Narrow chin, round eyes. The current picture she found more fascinating. Both of her parents were fat. Her mother's hair was dyed. Each of them held a pair of hamsters, and in between them was a guinea pig the size of a house cat. She laughed until she slipped off the

259

chair and onto the floor. She held her stomach. She looked like her father. She looked like her mother. She felt validated and humiliated, reckless and joyful, but most of all she wanted her real mom. The one in the nursing home who taught her how to raise three successful children. She turned off the computer without shutting down properly, went upstairs to the pantry, and opened some High River whiskey. She poured it into one of her mother's favourite teacups and took it to the front porch, where she waited for Birte and thought about how much she hated the snow.

30

June knuckle-rapped on the glass of the front porch door to get Birte's attention when she and Earle pulled up and got out of their car. Birte was wearing her travel shoes, blue suede, part sneaker, part loafer. She hurried up the walk, leaving Earle, in his fedora, to lock the car.

"Oh, a cup of tea," Birte said, as June sipped her whiskey. "I'd love one of those right now." She settled into the wicker loveseat as though the walk up the front drive had been exhausting.

"I can make you a cup?"

Earle brushed his feet on the doormat and kissed June on the cheek. He smelled like the Body Shop.

"Randy's down in his workshop," June said.

"Excellent. I'll pop down and see him." Earle tipped his hat, touching Birte's shoulder as he passed through.

"So?" June looked at Birte. "Tell me about it."

"Oh, Junie, it's everything we imagined. I'll show you some pictures." Birte unzipped her purse.

"Let me get your tea started." June went to the kitchen, plugged in the kettle, and dropped a pair of teabags into a *Wizard of Oz* teapot she'd found at Goodwill. She returned to the front porch, where Birte had lined up a row of pictures across the seat cushion. The rug had shifted and she was kneeling on the hardwood floor.

"Why don't we do this inside?" June suggested.

"Good idea." Birte collected the photos, grunting as she pulled herself up, and followed June into the kitchen. She sat at the island. June placed a mug in front of her.

"This is the first of two bedrooms," Birte pointed. "Where you and Randy will stay when you come to visit." She beamed.

"Looks amazing," June said.

"Earle and I were thinking, how would you like to come for Christmas?"

Christmas was a long way away. She had no idea what Christmas would look like this year. It occurred to her that the Figgs had never been apart at Christmas. That though there was fighting, and people watched movies with gratuitous violence and didn't shower, they still exchanged gifts and drank freshly squeezed orange juice. This year, Jaxx would have a stocking. He might be crawling by then or have teeth. Would Vanessa come home? Or would she spend the morning in her own house with Leslie? Would they put up a tree? Would it have tinsel? Would Jerry have his own stocking?

"I don't know," she finally replied. "But if not Christmas, perhaps New Year's or any other time in the dead of winter."

"Well, the offer's out there." Birte helped herself to milk from the fridge.

June handed her a spoon. "It's very exciting. We should do a toast."

"With tea?" Birte chuckled.

"With whiskey." June took Birte's full mug of tea and poured it down the sink, and filled it with whiskey.

Birte turned red.

"It'll help you relax on the plane," June offered, holding her teacup at chin height. Randy and Earle appeared at the top of the stairs.

"That's some table." Earle shook his head. He pulled a cellophane-wrapped candy from his pocket and slipped it in his mouth. It was the colour of red Lego.

"Gentlemen, you're just in time," June announced.

Randy looked enthused. He loved a good toast. He loved a bad toast. "Wait, wait!" He grabbed two glasses from the cupboard. June splashed whiskey in both, then picked up her cup again.

"To Birte and Earle, snowbirds."

"I've always wanted to be a snowbird!" Birte said. She took the smallest of drinks and then clapped her hands.

"And to June and Randy," Earle said. "Grandparents."

"Oh, yes!" agreed Birte. She pretended to take another drink, but June could see that nothing went down.

Grandparents, she thought. It was one of a number of things they could have toasted. *On finding your birth parents. On finding your birth parents are still together and enjoy hamsters. On finding your son. On finding your son, who is dead. On learning your daughter is a condo owner, college student. On discovering your oldest son gifted his grandmother a therapeutic robot.*

Birte collected her pictures, but Earle asked for them before she put them away. Randy leaned over Earle's shoulder and listened intently as Earle detailed the condo's special features.

"So, what's new with you?" Birte asked. She had got herself a new mug and filled it with tea.

June glanced at Randy and then back at Birte. "Absolutely nothing," she said. "Not a thing."

The foursome chatted for close to an hour about what the weather would be like in Phoenix and whether they were allowed to bring their own pretzels on the plane. Birte insisted on seeing Jaxx before they left, and when she did, sang a horrible lullaby in broken Norwegian that made Derek pull a toque over his ears. They hugged goodbye, and then cross-hugged so that everyone had touched each other equally. Randy and June waved their guests away from the front porch.

"Have fun," June hollered, though they were well out of earshot.

Randy ate a candy similar to Earle's, but green. "How come you said there was no news?"

"I'm tired of news," June replied. "I don't want there to be any more news for a long time."

He moved the candy around his mouth so that it bulged from his cheeks in sporadic places. It irritated her, the way Vanessa's chewing gum used to. "Stop that."

"What?" But the candy temporarily lodged in his throat. Green-tainted spit the texture of corn syrup dripped down his chin and into his beard. He wiped it away with the back of his shirt. "I almost choked."

"I'm going to bed."

"But it's still early," he protested.

"Maybe," she replied, "but it's been a forty-eight-hour day." She blew Randy a kiss and went to the kitchen to clear away the mess. He followed behind. She knew he'd reached into the air to catch the kiss.

"Birte invited us to Phoenix for Christmas." She emptied the teapot.

"This Christmas? We've never spent Christmas away from the kids."

"I know."

He looked troubled. She knew his sentiments without having to ask.

"I suggested New Year's instead."

"New Year's!" Randy repeated.

Derek hollered from upstairs. "Mom? Can you bring me up a bottle?"

Randy said, "I'll make it."

Jaxx was awake and crying, his voice sounding weeks older than it did at birth. Slightly less desperate. Randy placed the bottle in a cup of warm water to heat.

June opened the dishwasher. "Here." She handed him a pair of wine glasses that he placed in the cupboard over the fridge. "Do you know where we're going tomorrow?"

He shook his head.

"Why don't you go figure that out?" she suggested, noting the only Red Deer they knew was Gasoline Alley — a strip of fast food restaurants and gas stations off the highway, where the queues were always long and the bathrooms smelled like infectious disease.

"Good idea," he said, a bit sullen.

"And get directions to the cemetery and his high school. And anywhere else you want to visit." June pulled a large bread knife out of the dishwasher and held it by her leg as Randy cupped the back of her head and pulled her into his face. She could smell the green of his hard candy.

"I love you."

"I know," she replied.

He took the knife from her and slid it into the knife block before disappearing down to the basement. She pulled the bottle from the container it had been warming in and towel-dried the sides.

"Mom!" Derek called.

"I'm coming!" She kicked a pair of wool socks out of the way. Someone had discarded a cup on the landing. She noticed the blank space on the wall where the family crest normally hung.

Derek was sprawled on his bed, shirtless, with Jaxx on his chest in a diaper and a pair of leather slippers with fire trucks on them. The baby was content, sucking the part of his hand at the base of his thumb.

"Thanks," Derek said. "He's only sleeping an hour at a time."

"Like I said, he's probably going through a growth spurt." For a moment, she thought of her mom, because it was the same explanation she had given any time Derek or Tom had fussed. She smiled. Her mom had been such a wonderful grandmother. Cleaning bathrooms and making meals. Taking Tom out to play when Vanessa was born, and then Tom and Vanessa when she brought home Derek.

"Do we all have to go to Red Deer?"

"Yes."

"But what if he wakes up every fifteen minutes?"

"Then he wakes up every fifteen minutes."

Derek maneuvered himself onto his side, revealing his six-pack. Was he working out or stressed? June wondered. She handed him the bottle. She noticed his nails had been chewed halfway down his fingers.

"Are you getting enough to eat?" she asked. "Are you hungry?"

"I'm starving." He yawned.

"Okay, let me get you something to eat."

She picked up the socks on the landing, placed them by the door to the basement, and made Derek a roast beef sandwich. She sliced up an apple like he was seven and put everything on a tray. It was the same tray the kids used when they had after-school snacks in the living room.

"Thank you," he said, as she placed the tray on his desk, which was littered with crumpled receipts, lip balm, and a small wooden pencil.

"You're welcome, Derek."

He reached from the bed, took half the sandwich, and ate it with his head on the pillow. "Happy Mother's Day, Mom."

31

The next morning, Randy woke everyone up at eight, except for Derek and Jaxx because June insisted they sleep until they woke up on their own.

"What time should I tell Leslie to come?" Vanessa stood at the counter, spreading Nutella on burnt toast. Her black hair was big and twisted. Medusa.

"Leslie's coming?" Tom ate chunks of pineapple with a cocktail fork.

"Of course she's coming," Vanessa replied, like it was obvious.

"I thought it was a family trip."

Vanessa glared at Tom. "Well, she's family to me, and if she's not welcome, I'm not going."

"No one said anything about not being welcome, Vanessa." June intervened. "I think your brother's just thinking about your father. You know this is not going to be easy for him."

"Fine. I'll stay home."

"Vanessa, don't be like that." June had heart palpitations. This was not how she wanted to kick off the day.

"Like what?"

"Selfish," Tom said.

"I was thinking more *extreme*," June clarified. "I'm sure your father won't mind if Leslie comes, but you should mention it to him first."

She scowled and thundered over to the top of the basement stairs. "Dad, do you care if Leslie comes to Red Deer?"

"No," he shouted.

"See?" She made a childish face.

"We're leaving around nine."

Derek appeared at the bottom of the stairs. "Who the hell is yelling down here? I was trying to sleep."

"Vanessa," Tom said, jabbing his fork into the last chunk of pineapple.

"I wasn't yelling," Vanessa yelled.

"See," Tom pointed. "Yelling."

"I'm not going." Vanessa stomped on the foot pedal of the garbage can so the lid flung back with a crash. She dumped her toast crusts and tossed her plate on the counter. The plate broke in half.

"Tom?" June said.

"Tom?" Tom said. "Are you serious? She's the one breaking plates."

"Can't you all just cooperate for once?" June raised her voice. "Today is not about you. It's about your father, and you're all going to shut up and behave like good people who go to church."

Tom and Vanessa laughed.

"I'm serious," June said. "You're going to come on this trip, and you're not going to swear or ignore each other or complain about anything."

Randy was at the top of the stairs. He had a khaki camera bag that looked like a cooler slung over his shoulder, and a handful of papers that June could tell were Google maps. "What's going on?"

"Nothing," said June. "The kids were just saying how much they were looking forward to this trip."

"Good," said Randy, "because I think I'm just about ready."

"I'll get Jaxx," Derek yawned. "He needs to eat before we go."

June put fresh water in Jerry's cage and filled his food bowl. She stroked the top of the bird's head. His innocence made her heart swell. "Vanessa, Jerry's cage needs tidying."

Vanessa texted furiously on her phone. "Leslie's car won't start."

"You mean you weren't planning on coming in the van?" Randy's shoulders slumped.

Vanessa looked at her father. His gas station sunglasses were propped up on his head.

June saw Fergus's obituary on the top of his stack of papers. Vanessa noticed this too.

"Yes," Vanessa stammered. "She was just going to drive over here first."

"We can pick her up," Randy said. "That's no problem."

"I'm going to get dressed."

June stopped her. "Cage first."

A gargantuan sigh and Vanessa mobilized, cleaning up the broken plate in the process.

June made Jaxx a bottle.

"Do we have any apples?" Randy packed a grocery bag with granola bars and a can of nuts.

"There's a bag in the pantry." June pointed with her foot.

It was 9:40 by the time they were loaded into the van and parked in front of Leslie's older-looking apartment building. She was waiting on the front step with a faded MEC backpack that had all sorts of strings hanging off it. Her blond hair was hidden beneath a grey beret, the knees of her pants patched. Her army boots still shone a hint of polish from a parade square long abandoned. She waved when the Figgs pulled up. A bus behind them honked.

"You can't pull over here," Vanessa said, holding on to Randy's headrest. "Go in the driveway."

Randy pulled forward. The bus honked again. He turned into the driveway and stopped on the side of the brick building.

"Hello." Leslie slid open the door. She put her pack on the floor and belted into the seat next to Vanessa. Jaxx whimpered from the back row.

"I think we're ready." Randy smiled and made an eight-point turn to get out of the driveway.

June watched Leslie pull a thermos out of a side pocket and carefully unscrew it as to not disturb Vanessa, who had rested her head on Leslie's shoulder. Tom was slumped forward in the back, eyes heavy from last night's shift. Derek had his arm around the car seat and was staring at his son. June was struck by the purpose of the trip. They were going to say goodbye. Randy would not be looking at his son, but standing on top of him. They would all be standing on top of him. They would look at the gravestone and their feet might get wet if the grass was damp and long.

Randy turned on the radio. A documentary about people eating monkeys was playing. It made June feel sick. She probably hadn't eaten enough. She unwrapped a caramel from her

271

purse, but only thought of the monkeys skinned and stacked at the market. She gagged. "Can you change the station?"

"Pardon?" Randy was in a daze.

"I don't want to listen to the monkeys anymore."

"Sorry." He fidgeted with the dial. "I wasn't even paying attention." He shut the radio off. "What if we get to the grave-site and there's people there?"

"I doubt it'll be busy on a Monday."

"But what if it is?"

"So what?"

He rubbed his chin.

The traffic on Deerfoot Trail was light heading north. They zipped along in the right lane with no one to pass.

"What if it's locked and we can't get in?"

"They don't lock cemeteries during the day," June said. "That's only at night to keep weirdoes out."

Tom snored in the back. A low and tolerable snore that June found rhythmic and soothing.

"Are there headphones up there?" Derek asked.

Randy checked the console. "None up here."

"I don't want to listen to that." He nudged Tom with his elbow.

"Let's play a game." Randy stretched his neck to look in the rear-view mirror and smiled.

"I'm not playing a game." Vanessa took off her seatbelt, shifted, and put it back on.

"Come on," Derek urged, mockingly. "Games are fun."

"Why don't you put the radio back on?" June suggested.

"I'll play a game," Leslie offered, twisting the lid back on her thermos. "How do we play?"

Vanessa sighed. "Fine, I'll play. Someone wake up Tom."

Derek elbowed his brother. Tom stretched his arms over his head, fingers splayed on the car ceiling. He cleared his throat.

"Great," Randy said. "You can play too."

"Sorry, did I just wake up in 1995?"

Randy ignored Tom's comment and proceeded to explain the rules. "I'll pick a topic, for example, *food*, and then we go through the alphabet thinking of foods. Apple, banana, cauliflower . . ."

"Monkeys," June said, picturing their skinned pink bodies in a wheelbarrow.

"I'll go first," Vanessa said. "What's the topic?"

"Professions," Randy said.

"Asshole," Vanessa replied.

"They have to be real jobs, Vanessa," Randy said. "That doesn't count."

"Fine. Anaesthesiologist."

"Bartender," said Leslie.

"Carpenter," Derek yawned.

"Two points for Derek," Randy beamed.

"Dickhead," said Tom.

Vanessa laughed.

"A driller then."

"Electrician," Randy offered.

June looked out her window. The sky was big and cloudless and faded blue, where it almost wasn't blue. Like a white garment washed with a new pair of jeans.

"June?" Randy gently smacked her arm.

"What?"

"You're F."

"Forester," she said with immediate regret. Randy would think of Fergus, but when she looked over at him she could tell he was figuring out what letter he had next.

"Gynaecologist," said Vanessa.

"Sick," Derek replied.

"It's not *sick*," June said.

"Mom, I watched his birth."

"Horticulturist." Leslie sipped again from her thermos.

"This game sucks," said Derek. "Can't we play something else?"

"How about *Who Am I?*" Tom said flatly.

"How do you play, son?"

"Dad, I was joking," Tom replied. "These are kids' games."

"What about *I Never*?" Vanessa suggested.

Randy changed lanes to pass a horse trailer. "What's that one?"

"It's a drinking game," Derek said.

June did not listen to the rules. She thought about her birth parents. The thought of them still being together made her swoon, but it also made her want to hit someone. In the picture, they looked like lovers. She bet they had pet names for each other. Doris looked like the kind of woman who made hot breakfasts for her husband. He probably rubbed her feet at the end of the day. She wished she'd been able to witness it growing up. Her adopted parents no doubt loved each other. They were kind and respectful, but not the kind of lovers that made babies in snow forts. Lovers, too, the way she imagined Randy and Glenda. Helpless and innocent and making love under a homemade blanket. Or Birte and Earle, who were touchy and big. Birte even said they sometimes showered together. That it was erotic. For weeks

June couldn't get their wet squat bodies with all their flaps and folds out of her mind. June was too thin to shower with Randy. She had to stand under the stream of water or the backs of her arms would get cold. Randy would take up too much room and he would try to touch her. It would annoy her, not arouse her. Maybe she had a problem. Maybe she had to loosen up and have sex in the snow or in the pantry beside the recycling.

"I never had sex with a teacher," Vanessa said.

"Vanessa!" June gripped the handle above the window. Maybe she needed to have sex with a teacher.

"Don't panic," Randy assured her. "It's a game. You only drink if you *did* have sex with a teacher."

June looked in the back. Derek took a long swig of root beer.

"Derek!" she cried. "Tell me you did not do that. That's illegal! That's statutory rape."

"Not if it was last year."

"Okay," June said. "This game is over. It's inappropriate and upsetting."

"I never spent a night in jail," Derek said.

This time it was Tom who took a drink of water.

"You went to jail?" June was horrified.

"Remember that time Tom said he was going paintballing with his friends?" Derek said.

The vague memory resurfaced.

"He was in the drunk tank because he passed out at the fuck park with no pants."

June covered her eyes, feeling marginally relieved that he was only picked up for public drunkenness and not for trying to do inappropriate things under the slide in a basset hound costume with an elderly person.

"Where were your pants?" June said.

Tom shrugged. "I lost one of my shoes, too."

"Put on the dead monkeys," June ordered.

Randy turned on the radio, but lowered the volume. June strained to hear the conversation, but it was no longer about eating monkeys in Bioko. It was a documentary about homophobia in the NFL. She switched it off.

"I never had a relationship with someone who was married."

June closed her eyes. She wanted the game to end, but when she reopened her eyes, both Randy and Leslie were drinking.

"Randy!" June flicked his ear.

"Ouch. I didn't know she was married."

"Neither did I," Leslie said.

June crossed her arms. "When did this happen?"

"Long time ago. Before Glenda."

"I don't want to hear any more." She looked out her window again for some sort of landmark. They were only in Didsbury. Red Deer was at least another forty-five minutes away.

"One more round," Randy said.

From the back, Tom yelled, "I never had a threesome."

Randy took a drink. "Sorry," he said, "just thirsty."

Vanessa took a long exaggerated sip of her iced tea.

"Nice," Derek said, patting her shoulder from the back seat. "I'm jealous."

"That's really awful." June shook her head. "I'm so sorry for you, Vanessa. That's just really wrong."

"It was actually quite liberating," Vanessa said.

"I think it's awesome." Tom took off his seatbelt. "Way to go, Vanessa."

June cried, "What is wrong with you people? Aren't you the

least bit embarrassed to be saying all of this in front of your parents? Didn't I teach you respect? Have you no shame?"

"It was Dad's idea to play," Derek said.

"In fairness to me," Randy said, "I just wanted to play a game. Everyone apologize to your mother for offending her."

In unison, "Sorry, Mom."

"And say sorry for being bad," Randy added.

Derek was the loudest. "Sorry for being bad."

June had a hot flash. Within seconds her skin was a slick mess. She pulled a map of Montana out of the glove compartment and waved it in front of her face. There was a pack of Clorets in there too. She punched one out of the blister pack and put it in her mouth. Bits of its shell flaked off on her tongue. It was hard, but she carried on. "Keep calm and chew old gum," she said.

"Keep calm and stay in the right lane," Randy replied. He smiled and rubbed her leg affectionately.

"It's not a new game," she clarified.

"Keep calm and have a threesome," Derek mocked.

Vanessa lifted her head, which she'd rested back on Leslie's shoulder and said, "Keep calm and be a single dad."

"Good one," Tom said. "How about keep calm and have a hot flash."

June stopped waving the map in front of her face. "Why don't you put on some headphones or something?"

"You told us we weren't allowed to ignore each other."

"Keep calm and put on some headphones." Randy grinned.

"Keep calm and look out for the deer!" Leslie shouted.

Randy's knee-jerk reaction was to swerve, though the deer Leslie was talking about was well off to the side of the road.

June placed her hand on her chest as if to slow down her heart rate. Her hot flash ceased.

"You have my permission to ignore each other," June said. "I'm turning the radio back on."

Classical music danced from the speakers like tumbleweed on a country road. It was exactly what she needed. She sank heavily into her seat and closed her eyes. When she opened them again, they were in Red Deer, parked outside the gates of the cemetery.

32

Red Deer Cemetery was written in metal on an arch that bridged two squat red brick buildings with white doors and wrought-iron hardware. It looked militaristic and official. A checkpoint. Near-black conifers bowed and bent over the site like protective hands. It was dark, though still morning. Randy followed the winding road through the gate. Loose gravel crunched below the tires and reminded June of backing over plastic shovels and water guns in the driveway.

"How do I know where to go?" Randy asked.

"You don't know where his grave is?" Vanessa asked. "We'll be here all day."

"I know he's buried on the west side." Randy looked left and right as he crept forward. "Section M or N." He pointed to his stack of papers in the netted console between him and June. "There's a map of the cemetery in there."

She picked up the papers and rifled through the stack until she found the map. Hundreds of rectangular plots were organized by row and labelled with a letter. June turned the page ninety degrees. "Assuming we entered down here, it looks like we turn left and then go all the way to the end."

Randy turned left, but the road ended abruptly and he was forced to turn again.

"Left or right?" He asked.

She paused. "Left." She tried to sound confident, but June was terrible at navigating. She longed for a new vehicle with a fancy GPS. Randy turned left as she recommended and drove to the end of the lane.

"Do I stop here?" He looked all around. "Should he be here?"

"Just a minute." June stepped out of the van, leaving the door open and took a few steps toward the edge of the grass in search of an aisle marker like at a grocery store. CEREAL, CONDIMENTS, CAR ACCIDENT VICTIMS. This is ridiculous, she thought to herself. She turned three hundred and sixty degrees to take in the setting, and noticed a small building across the way. *That must be on the map.* She got back inside the van. Randy was flipping through papers.

"See if you can find that building." June gestured with her thumb.

"Can I interrupt?" Leslie said, unbuckling her seatbelt. "You need to turn it this way," she said, spinning her finger counter-clockwise. "See that road over there? That's this one on the map. See how it curves? We should have turned left back here."

"I couldn't find him alive and now I can't find him dead either." Randy was agitated.

"Here," June said, "let me see the map again." She grabbed it out of his hands and tried to make sense of Leslie's directions but she might as well have been looking at a map of Machu Picchu.

"Can I drive?" Leslie asked.

"Sure," Randy said, frustrated. He unbuckled his seatbelt and squished in beside June.

Leslie moved to the driver seat and studied the map for a minute or so, looking out the windows in ten-second intervals. Eventually she put her seat belt on and began backing up.

Randy's body was heavy against June, and she nudged him. "You're squashing me."

He adjusted his weight and put his hand on the glove compartment to steady himself. His neck was stretched long and alert as though they were on a safari and he was hoping to spot the giraffe before anyone else. The back seat was silent. Tom and Jaxx were asleep. Derek was scrolling his phone, and Vanessa appeared to be picking and eating the chocolate chips out of her granola bar. The van wound through the cemetery, backward at first, and then forward like they were in a maze. June thought of the puzzles Derek had done as a child. The mish-mash of loops and lines and dead-ends. The instructions. *Help Fluffy get to his doghouse. Help Randy find Fergus's grave.* Leslie pulled over and put the van in park. "The M's should be there and the N's just to the right."

Randy climbed over June and rolled out of the van, jogging toward the first row of graves that Leslie identified as being part of section M. Derek elbowed Tom to wake him up, then stepped over him. He passed Jaxx's carseat over to Vanessa, who passed it back once Derek was outside. June straightened her pants, which were bunched and stuck to her legs, and watched as Leslie chivalrously helped Vanessa step out of the van by taking her hand. *Big Gay Prom,* June thought. They wandered off towards the N graves. Tom was last out of the van. He stretched his arms over his head. The laces of his sneakers were loose and untied, his hoodie unzipped. He looked slimmer beneath all the looseness. He headed in Randy's direction. June stood beside Derek, who was bent over the car seat, tucking a receiving blanket around Jaxx's shoulders. The baby's head lay low on his chest like his neck was too weak to support it. Candy apple on a stick. His deep-sleep weight pulled down his lower lip so he looked disgruntled rather than peaceful.

"You go, if you want," June told Derek. "I'll wait here with him."

Derek nodded and headed toward the larger section N.

June breathed in the fresh air, which had an odd sweetness one would not associate with a burial ground. Pre-summer Alberta air. Green with a dash of ice. A mojito. Randy was jogging faster now, slowing down only to read the tombstones. But it was Vanessa who found him. She waved both arms over her head. It looked as though she was on her tiptoes.

"Here!" She cupped her hands around her mouth and said, "Charles Fergus Zacharellis," into the wind.

Randy ran, weaving through stones with the agility of a bike courier until he reached Vanessa. June ran too, but at the pace of a six-year-old, the car seat swinging and thumping against her leg. She was certain it would bruise. Derek met her halfway and pulled the car seat all the way up to his waist. When June reached Fergus's grave, Randy was bent over, perpendicular to the plot, hands on his knees, out of breath. Gasping. When he stood up, he looked dizzy. His glasses had fallen to the end of his nose and his eyes were flooded. She'd never seen such a mass of tears collect without falling and she thought of that casino game where the coins were continually pushed to an edge but never seemed to fall. She'd never seen them fall. Then Randy stumbled and let out a breath. A baritone one. Like cracked pavement. A pain breath. And as he staggered forward to the grave, his live children all took a step back. It was June who moved in when he fell to his knees. She remembered that feeling from her father's death. Of not being able to stand. Of being amputated by grief. Randy wailed like a cow separated from its calf. He carried on for several minutes, starting and stopping, clutching his stomach. June found herself glancing left and right to make sure no one was watching. The kids shifted uncomfortably, unsure whether to watch or hide or speak. They looked at one another with a mix of horror and embarrass-ment and sympathy when Randy walked on his knees, toddler style, over to the tombstone and wrapped his arms and one leg around it like he was trying to mount it. It was the leg that did June in. It was lifted at a high and awkward angle so that his pant leg fell up his shin revealing several inches of hairy skin and his signature wool sock. Vanessa cringed. Derek looked at June, eyebrows raised, hands up in a gestured plea for her to intervene. Tom cried. Sensitive Tom. June knelt down behind her husband, unsure of what to do. Out of the corner of her eye, she saw Leslie give Vanessa a sizeable nudge. Elbow to hip. It bumped Vanessa a step to the right, and then Vanessa jog-walked to the van. She returned holding a gift bag with straw-like handles. She cleared her throat.

"Dad?" she stuttered. "We, uh, have something for you."

Randy let go of the tombstone, all parts at once, and fell to the ground. June grabbed his elbow and tried to help him up, but was unsuccessful. Vanessa continued her speech.

"We wanted you to remember that even though you never got to meet Fergus — Charles — that you're still his father."

Randy wiped his face. Vanessa made eyes at Derek for him to jump in.

"And, uh, we wanted to commemorate that, so we made you something."

Randy looked at June for a hint, but she was in the dark, and shrugged. Derek reached over and took the bag from Vanessa. He pulled out the family crest. June was looking at the back of it, but she knew what it was. The brown paper, the green marker someone appeared to have tested in the corner, the drooping twine that was fixed too low on the frame, preventing it from ever being hung flush. Never quite perfect, like the wingless birds embroidered on the front, like the three children gathered in front of her now. Derek shook his head in an attempt to get his hair out of his face and then turned the crest around to show Randy. Yes, there it was. The fat swallows, the gold leaves, the shield, the fist. The green velvet background almost a match for the spruce at the edge of the lane. But there was something different. In the top right corner, a fourth bird was fixed to the velvet back. It was about the size of a bumblebee, round and petite, and had been carved out of wood. And it had wings.

"That's Fergus," Vanessa said.

Randy stood up. All the way up. Chest proud, chin lifted, proper. He took a deep breath and reached out his hand like he was about to receive a prestigious gift — a Nobel Prize, a Victoria Cross, a kidney. *Please don't salute*, June thought, which is exactly what Randy did next. Derek gave a sick look, but when Randy didn't put his hand down he saluted back. Randy took the crest in both hands. He gently ran his finger over Fergus. The ridges of his wings, the dull point of his beak, like the tip of a crayon, his tiny head, which was smooth and curved like a jujube. The only thing left was for Randy to give a speech. But instead he looked at each of his children.

"You're all," he said, "just right."

Leslie had detached herself from the family at this point. She wandered the cemetery a safe distance away, her hands clasped behind her back the way June imagined people strolled the English countryside. Jaxx woke up and started screaming. His separation/distress call. Looking for his mother. June bent down to unbuckle him and whispered, "Your daddy is your mommy and he's just right." She held him to her chest and danced a lullaby. Derek took the empty seat to the van. A car lumbered up the lane on the other side of the cemetery. A loan man got out of the vehicle and carried a single stiff white flower. He stopped in front of a squat tombstone. June watched as she swayed away from Fergus, from Randy. Vanessa had joined Leslie now. They walked hand in hand. It was Tom who stayed with Randy. He stood shoulder to shoulder with him, and June found herself falling in love all over again. Not with her husband, but with her firstborn. With Tom. For though he was crude and eccentric and a little perverse, he was also warm. A glowworm. Unassuming and effective. Jaxx started sucking on her windbreaker.

"I think someone's hungry." She cradled his head and walked him to the van. Derek was already mixing powdered formula with a thermos of warm water.

"Hey bud," he said. "Let's get you fed." He screwed the top on the bottle and gave it shake, his wrist snapping with each up and down jerk. "Is Dad going to be okay?"

"He will." June passed Jaxx over to Derek. "You know your father. Forever optimistic."

"I know. It's just . . . I can't imagine not being with my son or never knowing him."

"That's why you have to hang on to him, Derek. Don't let him go."

He nodded. "Can we get something to eat after this?"

"As soon as your father's finished up." June paced back and forth along the road, keeping an eye on Randy. After ten minutes or so, Tom left his side and returned to the van. June summoned for Vanessa and Leslie to come.

She asked Tom, "How is he?"

"He's singing," Tom replied.

"Singing?" June said. "I can't hear him."

"Very quietly. Seemed kind of personal, so I left."

"Tom," June said. "Thank you."

"For what?"

"Paro."

He nodded. She squeezed his hand before he pulled it away and brushed his hair out of his face.

"Why don't we get in the van and wait?" June suggested. "Could one of you look up a place to eat?"

Derek changed Jaxx on the driver's seat, then carried him to the back row and buckled him into his car seat. Leslie wrote in a pocket-sized notebook while the kids tended to their phones. Through the windshield, June watched Randy rest his cheek on the top of Fergus's gravestone, his body bent ninety degrees. He stayed there for some time and then lifted his head and walked away. He was quiet when he got to the car, handing June the crest. She ran her fingers across the velvet, the embroidered details, the tiny bird. It must have been Leslie, she thought, to have carved a bird so fine. Randy started driving, and after fifteen minutes they were still circling the cemetery. Leslie piped up and guided Randy through the rest of the graveyard, until they arrived back at the red brick entryway.

"Goodbye, Charles," Randy murmured. "Fergus."

"What did you leave behind?" Vanessa asked. "At his grave-site?"

June hadn't noticed Randy left anything behind.

"A baseball," he replied.

"I knew it," Vanessa said.

"Hey look, there's a diamond right there." Derek pointed. "Maybe that's where he played."

"Maybe," Randy brightened. "I mean, it's certainly possible." He reached for the stack of papers between himself and June and pulled one of the several maps he had printed on top of his lap. Fergus's high school, June noted. They drove through a suburban area that seemed to be run by preschoolers. Hoards of them on tricycles with and without helmets. Kids in trees, on doorsteps, strapped inside three-wheeling strollers.

"What a great neighbourhood," Randy mused, until the van was pelted with berries or apples, causing everyone inside to duck. He blew the four-way stop at the end of the street and drove to the high school.

"That's it." He parked on the street outside of the building, which was big and red and resembled a college. "That's where he went to high school."

"Neat," Tom yawned from the back.

"He might have run that track," Randy suggested. "Or climbed that tree."

"Kids in high school generally don't climb trees," Vanessa said.

"Then maybe he had a picnic under it. That would be a lovely place to have a picnic."

"Or get stoned," Derek said.

"Or laid," Vanessa added.

"Vanessa," June cautioned.

"Well, it's true." She shrugged.

Randy pulled back onto the road, and they drove aimlessly through Red Deer. June was getting hungry. She wanted to tell Randy to stop so they could eat, but he continued to point out all of the places Fergus may have frequented. *He might have gone swimming in that pool. He might have bought gas at that gas station. Maybe he took his dog to that vet. It's open twenty-four hours.* The kids used restraint. They tried their best to nod, or smile. Responding back with comments such as *maybe* or *who knows?*

"I'm getting kind of hungry," Tom said, but Randy continued exploring and soon enough they passed a Subway. "Maybe he ordered a sandwich from there," Tom said.

"With extra olives," said Vanessa.

"I like olives!" Randy blurted, smiling into the rear-view mirror.

"Perhaps he took his sandwich on a picnic," Derek said.

Tom pointed, "To that park over there."

"And he threw the wrapper in that garbage can."

"And crossed that street."

"And used that porta potty."

There was construction up ahead. "You have to merge into the left lane," June said, motioning for Randy to move over. But it was like talking to stuffed animal with a smile sewed to its face. "Randy," she said louder, "this lane ends." He swerved, clipping a pylon and knocking it over. The car behind them honked. Randy waved.

"Can we please go eat now?" Vanessa asked.

"Yes," Randy agreed. "I'm rather hungry."

"Not Gasoline Alley," June said, suddenly aware of the highway running parallel to them.

"Sorry," he said. "I figured it would be easy."

They pulled into a Wendy's/Tim Hortons and filed out of the van. Inside it smelled of beef and toilet. June lined up at Tim Hortons to get herself a coffee and a bagel, while the rest of the Figgs, and Leslie, clambered into the Wendy's queue, which seemed to be mixed with the bathroom one. June wondered if her birth parents took road trips, and whether they'd ever stopped here in Gasoline Alley, contemplating between a Wendy's cheeseburger and a disappointing Tim Hortons sandwich. Maybe they had an RV and they let the hamsters out for fresh air in the strip of grass beside the drive-thru. She didn't even know if they still lived in Calgary.

Lunch was quiet but for the folding and unfolding of packaging. Vanessa pulled a pickle slice the size of a Band-Aid off her cheeseburger, wiped it clean of sauce, and put it her mouth. "It's kind of weird to think Tom's not the oldest."

"True," Derek reasoned, "but if it had worked out with Dad and his mom, we wouldn't be here to consider that."

"Not necessarily," Vanessa replied. "Maybe they would have split up even if they got to keep him."

Randy strained to sip his Frosty through a straw, instead of using the spoon. The conversation continued around June, but her mind got tangled up in Glenda's immense hair, which was longer and thicker each time June thought of her. She had it cresting at her hips, and as gnarled as a yak's, but still she was a siren. She imagined Randy being pulled into it, tucked underneath into that sweet spot. That secret place beneath the boughs of a heavy tree, where the ground was soft and love and make-believe could be made. She wondered if he longed for her in the way Jaxx longed for Marissa. The way she longed for Doris. That connection of creating life with someone and the desire to preserve it. Like the newborn ascending his mother's body to find drink and wholeness and belonging. Didn't he want that with Glenda? Shouldn't Derek want it with Marissa? Shouldn't she want that with Randy?

"Do you still think about her?"

Everyone at the table looked up.

"Me?" Derek asked. "Do I still think about Marissa?"

"Randy," she said.

"Do I still think about who?"

"Glenda."

He shifted in his seat and moved his Frosty to the side. "Sure," he said. "I have to assume she feels the same blackness I do. Few people can say they lost their son twice."

Silence followed his comment. June stared at a swath of discarded bacon on the floor and thought about blackness. Randy was colour. The balloon house from *Up*. Skittles. South America. He didn't even own black socks, and yet he spoke of black like it was a part of him. Internal. Onyx ribs suspended from a white clavicle. Charcoal menisci distributing weight. Black matter. And she understood that it would be with him for life. Adoption, loss.

"We should probably hit the road," Randy said. "Give Tom a chance to get home and relax for a bit before he goes in to work."

33

When the van returned to the Figg house, the family dispersed like strangers stepping off a subway. She didn't keep track of who went where or what they were doing. Bodies just moved around her. Up and down stairs, in and out of rooms. Eventually she heard the radio come on in Randy's workshop. The clambering of planks, which sometimes had a soothing effect on her, because she thought it sounded like applause.

She went to the computer and opened an email from Birte that had just come through. It was a photo of her and Earle holding up the keys to their new condo. June noticed how visible Birte's scalp was through her fine hair. Her chest and shoulders looked sunburned. Earle simply looked wet. It was May in Arizona. She smiled.

There was another email from Doris. The message's background was purple, a line of digital sunflowers waved from the bottom of the message like kelp under water. Breathing emoticons flickered throughout her invitation to meet. She still lived in Calgary. Doris suggested a park, where they might go for a walk or grab a coffee and "find a good bench."

June wrote back. *How about Bowness?* By evening, the details were set. They would meet at 11:00 a.m. Her father was out of town and would not be attending. They would not have a picnic or dress up as Furries or bring hamsters. They would go alone. Doris would be wearing a yellow neck scarf and would stand by the paddleboat rental office. June said she would carry a red purse.

She changed into light pyjamas and tied herself into her robe. She stood at the entrance to Randy's workshop, where the family crest was now fixed to the wall. He was leaning over one of the table legs he was working on as though it were a crutch.

"What do you think?" he said, spinning it around.

"Pretty fancy."

"It is, isn't it? I want to do more stuff like this. Custom. It's fun."

"It wouldn't hurt for you to see Glenda," she said. "Maybe it will help."

"I'm fine," he insisted. "It was him I needed to see." He leaned the table leg against one of the built-in counters that lined the back wall of his workshop. "I'll finish up in a bit."

Upstairs, Vanessa came barrelling through the back door with several empty moving boxes. She was out of breath, and her hair was dishevelled. She dropped the load to her feet. "That took forever," she whined. "I had to go to four different places." She stomped across to the fridge, palmed a head of lettuce, and took it over to Jerry. She whistled at him while ripping off sheets of green-yellow leaves until she'd created a hearty stack.

"You're packing already?" June asked.

"Yeah," she replied, placing the lettuce in Jerry's cage. "I work every day this week because I took today off."

"Do you want some help?"

Vanessa looked suspicious. "Why?"

"What do you mean, why?" June asked. "What's wrong with offering to help you prepare to move into your first house?"

"It's just weird. But, whatever, help if you want, I guess."

June was pleased she had something to pass the time. "I'll start by taking some of these."

June managed three boxes and walked up the stairs. Vanessa trailed behind with another four boxes and Jerry on her shoulder, his claws embedded in the ribs of her faded black tank top. It had probably been four years since June spent more than seconds in Vanessa's room. There were heaps of darkened clothes separated into piles, and trays of metal jewellery that looked like the hardware in Randy's workshop. At least three boxes of black hair dye were filed on her shelf like books. But beside the closet, tucked behind the door, was a series of framed watercolour paintings, displayed floor to ceiling, like a family growth chart. The colours were vintage and sweet like a bakeshop. Peach and lavender, tea cup cream. Cartography blue.

"Did you do those?" June asked.

"Yes," Vanessa grumbled, cheeks flushed. "I guess I should start with my book shelves." She kicked a banana box with the outside of her foot.

"They're really quite good," June said. "And they're in colour."

"Not everything I own is black," she said, placing a trio of unused beeswax candles into the box.

"Are you taking them?"

"Planned on it."

June pulled items from the second bookshelf and let them fall messily into the box.

"Mom," Vanessa said. "Be careful. Some of that is delicate."

"I remember the time we went to Kelowna and your father and I let you pack your own suitcase."

"Sounds reasonable," Vanessa said, wrapping an ornamental red elephant in a hoodie.

"It was. You laid out everything on your bed and then you drew a diagram of where it would go in your suitcase. You even asked Dad for the measuring tape so you could be sure about the dimensions."

"Pathetic," Vanessa said.

"No, it was quite impressive. You stayed up an hour past your bedtime so you could pack until you got it just right."

"Sounds fucked up."

"You just went through a phase where you wanted everything to be perfect."

"Like I had OCD?"

"You just liked making things exact."

Vanessa hauled out the red elephant, rewrapped it, and returned it to the box.

"We thought you might become an architect."

Vanessa made an offensive noise and laughed, crouching down on her knees to get to the bottom shelf. June held up a shirt that was scrunched on the floor in front of her. "Laundry?" she asked.

Vanessa nodded and pulled out her phone, which had started to chirp from her back pocket. June could hear Leslie's voice from the other end. She continued to stack books into one of the boxes, sliding the remaining few spine-side-up so there were no gaps or open spaces. Nothing to shift around when they were moved.

Vanessa paced the room, pulling items off the wall above her dresser, running her fingers through the mass of jewellery on its surface. June gave the empty shelf a wipe with Vanessa's dirty shirt, and then shoved the box she'd been packing against the wall near the closet. She examined the watercolours, all of which were animals, but not quite. They may have been apparitions of animals, or spirits, or early versions of modern animals, like when horses were ugly midgets. When she looked closer, she realized that all the animals had detailed vaginas. She removed a wild cat, which had the smallest vagina of the lot, and left the room.

"I saw that!" Vanessa hollered.

"I know," June said. "I'm taking it."

June got a hammer and nail from the workshop and put the wild cat in the spot where the crest used to hang on the landing. She walked back to Vanessa's room and leaned against the doorframe. A few boxes, and already Vanessa's room was looking empty. Bleak. June had always thought Vanessa's room was dark and industrial and menacing. Gotham City. But it was much more bleak now. Cold and bare, and it made her feel panicky.

"Don't go," she pleaded. A desperate whisper.

Vanessa tossed a pair of slippers in a box. "It'll be good for me," she said.

June swallowed back tears and nodded. Vanessa sighed and pulled herself up from the floor. She tripped over a box and said *motherfucker*, then mumbled an apology. "It'll be okay, Mom," she said. "It's time."

June nodded again, and tucked a piece of Vanessa's hair behind her ear, only to discover it was caught on one of her earrings.

"Ouch," Vanessa said. She wrapped her arms around June. A hug to remember. Then she pulled away and ripped a poster off the wall.

June headed downstairs to return the hammer. She noticed Marissa in the family room. She was holding Jaxx on the couch, one of her legs propped up on the arm. Derek sat on the coffee table. It took a double take for June to realize Damon was there too.

"Hello, Marissa," June said.

"Hey, Mrs. Figg."

If there had been conversation, it had ceased when June entered the room, so she carried on to the basement, the hammer dangling from her hand.

"Marissa is up there with that guy you mistook for your son. They're just sitting there. It makes me nervous."

"Why does it make you nervous? You said it was good for Marissa to see Jaxx as much as possible."

"I know. And I still believe that. I just want him to stay here. Forever."

Randy changed the subject. "I need help."

June scanned the room. There were discarded bits of wood all over the floor and an array of tools lined up on the bench like surgical instruments.

"What do you need me to do?" June asked.

"Just need an extra set of hands."

They worked for the better part of the evening. At first June continued to think about Marissa sitting upstairs bonding with Jaxx, breaking his heart. Across from Derek, but beside Damon. Marissa, that narrow space where two circles overlap. What might have been a love triangle, now a simple Venn diagram. But eventually June became absorbed in the construction of the table.

Most of her time was spent holding things together, which she was good at. Randy praised her for her exactness. For her ability to keep things perfectly still, while he banged and manipulated pieces together. By ten o'clock they were weary. Even the radio, which had spent most of the night churning out high-stakes bludgeon-your-innards concertos by Mozart, had switched to a tired playlist. Like a migratory bird halfway across the ocean. Lullabies, they seemed. Where touch and warmth could pour you to sleep like warm molasses. They hadn't even stopped to eat.

The completed table was exquisite, and June ran the tips of her aching fingers, which were now a discoloured seal grey, across its surface. There were no chairs. She felt Randy, his chin exerting pressure on her bony shoulder, his wiry beard like moss, just thick enough to not make her flinch. He kissed her neck with the force of an average handshake, but his breath was far more intimate. It touched her like sunlight. He held her hips; he held her wrists. He touched the blades of her shoulders and made her feel like she had wings. Extreme ones with layers of silk-like feathers and an immense wingspan. He filled her with triumph, with loss, with hurt, with hunger.

They staggered out of the workshop like they'd spent too much time in a sauna. Heavy-footed, light-headed, and completely ravenous. Up the stairs. The house was quiet. Randy opened the fridge and pulled out hummus and artichoke dip. Leftover guacamole from someone's Mucho Burrito. June got the crackers. Rice ones, with black sesame seeds the size of fleas, and Melba toast. They spread them on the island and ate standing, crunching aggressively, barely talking. The way two people should eat after making love in a workshop, on a recycling table, in a snow fort with a muffler on top.

34

Tuesday morning June took a weekend shower. Long and complete, with moments of just standing under the water doing absolutely nothing. She shaved her legs with a disposable razor she'd been using for over a month and dressed in beige Bermuda shorts and an Eddie Bauer camp shirt with pearlescent buttons. A look she thought was both practical and put together. Park chic. Then Vanessa asked if she was going on a safari. She changed into jeans.

June rummaged through her closet for the red purse she had told Doris she'd be carrying. It was the last thing she pulled out of the bin where she stored her small collection of handbags. She did not remember the bag being porn-star red with a gold clasp big enough for a toddler to open. Why had she told Doris about the red purse? She tucked it under her arm and went downstairs to make toast. Derek was dressed in a pair of Carhartt pants and a faded T-shirt. Jaxx was propped up on his shoulder wearing only a diaper.

"Can you watch Jaxx?" he asked. "Marissa said she'd come watch him, but now she can't. Vanessa's at work and Dad went to Home Depot and I'm supposed to meet Leslie for a job at ten.

I really need the money."

June pushed the toast button on the toaster. She did not want to bring Jaxx to meet Doris. She wanted to go alone, so she could immerse herself in the moment and record the details in her mind. She wanted to be completely unrestrained and free to react in whatever way her body initiated. "Fine," she said. "But Derek, you have to sort this out."

"Thank you," he said, ignoring the latter part of her comment. "I'll go get him dressed."

On her toast, she spread Becel, and raspberry jam someone had taken from Denny's. Her stomach churned like a night ocean, dark and unpredictable. Nervous. She had planned a leisurely departure, but Jaxx changed that. She would need to pack supplies, and the car seat business would take twenty minutes. She would have to be reminded how to open the stroller and how to fit the car seat on it. Then how to remove the car seat and collapse the stroller. She would drive under the speed limit because he was precious cargo, and she'd need time in the parking lot in case she forgot how to open the stroller.

Derek returned. Jaxx wore a pair of cargo pants and a "Weird Al" Yankovic T-shirt. His leather shoes were decorated with friendly pirates. Derek kissed his mother on the cheek. "Thank you," he said, securing Jaxx in his car seat before slipping through the back door.

June looked down upon Jaxx. "I guess you're going to meet your great-grandma," she said, placing her plate in the sink. She brushed crumbs from her shirt. There was a blob of jam in the centre of her chest. June sighed. "Grandma will be right back."

She went down to the basement and pulled a clean shirt from the dryer. She noticed Percy back in the closet underneath the stairs. The horse stared nervously at her through the open accordion door. She petted his head and grabbed her ukulele. Maybe she could play Doris a song. Show her what she was working on, while Doris taught her about all the things that she could make out of snow. Back upstairs, Jaxx fussed in his car seat.

"We're almost ready," June sang, transferring items from her purse into the ugly red handbag. She pulled out *You Were Chosen* and hesitated. *Everyone has a birth mother.* Her heart skipped. She placed the book on the island.

June bent over Jaxx. "Should we go?" she cooed. Jerry whistled from his cage. She picked up the car seat and lugged Jaxx to the van, clicking him into the back row. A butterfly flitted past and landed in the hedge. She went back for her ukulele and locked the door.

June caught the tail end of rush hour and crept up the ramp to get onto the highway. She merged into traffic. A folk song played from the radio. A sea shanty. Jaxx whimpered. She nearly slammed on the brakes. Her ukulele slid from the passenger seat onto the floor. She had to get off the highway. She had to go back.

A pickup truck honked as she crossed lanes. She yelled *fuck you!* and then apologized, covering her mouth in shame. She took the next exit, circled back, and drove with the window down.

When June arrived at the nursing home, Yulu was eating a banana in the hallway. She had a Metallica tattoo on her neck.

"Mrs. Figg!" Yulu said. "Who do we have here?"

June placed the car seat at Yulu's feet, breathing heavy from its weight. "My grandson, Jaxx."

"Isn't he going to be a looker?" she said. "That strawberry blond hair. My, oh, my." She hollered to a nurse down the hallway. "Is Margaret back from physio?"

The other nurse must have nodded, because Yulu picked up the car seat and strode down the hall with June trying to catch up. "Your mother's going to get a real kick out of him."

Margaret was parked in front of the window in her wheelchair, as she had been on Mother's Day. Yulu whispered aggressively the way school kids did. "Hey Margaret, I have a surprise for you." She set the car seat on the bed and turned Margaret around with the jerk speed of a carnival ride. June was not prepared to see tears rolling down her mother's cheek.

"She cries sometimes," Yulu whispered, softly this time.

June took a Kleenex out of her pocket and dabbed the tears on her mother's face. They were still warm.

"This is your great-grandson," she said. "Derek's boy. His name is Jaxx."

"Derek," Margaret said.

"Yes. My son, Derek, had a baby boy named Jaxx. He's your great-grandson." June spoke slowly.

"Paro," her mother replied.

Yulu had removed Jaxx from the seat. She placed him on Margaret's lap, continuing to support his head as she sat propped on the edge of the bed. "Jaxx," Yulu corrected. "Baby. Margaret's great-grandson."

"Baby," Margaret said.

The room went quiet except for Yulu's heavy breathing, and a distant car alarm that went through two cycles of panic before it was disabled. Through it, Margaret looked pleased.

"Can you stay for a minute?" June asked.

"Of course," Yulu nodded, inching closer to Margaret.

June went back to the van and picked up her ukulele from the floor. She knocked away a French fry and took the instrument inside.

Jaxx was asleep when she got back to her mother's room. Margaret put her finger to her lips for June to be quiet, so June tiptoed toward the bed.

Yulu carefully transferred Jaxx from Margaret's lap, back into his car seat. She winked at June, touched Margaret's knee and slipped out of the room.

"I have a song for you," June said, lining up her fingers on the fret board. She began to strum. Margaret listened intently. June played the song once through, but she messed up the chords. She cleared her throat, reset her hands, and started over.

"Hakuna Matata," she strummed, trying to move her fingers more smoothly this time. She choked on the lyrics, their meaning too real, too right. She played the wrong chord again. Jaxx woke up and started crying. Margaret laughed.

June put down the ukulele, defeated.

Her mother reached out, touched June's hand. "I could never play the damn thing either."

35

June got back into the van. She gave Jaxx a soother. He popped it out of his mouth twice before he fell back asleep. She was supposed to meet Doris over an hour ago. June pulled out her phone to send her a message, but it rang before she had the chance.

"Hello?"

"Mom, it's me."

"Tom, I'm in a hurry here." June recklessly backed out of her spot.

"I want to go to China."

"China's really expensive."

"There's a seat sale."

June waited impatiently for a man with a cane to cross in front of her. "What about your business? Who's going to look after all your clients when you're gone?"

There was a pause. "I'll find someone," Tom said. "It'll only be for a couple weeks."

"Well, if you can find someone, great. Do it. I gotta go. I'm late to meet my mom. We can talk later."

June hung up and raced across town. There was construction. A family of ducks waddled across the road. All the lights were red. Once she found a parking spot, it took her three tries before she could open the stroller and set the car seat inside. She pushed Jaxx down a path and up a ramp to a stone bridge that crossed over the water. She stopped mid-way to look over the side and imagined Tom doing the same on the Great Wall of China, contemplating his life. She'd always wanted to try out his telescopic feather duster. For a few weeks, she could tolerate Go-Kleen Now! Operating his fancy high-speed floor buffer had to be better than learning the terrible ukulele.

June walked with trepidation down the other side of the bridge in the direction of the paddleboat rental office. She ignored everything in her wake. Chariot strollers carting blond children. An empty hot dog package. Someone walking a ferret.

The bench beside the boat rental office was empty, except for a plastic grocery bag. June plunked down beside the bag, out of breath, sweating. She looked around the park for any sign of Doris. Any sign of her birth mother's scarf. Anyone who looked like her. Nothing. *I'm too late.*

Paddleboats and geese clunked by. A little girl picked flowers on the bank of the pond. Her shirt was stained yellow. June peeked inside the bag. She knew right away it was Doris's hospital gown. It was chalk white, inventory stamped and equipped with half a dozen strings. It reminded her of the paper doll cutouts she'd played with as a child.

June unfolded the gown until she uncovered the stolen handprint. It was impossibly small, her pinkie as thin as a dandelion stem and disproportionate to her other fingers. She examined her hand to see if it was still that severe. The woman with the one small pinkie. June placed her hand over the print, and then brought the gown to her nose. It smelled like sheets, but if she strained hard and really inhaled, she smelled life. Lemon, tears, oven, hamsters, the colour blue. The elusive scent of her birth mother. June had been chosen, but she had also been wanted. The *girl with the one blue hand*, no longer her adoption story. Just her story.

Out of nowhere, Jaxx screamed himself awake. A nightmare in the park just after noon. Another one of his traumatic calls, as though someone had told him all the world's milk supply had gone dry. June undid the straps, which bore down on his warm rising chest. A panicky wisp of a boy, and she brought him to her own chest so that he knew he was wanted too.

Acknowledgements

Many thanks to all those who believed in *The Figgs*. This family fought hard to exist. Hats off to my extraordinary editor and publisher, Kelsey Attard, for giving the Figgs their wings, and to my agent, Jill Marr, of the Sandra Dijkstra Literary Agency, for throwing this family out of the nest. The Figgs have added you both to their family crest.

Props to my early readers: Betty Jane Hegerat, Kim McCullough, and Diane Wallace, and the first champion of *The Figgs*, Hilary McMahon. Something comfortable to sit on, grape Kool-Aid, and guacamole to Brad Somer, Cassie Stocks, and Judith Pond respectively, for reading later iterations of this book.

High fives and fist bumps to my magical critique group: Brad, Judith, Leanne Shirtliffe, Chase Baird, and Nancy Hayes for your thoughtful and sometimes mean criticism, counseling, and friendship. Surely, me mushroom, I've put you all in my family crest.

Kudos to my book designer, Natalie Olsen, for capturing the essence of this book, and gratitude to the blurbers, who took the time away from their families, to get to know this one.

Mad love to my own family: Dave, Pippa, Hugo, and Odessa, who have all embraced the arduous role of husband/child of a writer with patience, wonder, and support. My Mom, Dad, Reta, and sisters, Amy and Amanda, and all my extended family and friends far and wide who enrich my life with their presence. Love to my best girls, Bianca Johnny, Jennie King, and Amanda Maclean. And bananas to my dear rabbit Alfie for getting up with me at five and eating the shitty first draft.

Also thanks to the Writers' Guild of Alberta and the fearless writers across the province that quietly and boldly do their thing.

Finally, to the readers. Thank you for choosing to spend time with *The Figgs* and giving me the greatest gift an author could hope for: an audience.

"Bears all things, believes all things, hopes all things, endures all things." 1 Corinthians 13:7

Ali Bryan's first novel, *Roost,* won the Georges Bugnet Award for Fiction and was the official selection of One Book Nova Scotia 2014. Her non-fiction has been shortlisted for the Jon Whyte Memorial Essay Prize and longlisted for the CBC Creative Non-Fiction Prize. She is a certified personal trainer and lives with her family in Calgary.